Books by Raine Thomas

Daughters of Saraqael Trilogy
Becoming
Central
Foretold

Firstborn Trilogy
Defy
Shift
Elder

The Prophecy (An Estilorian Short Story)

ELDER

Firstborn Trilogy Book Three

by Raine Thomas

For my nephew and godson, Nathan, the fellow elder of a new generation. You're a true inspiration to me and I know you'll inspire many others in the years to come.

Acknowledgements

There have been so many people who have helped me in the course of the Estilorian series. I'll begin by thanking my husband and biggest supporter, Kevin. You're the reason I can work a full-time career and still have time to pursue my writing dreams. Thank you so much for everything you do!

The rest of my family is also an amazing source of support. My mom, Diane, is one of my first beta readers for every book, as well as a vocal cheerleader. My dad, in-laws, grandmother, siblings and cousins all buy and read my books even when they could get them for free. My aunts like to debate which of my male characters are their favorites (I told you that you'd love Zachariah, Auntie Linda!). With all of this to bolster me, how could I fail?

I can't neglect to thank some of my fellow writers, some of whom serve as beta readers, some who offer me support with advice and a friendly ear, and some who do both: Bethany Lopez, Roy Bronson, Leif G.S. Notae, Tiffany King, Carol and Adam Kunz and Marilyn Almodovar. I can't thank all of you enough.

Lastly, thank you to my readers. Although I'm moving on to other projects, you have made the Estilorian world a joy to live in for the past two years. You're the best supporters out there, and I appreciate you more than you'll ever know!

Author's Note

A warm welcome to those readers who are new to the Estilorians! Please note that the Firstborn trilogy serves as a follow-up to the Daughters of Saraqael trilogy. For an overview intended to bring new readers up to speed or refresh the memories of those who have already enjoyed the Daughters of Saraqael trilogy, please read the following Glossary. Happy reading!

Glossary

Estilorians (Things You Need to Know)

Daughters of Saraqael – Amber, Olivia, and Skye, triplets born to the Corgloresti, Saraqael, and their human mother, Kate, as a result of a ritual outlined in a powerful scroll. They're the first and only half-human Estilorians, which allows them to carry children…something full Estilorian females can't do. Amber is avowed to the Gloresti elder, Gabriel; Olivia is avowed to the Gloresti, James, and Skye is avowed to the Gloresti, Caleb.

Estilorian – A being that physically resembles a human, appearing no older than 40 human years old (most look like humans in their late teens or early twenties). Estilorians can fly, and have specific powers based on their class. They can live forever without aging if they're not mortally wounded. Their eyes, wings and markings—if they have any—are always the same color, and identify their class.

Estilorian Plane – About two millennia ago, the nine Estilorian elders created a separate plane of existence to remove themselves from humanity, making their kind the objects of human myths and legends. All Estilorians live on this plane, and humans cannot travel to it. Estilorian society hasn't evolved like human society, and doesn't have such modern inventions as electricity, vehicles or modern weaponry.

Estilorian Classes (Alphabetically)

Corgloresti – *Soul Harvesters* – Identified by their silver eyes, wings and markings, these Estilorians travel between the planes of existence to facilitate the transfer of dying human souls to the Estilorian plane via The Embrace…the only method full Estilorians have to reproduce.

Elphresti – *Lords of Wisdom* – These Estilorians, identified by their black eyes, wings and markings, maintain the highest levels of authority among their kind. In human terms, they would be considered judges or beings in similar positions of authority.

Gloresti – *Defenders* – Gloresti bond with Corgloresti who are on the human plane to protect the Corgloresti. Gloresti are highly trained to defend and are identified by midnight blue eyes, wings and markings. Aside from the Corgloresti, the Gloresti is the only class that can travel to the human plane, but only in emergencies.

Kynzesti – *Elementals* – Having half-human mothers, the Kynzesti are identified by deep blue-green eyes, wings and markings. Unlike other classes, they are only created through biological childbirth. The youngest of all Estilorian classes, the extent of their powers and abilities is largely unknown.

Lekwuesti – *Hospitality Ambassadors* – The Lekwuesti are identified by lavender eyes, wings and markings. Their primary focus is assisting their fellow Estilorians. They form exclusive pairings with other Estilorians to provide them items of "creature comfort," such as food, clothing, accessories, furniture, etc. All other Estilorians rely heavily on this class.

Mercesti – *The Dark Ones* – Once lauded for their skills in strategy and innovation, this class is identified by red eyes, wings and markings. The nature of the Mercesti changed dramatically when Grolkinei assumed power by killing the class elder, Volarius, out of hatred and rage. Estilorians now convert into Mercesti if they kill or intend to kill another Estilorian for any reason other than defense. Because they are formed largely of beings that used to belong to other Estilorian classes, some Mercesti maintain remnants of their former skills and abilities.

Orculesti – *Advisors* – Identified by dark green eyes, wings and markings, the Orculesti function as advisors regarding humankind. They work with paired Corgloresti and Gloresti to provide a mental connection between them when they are separated by the planes of existence. This class can read the thoughts of other Estilorians who aren't strong enough or trained enough to prevent it, and use their mental powers to suppress the thoughts and abilities of others.

Scultresti – *Creators* – The Scultresti are identified by brown eyes, wings and markings. This talented class creates all forms, including those that Corgloresti assume on the human plane when they transition there. They also create new Estilorian forms for human souls to inhabit when they are Embraced by Corgloresti, and are responsible for producing new animal and wildlife on the Estilorian plane.

Waresti – *Warriors/Lords of the Flame* – Identified by burnt orange eyes, wings and markings, the Waresti are dedicated to the overall protection of Estilorians from the Mercesti and other dangers. The most physically strong of all Estilorians, these warriors are markedly muscular and highly skilled with weapons and all forms of attack.

Wymzesti – *Intuits* – Incredibly charismatic, the Wymzesti have deep purple eyes, wings and markings. With the ability to read body language and intuit actions based upon past behavior, this class can predict events before they happen. Like the Orculesti, this class has the ability to manipulate thoughts and decision-making of those who aren't strong enough to resist them.

Kynzesti Family Tree

Parents: Amber and Gabriel
Children (in order of birth): Clara Kate, Joshua, Zara, Corliss, Riley, Kiera

Parents: Olivia and James
Children (in order of birth): Sophia, Keane, Leigh, Elle, Will, Paige

Parents: Skye and Caleb
Children (in order of birth): Tate and Tiege (twins), Nicholas, Abigail and Adam (twins), Grace, Quaid, Emma

Glossary of Terms

adelfi – A term of respect applied to Olivia and Skye, the sisters-in-law of the Gloresti elder, Gabriel.

adelfos – A term of respect applied to James and Caleb, the brothers-in-law of the Gloresti elder, Gabriel.

archigos – A term of respect reserved only for the class elders.

Avowed – The strongest connection two beings can have. An avowed pairing is made when two beings exchange heartfelt vows of love. It results in shared thoughts and feelings and can never be undone.

Central – The primary area where most Estilorians live, similar to a capitol city. Floating above the ocean and surrounded by heavy enchantments, Central is inaccessible to Mercesti. Also called *home base.*

Elder – The oldest and most powerful member of an Estilorian class; an elder must have inherent abilities that blend cohesively with the other elders.

Kragen – A beast that crossed over to the Estilorian plane when it was formed; humans called these creatures "dragons."

kyria – A term of respect applied to Amber, the wife of the Gloresti elder, Gabriel.

Mainland – All of the area outside of Central/home base. This area is not protected like Central, and as such is sparsely populated by Estilorians other than the Mercesti.

Markings – Estilorians develop markings on their skin, similar to tattoos, when significant events occur. For example, Gloresti develop a midnight blue marking when they pair with a Corgloresti, and the Corgloresti receives an identical silver marking. Also, Estilorians may have markings around their eyes, indicating they have a second ability.

Prologue

"LET ME GET THIS STRAIGHT. YOUR DAD IS GABRIEL? AS IN, *THE* GABRIEL mentioned in the Bible?"

"Yep."

"And he and I were once the equivalent of best friends?"

"Yep."

"Holy crap."

Clara Kate stifled a laugh as she watched Ini-herit process this news. His gray eyes were wider than she'd ever seen them. The only sound was of the rain pelting the roof of the large tree house located in the backyard of their human guardian, Mrs. Clara Burke. Despite the fact that they were eighteen and the tree house was meant for younger kids, it was a place they visited whenever they wanted some time away from everything else. They'd even camped in it a few times.

Now, they sat against one wall with their legs sprawled in front of them and their hands joined. He studied her for a moment. When she just quirked an eyebrow, he let out a long breath.

"Wow."

Her lips curved upwards. "You believe me."

He continued to look at her without responding. She knew his features as well as her own after these past few months with him on the human plane, but that didn't make her less interested in gazing at them. His aristocratic nose, long-lashed eyes and full lips would have made him what others called a "pretty boy" if not for the rough, honed edges of his cheekbones and jaw line. He wore his dark hair longer than Mrs. B would have liked, but he usually pulled it back into a ponytail out of deference to her. At the moment, he had it unbound and it brushed his shoulders in beautiful waves.

"I do believe you," he said at last. "Though heaven knows why."

"Well, you're the Corgloresti elder. It's a class founded on faith. Even though your Estilorian memories and abilities have been suppressed while you re-learn human emotions, you retained your core characteristics."

"So when I call you Angel, it's not so much a nickname as a fact."

Shaking her head, she nudged him with her elbow. "I told you we're Estilorians, not angels."

"What if I want to be an angel?"

"Oh, you're no angel," she said. He grinned wickedly, making her heart work overtime. "Angels are just one of the mythical creatures humans created based on their memories of Estilorians. When we separated the planes a couple of thousand years ago, humans documented their experiences with us in a variety of ways. Art, literature, music…you name it. In essence, we became human myths and legends."

"Being a legend doesn't sound so bad." He paused, looking thoughtful. Then he asked, "And I'm how old?"

"Well, you were around before the separation of the planes."

"Get out."

"It's true," she said, laughing at his expression. "On the Estilorian plane, you'll look about the same age you are now, though. Maybe a few years older. Estilorians don't age, and many of the elders are the youngest in appearance."

"You said I'll look different when we transition. How different?"

She was pleased by his apparent acceptance of what she'd shared with him. They had been discussing this for hours, ever since she received word that they had to return to the Estilorian plane. She knew she wouldn't be commanded back unless something big had happened. Maybe her mother had gone into premature labor or something. Whatever the reason, she couldn't refuse the command.

"I don't know," she responded. "We don't have photographs on the Estilorian plane, and you left before I was born. I've never seen your Estilorian form."

"Well that kinda sucks."

"Why? Do you think you'll end up looking like Brent?" She batted her eyelashes at him.

He shoved her shoulder. "Ha. You can have that blond Viking with the IQ of a sock puppet. Who needs enough muscles to lift a car, anyway?"

"Yeah." She sighed dramatically. "Who needs 'em?"

He rolled his eyes and swung an arm over her shoulders. She felt the taut muscles there and knew he didn't really have a complex about Brent's steroid-induced physique. It was Brent's unwanted attention toward Clara Kate that had brought her and Ini-herit closer together, so he was a frequent butt of their jokes.

"But you'll look the same?" he asked.

"Yes," she said. She'd already discussed this, but didn't mind reviewing it if it helped ease his worry. "I've been able to transition between the planes without changing forms since I was three. I'm the only Estilorian who can, actually. No one knows why."

She didn't bother describing the uproar she'd caused the first time she did it. She barely remembered the experience. One moment she'd been sleeping in her bed at home. The next she was in a hospital on the human plane answering a million questions from the humans who found her. As a result of her impromptu transition, the protections around her homeland had been strengthened considerably.

"You'll look similar to how you do as a human," she explained. "*Archigos* Zayna, the Scultresti elder, did her best to mimic your Estilorian features in your human form to make the transition less psychologically stressful on you. Your eyes will be more silver than gray, and you'll have a bunch of silver markings on your body from past pairings with Gloresti. And I think your hair will be longer, based on what I've heard."

"Based on what you've heard?" he repeated. He reached over and traced the line of her jaw, causing her to shiver. "You were curious about me before you ever came here, weren't you?"

"Yes," she said breathlessly. His touch always did this to her. "I couldn't wait to meet you."

"And now that you have?"

"You're everything I ever dreamed of and more. You know that by now. I love you, Harry."

He leaned down and kissed her. It was every bit as potent as the first time. She reached up with her left hand and wove her fingers through the soft hair at the nape of his neck. Her tongue pressed eagerly against his as he deepened the kiss. Bliss such as she had never envisioned coursed through her.

Eventually, he pulled away from her. They both had to catch their breath. His eyes were dark with passion.

"I love you, too, Angel."

Her heart soared. This wasn't the first time he'd said it, but it never got old. She caressed the side of his face, enjoying the feel of stubble beneath her sensitive fingertips.

"What will we tell Mrs. B?" he asked.

She sighed. "We'll have to tell her some form of the truth. She won't see you again…at least, not in this form. She went through this nineteen years ago with my parents. She'll understand."

"I'm worried about her," he confessed.

"I know," she said. "Me, too."

They'd both observed how tired their guardian seemed lately. She had told them that she was retiring once they left for college in the fall. She'd been a foster parent for nearly forty years, ever since her beloved husband, Henry, was killed in the line of duty when she was twenty-eight. She'd been unable to have her own children, so she decided to raise those kids who needed a good home. But the time had come, she said, to hang up her hat.

"She's been going to the doctor more frequently," he said, running his fingers through her hair. "She won't tell me what they say."

"We'll get some answers after we transition," she promised. "We have contacts in the human medical field. My friend, Quincy, will probably be coming back here soon to harvest more souls. He usually transitions after the Kynzesti are born. I'll ask him to look into it."

"Okay."

They sat in silence for a moment. Clara Kate rested her head on his chest, listening to his heartbeat. "We have to leave soon," she said eventually. "Within a day or two."

"That soon?"

She nodded. "There's something going on. They wouldn't tell me what, but we're both needed right away."

"Wow."

"Yeah." Lifting her head, she looked again at his lips, then caught his gaze. "Harry, when we transition…things might be different. We'll both have responsibilities, and I'll have my family around me every moment of the day. And, well…I've decided that I want our last bit of time here on this plane to be memorable."

He lifted a dark brow. "Memorable?"

"Yeah." She shifted and ran one hand slowly up his chest, following the lines of his well-toned midsection through his T-shirt. When he drew in a sharp breath, she smiled. "Memorable."

Before he could say anything else, she rose up and turned to face him, straddling his thighs. Then she kissed him, long and deep. His hands soon began to roam, causing unbelievable flares of pleasure.

What she wanted was reckless. Foolish. Unlike anything she would normally do.

But she wouldn't be swayed.

"I don't—" he managed to say as she pulled away from his mouth and ran the tip of her tongue along his sensitive ear lobe. "I'm not prepared for—" he stopped again when she bit down lightly on his neck. Then she reached under his shirt, producing a tormented groan. "My wallet's—in the house."

"Do you want this?" she asked, pulling back so she could catch his gaze.

"Dear Lord, yes."

"So do I. This feels right, Harry. I haven't ever, you know, menstruated." She blushed after that confession, but purposefully ignored it. "I can't get preg—"

He reached up and gently touched her lips. "Thank you. I promise you, Angel…no matter what occurs when we transition to the other plane, I'll never forget this moment. You're everything to me. Whatever happens, we'll always have each other."

PART I:

PROMISES

Promise [*n.* **prom**-is]: A declaration that something will or will not be done, given, etc. by one; an express assurance on which expectation is based: *promises that an enemy will not win.*

Chapter 1

"CLARA KATE. WAKE UP, CLARA KATE. C.K.?"

Blinking away the memory that haunted her dreams, Clara Kate responded to the prodding of her cousin, Sophia, with a low moan. She'd only slept for a couple of hours. She felt like she needed to sleep for a couple of months.

"It's time to get up," Sophia said, rubbing Clara Kate's arm. "Tate and Ariana need us."

That had Clara Kate pushing herself into a sitting position and rubbing the sleep from her eyes. She realized it was still hours before dawn. Her breath floated in a white vapor around her head as she tried to get her bearings.

"*Archigos* Sebastian is preparing some food for everyone if you're hungry," Sophia said. She reached over and removed a dead leaf from Clara Kate's hair. "And I'm sure we can get him to help you feel more…refreshed before we go."

"I look that good, huh?"

"You look like you traveled almost three days without sleeping. Oh, wait. You did."

"Hah. Guess that explains this persistent headache," Clara Kate said, rubbing the bridge of her nose. "It's been nagging me."

"We've all pushed ourselves hard these past few days." Sophia reached over and touched Clara Kate's forehead with the back of her hand. "You do look a little pale. Maybe you should have Ini-herit—"

"I'll be fine," Clara Kate interrupted. She offset her rudeness with a small smile. "I'm just exhausted. Using my abilities to imbue so many weapons and then fighting all of those Mercesti really took it out of me. The lack of sleep leading up to that sure didn't help."

"Yeah." Sophia lifted one corner of her mouth, but her eyes continued to reflect her concern. "Some food will probably help, too."

"Sure. I'll get some in a minute. I've got to find a bit of privacy first."

"Okay."

Clara Kate got to her feet, fighting back a groan of discomfort. She seemed to hurt everywhere. She staggered as a wave of dizziness hit her. Sophia reached out and offered her a steadying hand.

"Hey…I know we tease you about your lack of grace and all, but don't go trying to earn extra credit," Sophia joked. After a brief hesitation, she added in a quieter voice, "You know, Quincy could always do a little checkup, just to make sure—"

"Thanks, Soph, but I'm really okay. I'll join you shortly. Save a piece of bacon for me, okay?"

Sophia nodded. "Sure."

A twinge of guilt struck Clara Kate as she watched Sophia turn and walk back to rejoin Quincy, who stood conversing with a number of other beings near a small campfire. The pair had only just avowed themselves to each other. It had been many years coming, even if the timing was odd, what with them in a race to save Tate and Ariana and recover the pieces of the Elder Scroll stolen by the Mercesti, Eirik.

She was thrilled for Sophia and Quincy, though. They should be off celebrating, not dealing with all of this.

Sighing, she moved deeper into the forest so she could attend to her personal needs. She made sure to stay where she could see some Waresti scouts through the trees. Their group had made camp within a thick forest not far from the ancient Estilorian library, which meant there was always a possibility that some of Eirik's followers skulked about in hopes of taking one of them unawares. Clara Kate was far from defenseless, but after everything that had occurred over the past nine-plus weeks since she returned from the human plane, she knew all too well to expect the unexpected.

Once she finished relieving her full bladder, she rose to cleanse her hands and face with a cloth Sebastian had provided. Just standing up made her entire body hurt, including parts of her that had no business hurting. As she told Sophia, she was sure it was her extreme exhaustion that had worn her down.

Her cousin's concern was thoughtful, but Clara Kate knew that if Quincy did examine her and decided she needed treatment for her exhaustion, he would tell her to have Ini-herit heal her. That wasn't an option. She truly couldn't bear the thought of Ini-herit touching her.

Even if he did have the power to heal, it wasn't worth the pain of enduring a touch that was no longer filled with love for her, but with no feeling at all.

From a discreet distance, Ini-herit watched Clara Kate collect herself and then make her way back to the center of camp. He followed, taking care to remain far enough from her that his surveillance would go unnoticed. Although he wasn't sure why, he'd felt a powerful need to see to her safety ever since he met her. Maybe because he hadn't even known her a few days before she had almost fallen off a cliff.

Whatever the reason, he often found himself trailing after her like this. He was careful to keep his distance, having learned that she didn't welcome his presence. Not understanding why, he'd asked her about it not so long ago.

"Do you really want to know?" she had asked.

He nodded. She had intrigued him from the moment he first saw her after his transition. He couldn't say what it was, exactly. But her reaction upon meeting him for the first time had struck him as odd, and he caught her staring at him quite often.

She had taken a deep breath and said, "Okay. We were in love on the human plane and you forgot me when you transitioned back."

He hadn't known what to say. As if sensing that he wasn't going to reply, she added, "So, since I'm still in love with you and you don't know me at all, it's been a bit awkward."

Awkward. He wasn't sure what that meant. Still, he could acknowledge that he wished he hadn't caused Clara Kate what was obviously negative feelings regarding him.

Since then, she had done her best to avoid him. He hadn't pressed her, not seeing any need. But he did allow himself to succumb to this strange compulsion to protect her.

As he neared the group around the campfire, she glanced up and caught his gaze. The firelight reflected off her arresting features. He'd realized upon meeting her that she was a blend of her parents in appearance. Her shoulder-length brown hair had the wavy texture of her father's. She also had his strong chin and lopsided grin. The dimple in her left cheek and her full, heart-shaped mouth mirrored her mother's. But her compelling, deep blue-green eyes, accented by the deep blue-green estoile markings symbolizing her second power, were all her.

Those eyes now reflected more of the negative emotion she held toward him as she quickly looked away. Sophia glanced between them and then reached out to link her arm with Clara Kate's.

"I sent scouts across the mainland to spread the word about Eirik," said Derian, the leader of the Mercesti allies who had escorted Sophia to the library. His words rolled from him in what humans called a Scottish accent. "If anyone catches sight of him or Tate or Ariana, we will hear about it."

"Thank you," Zachariah replied. The polite phrase was new for him. Ini-herit wondered if that had anything to do with his recent avowing to Clara Kate's cousin, Tate. As if sensing his thoughts, Zachariah's red gaze turned to him. "We have been studying your medallion, *archigos*. The map that Saraqael mentioned doesn't make any sense to us."

Ini-herit had also studied the medallion that he had worn around his neck for as long as he could remember. Just after they lost Tate and Ariana in the library, a manifestation of Saraqael appeared before him, Zachariah, Sophia, Clara Kate, and Tate's twin brother, Tiege. Saraqael had informed them all that they were among the eight beings required to activate the powerful Elder Scroll, news that Ini-herit hadn't expected. He'd been one of the nine elders who created the scroll, after all, and they hadn't intended for the elders to be the ones required to activate it. The line from the scroll that supposedly pertained to him did seem rather fitting, though.

One with too much self-control.

He looked again at Clara Kate, but she refused to meet his gaze. Then he glanced at the medallion, which rested in Zachariah's hand. Saraqael had also revealed that the medallion bore a map to the last scroll piece. Although Ini-herit had hidden the piece many centuries ago, his memory of that experience had been erased for the safety of all Estilorians. Apparently, he had decided to keep a map to it. That map did little good, however, if it couldn't be read.

"I have not been able to remember anything about the map," he said at last. "Have you reconnected yet with Tate so we can go in pursuit of her and Ariana?"

He didn't recognize the expression that passed briefly across the Mercesti's face, but he knew that Zachariah's responding, "No," was issued in a quieter tone than he had previously used. Ini-herit realized that he had somehow upset the other male.

"Ini-herit," said the Orculesti elder, Malukali, "Knorbis and I would like to scan your memories. Perhaps with our combined efforts, we can uncover information about the map."

Seeing no reason to object, he responded, "Of course."

"Good." Malukali waved at a nearby fallen tree. "Why don't you come over here and sit?"

Once he moved to comply, she and Knorbis stood on either side of him. The married couple had the most powerful mental abilities of any beings on the plane. If anyone had a chance to retrieve this particular memory, they did.

"Try to relax," Knorbis instructed as he and Malukali placed their hands on either side of his head. Dark green and dark purple light glowed as they exercised their powers. "Do your best to focus on the medallion. Try to visualize the symbols on it as well as the scroll piece. Maybe it will jar something loose."

Ini-herit nodded. But as he felt them invade his mind, his gaze wasn't on the medallion. It was on Clara Kate.

"I didn't expect to have to hike up a mountain when you told me about this transition," he said.

They stood in a small clearing holding hands. The northern lights glowed in the sky above them. A light sheen of perspiration coated them both.

She laughed. "If I had, you wouldn't have come."

"Truer words were never spoken."

"Well, we're here now. No harm, no foul."

"So you say." He grinned. "All right. Now what?"

"Now we're going to transition. I'll wait until you're gone before I go. It'll be quick and painless for you."

"That's a relief. I'd hate to reach the other side and have you see me crying like a girl."

She gave him a light shove, but her lips curved into a smile. "Yeah, yeah." Then her expression sobered. She took a deep breath. "Look, Harry—"

"I've already promised you that I'll get through this," he interrupted. "I won't forget. I'll have your love to see me through."

Her smile wavered, but she nodded. "Okay."

"Might as well have a grand send-off, though," he said.

He pulled her close and kissed her. Then he kissed her again. When he finally parted from her, he reached up and brushed her hair away from her face. The look in her eyes had his heart dancing a jig in his chest. He smiled, sensing the time to transition had come.

Taking her hands in his, he asked, "You said the most significant way that Estilorians can bond is through an avowing, right?"

"Yes," she said.

"Okay. Then here's my other promise to you: the first chance we have when we get to the other plane, I'll avow with you."

Returning from the memory, Ini-herit glanced around at everyone staring down at him. The green and purple light faded. When he looked up, he saw Malukali and Knorbis exchange glances over his head.

"Did you find out anything about the map?" Quincy asked.

"No," Malukali replied, shifting her gaze to Ini-herit. "I'm afraid not."

"Why don't you try again?" Tiege pressed. He shared equal concern for his twin and the female Lekwuesti, and Ini-herit knew he was anxious to get to them.

"Not right now," he said, getting to his feet. "I need a moment to…recover."

Ini-herit turned and walked away from the group, the remnants of the uncovered memory swirling through his mind. There had been moments in that memory when he felt things that he'd never before experienced. Now, those feelings had lost all context.

He knew only one thing for certain: he had failed to keep more than one promise to the female he had claimed to love.

Chapter 2

METIS HAD NEVER HAD A TASTE FOR BLOOD. HER SINGLE CREATION, Deimos, however, certainly had.

She had been confident that she could surpass the efforts of her own creator, Tethys. After all, Tethys had conducted her experiments before the separation of the planes. Tethys' goal had been to create a female Estilorian who could bear children, since she was abandoned by a human male because of her infertility. Metis was the result of her efforts.

Well, Metis couldn't bear children any more than the next full Estilorian female, but she could assume the forms of those she killed, as she'd discovered when she killed Tethys. Since then, she had assumed numerous forms.

Her latest was the form of her own bloodthirsty creation. Deimos had been Metis' attempt at generating life in a nontraditional way. Typically, Estilorians relied on a number of beings from different classes—Corgloresti, Gloresti, Orculesti and Scultresti—to perpetuate their kind. Metis, however, had decided to assume a few of these roles in her own effort to create life. It hadn't worked out very well. In the end, Deimos had been far from stable. Still, she treasured him like a human would a pet. He was *hers*.

Just hours ago, she had been forced to kill him. She needed his unusual ability to teleport. Since he had been near death anyway thanks to the wretched Lekwuesti, Ariana, Metis had finished the job and assumed his form and his abilities. She was fortunate that his talent transferred to her, as that wasn't always the case.

Eirik's shouts that they needed to remove Tate and Ariana from the library before they were rescued had pressured her into the terrible act. Now, she watched the fearsome Mercesti as he sat across from her, staring at the two females they had abducted. They were both still and silent inside their cage. Metis had teleported them to the first place that came to her mind: the hidden lair where Tethys raised her. It boasted a unique laboratory. The large cage was intended to hold experiments. Deimos had once spent time inside it while she worked on gaining his trust.

The memory had her suppressing a desire to tear into Eirik's throat.

"I will not hesitate to slay you, should you ever attempt it," Eirik said. His red eyes moved to her, and she realized he had intuited her intent.

A snarl issued from her throat. She couldn't stop it.

One of his eyebrows—the one on the side of his face with a long scar running down it—lifted in response. "I wonder if you will convert entirely to Deimos' primitive nature should you remain in his form along enough."

She sneered at him. "I allow as much of my form's base nature to control me as I wish. You made me kill Deimos. I therefore hold you in very low regard at the moment."

"You did it as much to save yourself," he said, returning his gaze to the cage. "If you wish to garner a position of authority under me once I assume the powers of an elder, you had better work on restraining yourself."

This time, she consciously stopped the growl and instead bowed her head. "Of course."

After drumming his fingers on the table for another ten minutes, Eirik got to his feet and approached their prisoners. Metis remained seated. The scent of blood coming from the cage made it difficult for her to repress Deimos' urges. She felt it unwise to test her self-control, even if she would have liked nothing more than to kill both of the other females. In her mind, they had each contributed to her beloved pet's death.

"Ariana, produce something to rouse the Kynzesti," Eirik barked. When there was no response, he reached for a thick stick that Metis kept near the cage and used it to prod the Lekwuesti. "Wake up, female."

Awakening with a gasp, Ariana hurried to get out of the way of the stick. Her dark hair covered her pale face until she reached up with a trembling hand to push it back. Dirt, blood and a number of other stains covered the light blue gown she wore. After she had reoriented herself to her surround-ings, she reached for the other female in the cage and lifted her unconscious form, cradling her in her arms.

"Rouse her," Eirik demanded a second time.

"No," Ariana said in a whisper. "She's badly injured and needs the rest to recover."

"Metis healed her most significant injuries."

"Her efforts might have stopped the internal hemorrhaging that your followers caused, but Tate is still bleeding from a number of wounds. I know some of her bones are broken. Her face is one big bruise. I won't rouse her to this pain."

Eirik rattled the cage with a fierce expression. "You and the Kynzesti will get me to the third scroll piece."

"Or what?" Ariana asked wearily. "You can't kill either one of us if you want to find it. Deimos is no longer around to use as a threat against me. You have none of your followers here to keep us in line. Tate is so hurt that you can't even torture her to try and secure my compliance." She looked up from stroking the Kynzesti's matted hair to catch Eirik's furious gaze. "Quite frankly, at this point, I wish you would open that cage and let me out. I'll pick up a weapon and raise it against you. May the better one of us win."

Metis knew the female had a point. It seemed Eirik did, too. Rather than continue to issue empty threats, he whirled away from the cage.

"I can remedy that," he said. "Metis, you must teleport me back to the library. Choose a location several miles from it so that we do not encounter anyone who may still be lingering around it in search of the females. I will soon have all of the followers I need to keep these two females obedient."

"And once you have found those followers?" Metis countered. "It will take some time to lead them here."

"You will teleport me and several of them back here and the others will follow. I need only enough males to keep these two under control. I am not foolish enough to attempt to bring them both across the plane with you barely controlling your bloodlust. Even injured, the Kynzesti makes a challenging opponent. We need reinforcements if we are to fulfill our plans."

Metis nodded. She knew Eirik thought only of himself. He was using her as long as she proved useful and then he would attempt to kill her.

That was fine with her. Two could play at that game.

Ariana waited until Deimos—or rather, Metis in Deimos' form—took hold of Eirik and they both vanished. Then she cast a light and used her Lekwuesti abilities to bring forth some spirit of hartshorn and waved it under Tate's nose. Despite what she told Eirik, she knew this was their only chance to escape.

When Tate tried to pull her head away and issued a low moan, Ariana winced. She knew Tate was in a lot of pain.

"Tate, wake up. We have to try and get out of here before they return."

That seemed to get through. Mumbling something through a swollen lip and likely cracked jaw, Tate managed to push herself into a sitting position. Her hair, a long mass of brown, light blue, deep blue-green and sparkling dark blue curls, was stuck to half of her head with congealed blood. Unable to resist her Lekwuesti nature, Ariana produced a wet towel and began trying to clean her friend.

"You are connected to Zachariah now, right?" she asked as she worked.

Tate nodded. Ariana figured they were communicating through their mental connection. She wasn't sure how, but the couple had recently managed to avow themselves through their dreams. It was something she would have never believed possible if she hadn't seen it herself.

She had experienced many things over the past few days that opened her eyes to how self-involved and narrow-minded she had been. When she was invited to stay at the Kynzesti homeland after Eirik forced her to find the first piece of the Elder Scroll, she had accepted it like a lifeline. Everyone within the homeland treated her like a long-lost friend, helping her begin to heal from the abuse she had suffered at the hands of Eirik and his followers. Tate's twin brother, Tiege, had been particularly friendly and eager to help her learn to defend herself, something that promoted her healing.

Two weeks later, Zachariah showed up.

After everything she had endured while in the company of Eirik's Mercesti followers, she couldn't stand the sight of Zachariah. She knew he was the former Gloresti second commander and that he had been forced to convert to a Mercesti, but she hadn't been able to look past his class. In her still traumatized mind, it hadn't even mattered to her that enough of his Gloresti traits still existed that he was able to pair with Tate for her protection.

She had been so wrong. If it hadn't been for Zachariah's unconventional training methods, she wouldn't have been able to protect herself against Deimos' most recent attack. Zachariah had saved her life—twice now, actually. Gruff and unemotional he may seem, but she now knew what lay at his core.

"Do you know where we are?" Tate asked, turning Ariana's attention. She barely moved her lips.

"No."

Another span of silence followed. Ariana considered using her power to clean their clothing, but it would use a great deal of energy that they might need to escape. Instead, she just wiped Tate's skin as best as she could without aggravating her injuries.

After another minute, Tate asked, "Can you unlock this cage?"

Feeling useless, she answered, "No." Some more powerful Lekwuesti could pass through locked doors. She wasn't one of them. "The door was sealed by Metis with some kind of energy. I don't even think there's a key."

"Do you know where Eirik and Metis went?"

"Yes," she replied, wanting to kick herself for not thinking to mention it sooner. "Somewhere several miles from the library. Eirik wants to recruit more of his followers to escort us to the last scroll piece. Metis indicated that the library is quite a distance from here."

Another period of silence ensued. Ariana looked around the cage to see if there was anything near enough that they could reach through the bars to try and break free from the cage. Outside of the stick Eirik used to poke her, however, there wasn't a single thing.

"Did Zachariah say anything else?" she asked at last.

"Yeah," Tate said in grim tones. "Get the bloody hell out of that bloody cage."

Chapter 3

CLARA KATE COULDN'T HELP BUT WONDER WHAT MEMORY MALUKALI AND Knorbis uncovered when they scanned Ini-herit's mind. For a brief moment after he surfaced from the scan, she wondered if it was about her. The elders had exchanged a long look, and Knorbis glanced in her direction before looking away.

But she dismissed it as wishful thinking. Not long after transitioning back to the Estilorian plane and discovering that Ini-herit hadn't retained his human awareness, she asked her dad whether Ini-herit's memories from the human plane could be revived. He had explained that it didn't work that way. Ini-herit's memories as a human had formed while his Estilorian self was fully suppressed. If his human and Estilorian selves didn't successfully merge during the transition, the human memories would be lost. It had been a one-shot deal.

She had believed that their love for each other would be enough to get him through it. Her parents had done the same type of transition nineteen years ago with success, and it was their strong bond that made it work. They, however, had been together for six years on the human plane...not four months.

"Time to eat something," Sophia said, carrying a plate over to where Clara Kate sat beside the fire.

"Thanks, Soph," she said, reaching for the plate. She realized she was starving and gave the plate's contents a scan.

"Sure." Sophia sat next to her with her own plate. "Extra bacon for you."

"Thanks again." Clara Kate picked up a piece of bacon, but when she brought it near her mouth to take a bite, she caught its scent. "Ugh," she said, making a face. "Is this fresh?"

Frowning, Sophia said, "Yes. I just ate a piece. Is that one bad or something?"

"It smells gross." She set it to the side. "That's all right. This fruit smells delicious."

Sophia looked down at her own plate and moved the bacon around with her finger. Then she picked up a piece and sniffed it. Shrugging, she ate it as Quincy joined them with his own plate.

They finished their meal in companionable silence. Across the campsite, Malukali and Knorbis approached Ini-herit. Clara Kate watched them, wondering what they were discussing. Knorbis handed something to Ini-herit. The medallion, she realized as it caught the firelight. After a couple of minutes of conversation, Ini-herit nodded. When the two other elders once again raised their hands and their energy started flowing, Clara Kate figured they had convinced him to give the memory scan another try.

"Finish up those meals," Tiege said from behind them. His tone had all of them turning. "Zachariah just connected with Tate."

"Eirik and Metis have teleported somewhere within a few miles of this location," Zachariah conveyed as he paced near the fire. He glanced at Derian and Uriel, both of whom stood nearby. "We need to send out scouts and try to intercept them."

The other males nodded and turned to issue orders. Zachariah could only appreciate their responsiveness. He itched to hit the air in pursuit of Tate. Unfortunately, she was so consumed by pain that she could barely remain conscious. His connection to her felt faint, certainly not strong enough for him to follow in a rescue attempt.

He turned on his heel to pace back in the other direction. Running a hand through his hair, he said, "Ariana heard Metis tell Eirik that the library is located quite a distance from wherever they're being kept."

He was still adjusting to using contractions when he spoke. Many Estilorians who hadn't been exposed to the informal manner of speech used by modern humans didn't use them. He'd been living in the Kynzesti homeland for a couple of months now, however. That combined with his close connection to Tate had gradually resulted in the change.

"I sense that's true," he continued as everyone else joined them around the campfire. "My connection to Tate feels as though it reaches across a distance."

His gaze landed on Clara Kate. She stared across the clearing at Ini-herit. Her eyes were damp. After a moment, she looked over at Zachariah. When he tilted his head in consideration, she turned so that she wasn't facing anyone and did a quick wipe of her eyes. Figuring she didn't want him commenting on her emotion, he paced back in the other direction. He sensed Tate wondering about her cousin's reaction and silently urged her to focus.

"We have to go after them," Tiege said. "Now."

"We might not reach them before Metis and Eirik return with their reinforcements," Uriel replied. "It makes more sense to try and get to the third scroll piece. Eirik will bring Tate and Ariana to it, and we can rescue them then."

"That plan failed us yesterday," Zachariah argued, clamping down on the residual guilt and anger that threatened him. "We have no idea how to read the damn map to get to the scroll piece, anyway."

Everyone glanced at Ini-herit, who looked at Malukali and Knorbis. Zachariah bunched his fists and looked at the ground for a long moment before he also turned his gaze to the two mentally-attuned elders.

Don't blame them, Tate thought. *Knorbis wouldn't have kidnapped me and Ariana if Metis hadn't been torturing Malukali.*

Zachariah already knew that. It didn't change how he felt.

You and Nyx nearly died, he returned. *How can you expect me to forgive the being who almost cost me everything that matters?*

She didn't respond. He knew she read from his thoughts that he had only an hour ago sent his long-time kragen companion back to the Kynzesti homeland for healing by Olivia and James. Tate also knew, even if she was trying to buffer it, that he was absorbing some of her excruciating pain resulting from an attack that Knorbis witnessed.

No. Forgiveness wasn't going to be forthcoming anytime soon.

Malukali caught his eye. "We've been unable to recover the key to the map on the medallion from Ini-herit's memories. I don't believe we can make any progress with that right now."

"Then we have to use Zachariah's connection to Tate and fly to them," Tiege insisted. "We should leave now, before Eirik returns to them with a dampener in tow."

Tate's twin looked pale, his eyes shadowed. Zachariah knew that, like him, Tiege hadn't slept at all the night before…not after failing to save Tate and Ariana. Now, they exchanged a look. Zachariah briefly lifted his chin in acknowledgment.

"We still have a bit of the potion that I created to fly more quickly," Knorbis said. "We should administer that to as many of us as we can."

There were nods and words of agreement issued among the group. Zachariah stiffened over the Wymzesti's words, but even he couldn't deny the power of the flight-enhancing elixir. The potion had led Tate and Ariana into Eirik's clutches. Maybe it would help get them out, too.

With everyone in agreement, they broke into smaller groups as they prepared to leave. Zachariah watched Sophia and Quincy step into the forest, exchanging looks that told him they were probably communicating by thought. Knorbis and Malukali also moved to a far edge of the campsite. They had eyes only for each other, making him frown and look away.

Tiege shadowed Uriel, Harold and Alexius as the Waresti gathered to determine their flight path. Derian, his mate, Melanthe, and their group of non-hostile Mercesti joined them in the conversation, as did Clara Kate.

Spotting Ini-herit, Zachariah made a quick decision. He approached the elder. When the Corgloresti caught his gaze, he said, "I need your help, *archigos.*"

"Of course," Ini-herit replied.

Appreciating the elder's matter-of-fact manner, Zachariah walked further into the forest, trusting the other male to follow. He ignored everything else. Several times, his stride faltered as waves of agony hit him. He knew what he felt paled in comparison to what Tate did. It made him want to rip Eirik's heart out with his bare hands and feed it to him in pieces.

When he reached a quiet spot, he stopped walking. Another stab of pain had him gripping his side. He heard Tate whimper in his mind. His jaw clenched.

Observing this, Ini-herit asked, "Do you wish me to try and assess your avowed's condition?"

Zachariah nodded once.

"Normally, I would think your request impossible," Ini-herit said. "However, your connection to Tate is unlike anything I have ever heard of."

Without another word, he placed his hands on Zachariah's shoulders. His eyes glowed as his power surged forth. They stood in silence for several minutes.

"Her injuries are not life-threatening," Ini-herit said after a minute. "She has sustained three rib fractures, a fractured jaw, two periorbital hematomas, a nasal fracture, a distal radius fracture, pelvic trauma—"

"Can you heal her through me?" Zachariah ground out.

On the other side of their connection, Tate started crying. This was a type of pain he wasn't equipped to absorb. The excruciating ache in his chest had nothing to do with fractured ribs.

He decided that ripping Eirik's heart out was far too quick a way to end the bastard's life.

"I can certainly try," Ini-herit said. "You and Tate have an ability to connect unlike any other two beings, joining your consciousnesses in an almost physical way. Open yourself to my healing energy. Use whatever connection you have to send it through to her."

Zachariah nodded. As Ini-herit's silver healing energy encompassed him and continued building, he closed his eyes. Slowly, he felt Tate's pain ease. The ache in his chest subsided.

When the light finally faded, Zachariah again opened his eyes. Ini-herit slumped and would have fallen if Zachariah hadn't reached out to steady him. The display of power had cost the elder.

"The fractures have been healed," Ini-herit said as he bent at the waist with his hands on his knees. "I opted to focus on those rather than the more superficial and less painful bruising."

"Thank you, *archigos*. I am in your debt." He caught Ini-herit's gaze. "You will take some of the potion so that you'll be among the first to reach Tate. That way, you can finish healing her." When the elder didn't immediately respond, he added, "Please."

"Of course."

When he was sure Ini-herit was steady enough, Zachariah turned to head back to the center of camp. His gaze flickered briefly to the shadows, where Clara Kate stood.

"He's all yours," he said.

Clara Kate felt a flush build in her cheeks when she realized Zachariah had spotted her. Her attention had been caught by Ini-herit's silver healing light, and she hadn't been able to resist spying on them. Now, she shifted her gaze from the Mercesti's retreating back to Ini-herit.

Her blush intensified when his eyes met hers. Sure, Harry didn't look exactly like he had on the human plane. His skin was a bit darker, his hair was longer and usually worn in a braid, and his eyes were the Corgloresti silver she expected instead of gray. Rather than appearing eighteen, he looked closer to a human in his early twenties.

That just meant he was taller, more muscular and more *male*.

He still made her heart flutter every time she looked at him. Why wouldn't he? It wasn't like she could just turn off her attraction to Harry like a switch.

Ini-herit, she reminded herself as she took a deep breath and let it out. *Not Harry*.

The prick of tears caught her by surprise. She thought she'd mastered her emotions when it came to her new reality. Just then, however, it all felt like too much. She turned to go back to Tiege and the others.

"Clara Kate," Ini-herit said. "May I speak with you?"

Glancing up in surprise, she considered what to say. He hadn't made a point of communicating with her very much since the transition, and she'd been avoiding him as much as possible lately. Maybe this was a conversation they needed to have.

Reaching her decision, she nodded.

"I wish to apologize to you," he said as he approached.

She blinked. "What?"

"I feel I owe you an apology. When Malukali and Knorbis attempted to extract the memory about the map, they inadvertently triggered one of us on the human plane. The memory of you and me standing together before I transitioned."

Her breath lodged in her throat. Had her father been wrong? Was it really possible Ini-herit's memories could be revived?

"I made a couple of promises to you that I failed to keep," he said. "I could sense that we shared an emotional connection. I did believe that it would sustain through my transition. However, that is not the case."

She stepped away from him. The words landed like slices from a well-honed blade. How was it possible that her heart could break all over again when it had already been so thoroughly shattered?

"You will move on from this experience. You are young, after all," he said, his silver eyes reflecting nothing. "I hope that you can find it in your heart to forgive me."

She wasn't sure how her voice made it past the raw pain he had just ripped into her chest. But before she walked away, she managed to reply, "My heart is capable of all kinds of things, Ini-herit. But you have no right to ask anything more of it than you already have."

Chapter 4

ARIANA SHIELDED HER EYES AS TATE'S FORM GLOWED WITH SILVER LIGHT. When it finally faded, she blinked to clear her vision and then glanced at her friend.

"What was that?" she asked with wide eyes.

Tate smiled. "*Archigos* Ini-herit used his power to heal some of my injuries."

Giving Tate a closer study, Ariana realized that much of the swelling in her face had gone down, leaving only dark bruises to mark where she'd been injured. Tate wiggled her wrist, which was apparently now healed, as well. When she moved, it appeared less painful for her than it had been.

Deciding not to question it in light of everything else she'd witnessed, Ariana just said, "I'm very glad to hear it. I was so worried about you."

"Thanks, Ariana." Tate reached over to give her a sideways hug, the best they could manage in the cage. "And thanks for sticking by me. I know you didn't have to. I saw you nearly escape just before Eirik's goons dragged me over the library door and shattered the illusion. You could've kept going, but you didn't."

Ariana didn't know what to say. Tate's words had her fighting back emotion. She'd never thought of herself as anything other than a coward. "You would have done the same for me," she said at last.

Tate started to speak, but then she paused. "Okay, okay," she said with a wave of her hands. Once again catching Ariana's gaze, she said, "Sparky told us to stop chit-chatting and get out of this cage."

"I'm willing to bet he inserted a few rude words in there, as well."

"You betcha."

Ariana managed a small smile. "Well, that's easier said than done."

"Yeah." Tate looked around. "What's this stick-thing?" She reached through the bars, stretching almost her full length to get her arm out far enough, then pulled it closer.

"I think it's meant to keep caged creatures in line. Eirik used it to poke me earlier."

Tate shook her head and cursed Eirik under her breath. Then she said, "Hmm. It's thick and sturdy, but I don't know how we could use it to break out of this metal cage. Is there anything you can produce that could cut through metal?"

She'd been thinking about that for a long time. "Nothing has come to mind. I don't specialize in tools and weapons, and they're difficult to produce. Those I do know how to create wouldn't cut through these bars. I can only heat things hot enough to cook, not to melt metal." Reaching up, she pushed on the top of the cage, which was only about four feet off the ground. "I don't know how this thing is mounted, but it doesn't seem like we'll be able to budge it."

"My ability to produce water won't help us much, either." Tate lifted the bloodstained towel that Ariana had used and eyed it consideringly. After a moment, she said, "Sparky is trying to gather ideas on how we can get out. They've left the library to come after us."

"We can't assume they'll get back here before Eirik," Ariana pointed out.

"You're absolutely right," Tate agreed. "Eirik and Metis could return any time now. If we want to escape, it's up to us. So let's get the hell out."

Metis brought Eirik to an area she remembered about five miles east of the library. She had been tempted to teleport them to the library itself so that he would be captured or killed by the Estilorians searching for the two females, but she decided that would be unwise. She didn't know yet whether Eirik might be useful in fulfilling her own plans to obtain the Elder Scroll. She also wasn't sure that she was powerful enough, even in a bloodthirsty male form, to acquire the two scroll pieces he already had. No, she needed some assistance for that.

When they appeared in the meadow, she looked around to ensure they were alone. She realized the sun hadn't yet risen. A cool breeze blew across the tall, browning grass, carrying a noticeable stench with it. She imagined it was her and Eirik who smelled so foul, and frowned in distaste. She should have insisted that the Lekwuesti female clean them both before they left. Eirik was ever pressuring her to act before she thought.

"Where are we?" he asked as he studied the area. "I do not recall this place."

"We circled here when the Lekwuesti attempted to stall for time before finally leading us to the library," she explained. "It was the only location I could visualize well enough to get us here."

"How far are we from the library?"

"I am not certain," she lied. "It was difficult to calculate from the air."

He turned to study her. His red eyes revealed nothing. When his blond and red-striped hair blew into his gaze, he didn't even blink. "In which direction is the library?"

"To the west," she said.

"Then we should fly that way and search for my followers."

"Fly? There are bound to be Waresti scouts searching for Mercesti. If they see our red wings, we will make easy targets."

He released a deep breath of frustration. "Very well. Walk, then. But walk now. We must find some Mercesti quickly so that we can continue in search of the last scroll piece."

"How certain are you that this is truly the last scroll piece?" she asked.

He frowned. "What are you implying?"

"Simply that the Lekwuesti has lied to us on more than one occasion. Who is to say that she has not lied once again? What if the scroll is in five pieces? Or ten? How are we to truly know?"

His jaw clenched as he considered her words. "I shall have to torture her to discover the truth," he said.

Attempting to control her satisfied reaction, Metis suggested, "Why not have me do that while you find your loyal followers? I can plan to meet you here and transport you and those you have with you back to the two females. By then, I will have all of the information you need."

"You will succumb to your creature's bloodlust," Eirik argued. "You cannot be trusted to torture the females."

"Then, at the very least, you should allow me to return to the laboratory to keep an eye on them. Do you really trust them alone? What if they escape?"

She could see him warring over the idea. He didn't trust her, but the females were far too valuable to his cause. In the end, he reached for her throat, much as she expected him to do. As his hold tightened and cut off her circulation, she made sure to flail and cower as she was sure he wanted.

"If any harm comes to those females before I return, there will be no manner of death too painful for you, Metis," he growled.

"Of course," she wheezed, adding an urgent nod to punctuate the statement.

She couldn't help but consider the irony of his treatment of her when he sought to become an elder…the ultimate leader of his class. Who would want to follow him?

"Very well," he said, and tossed her from him. "I will meet you here within an hour. Do not be late."

"Of course," she repeated. She even bowed her head in submission, praising herself for her performance.

Then she closed her eyes and visualized her next destination, which was nowhere near the laboratory housing the females. This new destination was an isle far from the knowledge of most Estilorians. She had only visited it once with her creator, and that had been centuries ago. But this was a very memorable place.

The moment she materialized on the isle, she whipped her head around to glance in every direction. Not seeing any signs of movement, she breathed a sigh of relief. The last thing she wanted just then was a battle for her life.

She stood within the crumbling structure of an ancient temple. It had made the transition when the planes were separated, as had most of the structures on the isle. Since it offered her shelter from sight, she relaxed a bit and considered her strategy.

The help she sought was from an unstable source. If she wanted the best chance of recruiting aid, she should shed Deimos' form and assume her own. The last time she was here, she was still in her base form. The problem was, she hadn't figured out how to reassume a form once she had shed it. She chalked this frustration up to her creator's significant limitations.

Once she shed a form, she sometimes retained a portion of that being's abilities. Most of the time, however, she lost them. She believed that her success in retaining assumed abilities depended in part on the age and power of the being she killed. Her success also increased the longer she remained in the being's form. In that way, Eirik's query about whether she would convert entirely to Deimos' bloodthirsty nature was surprisingly insightful.

Because she had just assumed Deimos' form, she held little hope that she would retain his ability to teleport once she shed it. That would just not do.

A loud thud not too far away made her tense. Moving as quietly as possible, she edged around a large stone slab and moved closer to a gap between the columns lining the front entryway. Peering outside, she caught a glimpse of her goal.

"I smell you," said a deep, booming voice. "My next meal."

Deciding it was now or never, she replied, "Cephalus, you will not recognize my voice or my form when you see me, but I beg you to listen to—"

A resounding crack filled the air. Stone crumbled. Gasping, Metis looked to a point in the distance and teleported just as the roof caved in.

This was going to be harder than she thought.

Chapter 5

AS EIRIK HIKED ALONG THE FORESTED WESTERN TRAIL LEADING TO THE library, he considered whether it was wise to have Metis stay with the two females. She seemed in control of the strange impulses that controlled Deimos, and her point about the two females being unguarded was valid. Although Metis had described some of the impressive security measures in place around the laboratory, there was no saying that the two females or their would-be rescuers couldn't get through them.

He had witnessed several unusual occurrences since coming into contact with the Kynzesti female, Tate. It wouldn't surprise him if she had even more tricks at her disposal. If she could avow herself without coming into contact with the other being, after all, she could do just about anything.

Her avowed was almost certainly Zachariah. Because her secondary pairing markings were red, she had to be avowed to a Mercesti. Outside of those who followed him, the only Mercesti he had seen interact with Tate since he met her was the former Gloresti second commander. Zachariah had saved her life when Eirik tried to kill her after acquiring the first scroll piece. At the time, Eirik deduced that the rescue effort was an attempt by Zachariah to preserve the Kynzesti's life because he was also searching for the Elder Scroll, and he knew the female was needed to shatter the illusions surrounding it. He had been wrong.

He didn't know how it was possible that the pair had avowed at all, never mind through some kind of remote connection. The amount of love and commitment required to create an avowed pairing was beyond the ability of most Estilorians, especially Mercesti. Prone to emotions they might be, but not the ones most beings considered positive.

It was a puzzle, but one Eirik didn't care to solve. Somehow, Tate had avowed with Zachariah across a distance. All that signified to Eirik was that Zachariah was now an enemy.

Their unusual connection meant there was a possibility Tate could accomplish other things beyond the typical. It was a good decision to have Metis with her and Ariana while he searched for his followers, he decided. He just hoped she managed to contain her urges.

Rounding a bend in the trail quite a distance from the meadow, he spotted evidence of a campsite. Because it was tucked in among a tight cluster of trees rather than a clearing and there was evidence of a recent kill a short distance away, he reasoned that it was a Mercesti campsite. Non-Mercesti could connect with a paired Lekwuesti for food.

Holding a hand over the campfire's ashes, he felt heat touch his skin. That meant the others were near.

He studied the ground, then set off in the direction of the freshest boot prints. It took him little time at all to find the group he sought. They had stopped to evaluate some tracks, posting lookouts at several points in the nearby trees. A wise decision, Eirik mused, and was pleased to come across some of his more competent followers.

Emerging from the trees, he caught the eye of the Mercesti who raised a bow and aimed an arrow at his heart. Not saying a word, he continued walking toward the alcove as though daring him to shoot the weapon.

The moment he recognized Eirik, however, the archer lowered his arms and turned to speak to someone behind him. A second later, a large, bald male pushed aside two others and stepped forward.

"Friedrich," Eirik said as he stopped.

Bowing, Friedrich replied, "We are pleased to see you, my lord." When he again stood tall, he added, "I trust you will indulge me by answering a question to verify your identity. In light of the abilities of some of the companions you keep, I feel it best to be cautious."

Yes, Friedrich would do quite well on this next mission, Eirik decided. He might even make a good commander once Eirik assumed the power of an elder.

"You may ask and I will answer."

"Thank you." Friedrich paused for a moment, then asked, "What was the name of the Scultresti female whose cottage we raided last year?"

"How should I know? We never bother asking names."

Nodding, Friedrich said, "Excellent. And what was the most valuable item we took from her?"

"Some might say her life," Eirik replied, "but I particularly enjoyed the peach cobbler she had just sat down to eat."

"That was exceptional cobbler."

"Now that we have established my identity, we must get down to business." Eirik moved closer to the alcove and conducted a brief scan of the males standing there. He counted eighteen of them. "I require the aid of you and five of your best soldiers. We must make our way to the east, where we will be transported to another part of the plane."

"And when we get there, my lord?" Friedrich asked.

Frowning because he wasn't receiving blind obedience, Eirik clenched his hands and answered, "We will continue the pursuit of the last item I need to fulfill my plans."

The others all exchanged looks. Seeing this, Eirik found himself wondering about the status of his two most loyal followers, Bertram and Tycho. He had sent them on a mission to bring the Kynzesti and Lekwuesti to him, but the two males hadn't been seen since. For their sakes, he thought now, they had better be dead.

Friedrich once again looked at him. "May I speak with you privately, my lord?"

Not bothering to respond, Eirik turned and stalked back into the forest where he had emerged. He reminded himself that once he had the powers of an elder, his class would cower before him and beg to be given orders to fulfill.

"What is it?" he snapped once he was alone with Friedrich.

Raising an eyebrow, Friedrich crossed his arms over his chest and said, "I request more details about this assignment, my lord. I mean no disrespect, but so far on this journey we have engaged in two bloody battles and suffered significant losses. None of us really has any idea what we are fighting for. While I know you would only ever put forth this kind of effort for something important, we must convince the others or all will be for naught."

Clamping down on his fury and impatience, Eirik considered the other male's words. While he wanted the ability to command the world to do his bidding, he was smart enough to know that he had to work on maintaining control among his followers…for now.

"We are in search of one last element to an artifact that offers unique promise," he said at last. *At least, we had better be,* he silently added, thinking of Metis' comment that Ariana could have lied yet again. "Once I obtain it, I intend to lead our class to greatness." Seeing the other male's continued hesitation, he continued, "I will need a solid core of commanders by my side."

"What you state sounds rather like something Grolkinei would have attempted," Friedrich pointed out. "His efforts never did our class any good."

He referred to the male who had killed the original Mercesti elder, Volarius, and forever changed the nature of their class. The Mercesti had once been equals with the other classes, sought after for their skills in strategy and innovation. After Grolkinei murdered Volarius with his own sword out of blind rage, he dramatically altered that fact. He forced the Mercesti to either follow him or be killed. Many members of the class turned against each other, resulting in a dark period in Estilorian history.

Following Grolkinei's rash and deadly act, the only way a Mercesti could be created was by converting members of other classes. Any being who killed or intended to kill another being based on a reason other than protection converted immediately to a Dark One. There hadn't been a Mercesti created through the Corgloresti Embrace in over two thousand years.

"Grolkinei was a fanatic," Eirik responded. "He lost sight of the larger picture. There are more Mercesti on the mainland than any other class residing at Central. Estilorians retained more knowledge of negative human emotions than positive ones after the planes were separated. Fueling anger and jealousy to turn beings against each other has never been much of a challenge. With all of us united, we will be an unstoppable force."

"Again, I do not question your goals, my lord," Friedrich said. "I have known you for centuries, and we both stopped following Grolkinei for similar reasons. But if we are going to convince other Mercesti that our efforts are different than anything undertaken by Grolkinei, you will have to be more forthcoming with the details."

His nostrils flaring, Eirik snapped, "Since when have you known me to be so foolish as to trust just anyone with essential information, Friedrich? You know as well as I do that if word gets out about the artifact I seek, every Mercesti will want it."

Nodding, Friedrich said, "Your point is well taken. I do not need all of the details. Just tell me how this effort will differ from Grolkinei's and I will convince the others."

After a moment of consideration, Eirik decided he had no choice but to offer enough information to capture Friedrich's interest. His gaze steady, he intoned, "The answer is simple. Grolkinei never ascended to any level of greatness because he could not combat the powers of the elders. When I acquire what I seek, I will not only be able to compete against the elders…I will become one."

Chapter 6

ZACHARIAH WAS GLAD TO BE BACK IN THE AIR. KNOWING THEY WERE ON the way to rescue Tate gave him a sense of purpose. He gauged by Tiege's expression that the younger male felt the same way, even if his feelings also extended to Ariana.

They flew at a remarkable pace thanks to the elixir. There had been enough potion to enhance the flight of twenty-five beings. Beside him flew a group of Waresti warriors along with Tiege, Sophia, Quincy, Clara Kate, Iniherit, Uriel and Alexius. Their numbers would be enough to rescue Tate. Zachariah wouldn't allow otherwise.

As he flew, he intercepted her thoughts about her situation. Things weren't looking good. When she communicated the details about their prison, he frowned and looked at Uriel.

"They're trying to get out of the cage," he said. "All they have at their disposal is a thick wooden rod and a towel."

Out of the corner of his eye, he saw Clara Kate tilt her head in interest as she listened to the conversation. He glanced at her when she wobbled in the air. She blinked as if to clear her vision, making his brows draw together.

She looks so pale, Tate thought. He silently agreed.

"I can think of no way to use those items to escape a cage such as the one you described," Uriel said, recapturing his attention. "Maybe the Lekwuesti can create a serrated blade they can use to saw through the bars."

"She can only create kitchen utensils," Zachariah said. "Nothing strong enough to cut solid metal. It would take them a long time to cut the bars, anyway. They need a faster way out."

Uriel frowned. "They can't access anything aside from those items?"

"Not outside of the cage. The Lekwuesti can create hospitality items, but no tools or weapons and nothing hot enough to melt the metal."

Clara Kate flew closer. Zachariah and Uriel looked over at her.

"Have Tate get the towel wet," she suggested. "Then have her wrap the towel around two of the bars as well as the pole. If they use the pole as a handle and twist the towel hard enough, it should bend the bars."

Zachariah considered this, then exchanged a look with Uriel. They both nodded.

"Thank you," Zachariah said to Clara Kate even as Tate acknowledged the thought about the wet towel and explained it to Ariana.

"That was awesome, C.K.," Tiege said from Clara Kate's other side. He grinned. "Where'd you come up with that?"

"Something I picked up over the past few months," she said with a shrug.

"While you were on the human plane?"

"Yeah. Mrs. B wanted us to watch educational shows whenever possible. I remembered a show testing theories about escaping prison, and this was one way that worked."

Zachariah sensed that she didn't really want to talk about it. When her gaze moved to Ini-herit and then lowered to the ground, he understood why. Tiege must have realized the same thing, as he just nodded and returned his focus to flying.

Ask C.K. if she's okay, Tate thought.

Sorry, Beautiful. If it doesn't involve you, that kind of thing isn't in my repertoire.

She issued a mental sigh but didn't push him. He shook his head. She was forever imbuing his character with more nobility than he actually possessed.

Despite that thought, he glanced again at Clara Kate. She'd been flying without much rest for several days. The strain showed itself in her waxy complexion and bleary eyes. Maybe they should have left her back with Harold and Derian, he mused.

After a few more minutes of observing Tate's progress in his mind, he told Clara Kate, "Your idea appears to be working."

She smiled. "Great."

"Way to go, C.K.," Sophia declared from slightly behind her.

When Clara Kate turned in her cousin's direction, her eyes rolled back in her head and she briefly lost altitude. Zachariah reached out and grabbed her. Her eyelids fluttered as she regained her senses.

Looks like I don't have to ask her how she's doing, after all, he thought toward Tate. *I'd say it's pretty damn clear.*

"Are you all right, C.K.?" Tiege asked with a frown.

"Sure," she said a little breathlessly. She swallowed the fear that still stuck in her throat. "I'm just tired. Let's get to Tate and Ariana so I can get a real night's sleep, okay?"

Her joke fell flat, probably because her voice sounded so thin. Quincy flew up beside her. She clenched her jaw, but caught his gaze and worked on offering him the most normal expression she could. He studied her for a long moment.

"You're pale, C.K. I think it would be a good idea for you and me to stop for a couple of minutes so I can make sure everything is okay."

"I'm—"

"I know you're fine," he interrupted with a quick smile that didn't reach his eyes, "but I wouldn't be able to live with myself if I didn't take just a couple of minutes to be sure." He paused, glancing at Ini-herit. "If you'd rather—"

"All right, all right. I'll stop," she said, not wanting him to suggest that she allow Ini-herit to heal her. When Zachariah looked at her, she said, "We'll catch up with you soon. Don't stop on my account. It's just been a hard few days."

The Mercesti nodded, then glanced at Uriel. The Waresti elder said, "Alexius will travel with you."

"I'm coming, too," Sophia said.

Embarrassed over the fuss, Clara Kate just nodded and changed her course to find somewhere to land. She purposely avoided looking at Ini-herit, not wanting to see the lack of concern on his face. When dots danced in front of her eyes, she blinked and shook her head to clear them.

Okay, maybe landing was a good idea, after all.

Beside her, Alexius gave her a considering look. The Waresti second commander often saw more than most. She offered him a smile that she didn't feel to try and convey that all was well.

She'd gotten pretty good at lying lately, she thought. It was rather depressing. But who could she talk to about what she was feeling?

As the Orculesti elder, Malukali was the most in tune with emotion. But just like all of the elders, she shared thoughts with Clara Kate's father and Ini-herit. Sure, Malukali was capable of containing her thoughts, but what if she felt obligated to talk to them about what had happened? The very idea mortified Clara Kate.

A couple of times when they'd been at the homeland, she'd considered talking to her mom. She had a level head and was the most likely to listen to what Clara Kate had to say without injecting her own opinion or emotion into it. Clara Kate's biggest concern was that her mother might decide to take up her blessed sword and run Ini-herit through.

In the end, with everyone believing that Tate was dead and then getting involved in her rescue once they realized she wasn't, Clara Kate hadn't had time to talk to anyone. Once they returned home, she hoped to just bury everything and get over it.

Yeah, right. How did you get over losing someone you loved when they were still a part of your life?

She shook her head as they landed. One of the nice things about the Estilorian plane was how undeveloped it was. With the majority of Estilorians making their homes at Central, there was no shortage of beautiful forests on the mainland. They now stood on the outskirts of one.

"Come on into the shade," Quincy instructed, taking her by the elbow.

Knowing he was trying to keep her steady in case she lost her balance, she could only appreciate the action. Alexius stepped away from them and patrolled the perimeter of their location to make sure it was secure. Sophia walked on Clara Kate's other side, a faint line drawn between her eyes.

"Thanks, you guys," Clara Kate said, feeling her cheeks grow warm. "I'm sure there isn't any need for all this, though."

As he led her to a large boulder that had a nice curve in it for her to sit on, Quincy said, "Let's just make sure, okay?"

"Sure."

"I'll be right back," Sophia said. "I'll take this opportunity to enjoy a couple of minutes to myself."

Knowing Sophia was only doing it to give them privacy, Clara Kate offered her a smile. After her cousin walked off, she said to Quincy, "The silver accents in her markings and wings make Soph look like a beautiful, glittery fairy queen."

That made Quincy smile as he pulled something out of the satchel he wore. "She's always looked that way." He placed the ends of the Estilorian-style stethoscope into his ears and added, "But the color does suit her, doesn't it?"

"You suit her, Quincy. I'm so happy for you both."

"Thanks, C.K. That really means a lot. Take a deep breath for me."

She obeyed, repeating the process a few times as he placed the instrument on her chest and back.

As he picked up her wrist and held his fingers against her pulse, he asked, "How often have you been having the dizzy spells?"

"On and off for a few days."

"Not before?"

She frowned. "Well, there may have been one or two times in the past few weeks when I was working too hard in the training paddock. But they went away after I drank some water."

"Okay. Sophia mentioned that you've been experiencing headaches."

Sighing, she acknowledged, "On and off for a few weeks. I'm sure it's just stress, though. I've had a lot on my mind."

His silver gaze was steady as he pulled out a temperature gauge and inserted it under her tongue. "I've been your physician since I brought you into this world, C.K. You've never had a headache before."

She knew that, but hadn't wanted to put any importance on it. Now, she realized she should have mentioned the symptom to him sooner.

"I'm sorry, Quincy," she said when he removed the device from her mouth. "I've been a little distracted."

"I know," he said. The empathy in his gaze had her blinking back sudden tears. Seeing the reaction, he rubbed her shoulder. "I need you to tell me of any other physical ailments you've experienced that have struck you as unusual."

"Well...this for one," she said, pointing at the tear that trickled down her cheek. "I spend at least half of every day wanting to cry my eyes out. But having your heart broken tends to do that to a gal, right?"

"I'll go with yes. Anything else?"

She thought about it. "I've been more sore than usual, especially after training. Everything seems to hurt. Half the time I feel like I'm in someone else's form."

He was quiet for a long moment, holding her gaze as he sorted through her list of symptoms. She wiped away another unwanted tear.

"I have a personal question to ask you," he began.

Shrugging, she said, "Go for it."

"Did you engage in sexual intercourse while on the human plane?"

The blood in her face drained so fast her head swam. Why would he ask—?

Oh. Dear. *God*.

"I've never menstruated," she said hoarsely as her thoughts caught up with his. "I can't get pregnant."

"We don't know that, C.K." he said levelly. "The Kynzesti is a new class. None of you has had the benefit of an internal exam conducted with more thorough human equipment. There is always the possibility that your class has made an evolutionary leap and no longer has to experience the inconvenience of a menstrual cycle to be fertile."

"And you're only putting this out there *now*?" she exclaimed, surging to her feet. When she swayed, he reached out to grab her. "Holy light, Quincy! I wouldn't have—*we* would have—holy light!"

"C.K." He turned her so she was looking at him. His gaze was steady. "Could you be pregnant?"

Unable to speak, she just nodded.

"Okay," he said. "I'd like to do an exam to see if…well, to see. May I touch your abdomen?"

Once again, she nodded. When he lifted her shirt and pressed against her lower belly, she inhaled sharply over the tenderness there. He removed his hand and once again lifted the stethoscope-style instrument, this time holding it against her abdomen. Her womb.

She couldn't deal with this. There was no way fate could be this cruel.

But when Quincy removed the earpieces and caught her gaze, she knew.

"Hey, C.K., what's the verdict?" Sophia asked in a cheerful tone as she approached. "Are you going to live?"

Rather than answer, Clara Kate walked over to her cousin, grabbed her into a hug and burst into tears.

Chapter 7

IT TOOK A COUPLE OF MINUTES FOR TATE AND ARIANA TO GET THE WET towel into place and wrapped around the stick so that they could try to bend the bars. Ariana produced a metal rod that they used to reinforce the stick, which helped keep them from shattering the wood. It took time for them to actually make progress.

But it was working. They both had to use all of their strength to twist the stick once the towel got tight enough to cinch. Sweat dripped into their eyes as they worked on giving it yet another turn.

"What's the first thing you're going to do when we get out of here?" Tate asked. Her breath left her in a pant as she struggled with her end of the stick.

"Kiss the ground," Ariana said, gritting her teeth over the strain of pushing. "The free ground where I can go anywhere I please."

Choking out a laugh, Tate gave another push, bracing her boots against the side of the cage for additional leverage. "I thought you might say you're going to kiss Tiege."

"Tate!" Ariana gasped. Then she smiled despite herself. "I can't kiss him looking and smelling like this."

"Oh, I know what you mean. But Sparky is going to get one helluva greeting from me. I don't care if he ends up covered in blood and sweat. He'll just have to deal."

Ariana grunted as they managed to get the stick around one more complete turn. She appreciated the banal chatter to keep her mind off her outrageous fear. "Well, since you and Zachariah share thoughts, he'll now be prepared for that."

Tate winked at her as they started the next rotation. The bars groaned as they bowed. "Tiege won't care what you look like, you know. He loves you for more than just your pretty face."

"Ha." She was glad her exertion concealed her blush. Not meeting Tate's gaze as she gave the stick another shove, she asked, "Do you really think so?"

"Sure I do."

Her certainty brought a lightness to Ariana's heart. It seemed to give her another burst of energy, too. She angled her body to lift the stick as Tate all but sat on her side.

"Do you know that's why I was seeking you out on the day *archigos* Knorbis led us away from everyone?" Ariana asked.

"Really?"

"Yes. I wanted to see if you thought Tiege would be open to pairing with me as his Lekwuesti. I was too anxious to just ask him."

Tate raised an eyebrow. "His paired Lekwuesti?"

"See? That was Sophia's initial reaction, too." Ariana frowned as she shifted again. "After discussing it with her, I wanted another female's opinion. Do you not think he'll want me, then?"

"He wants you, all right. Just not as the Lekwuesti who sees to his hospitality needs."

Before Ariana could pursue the conversation any further, Tate stopped pushing and sat back on her heels. Nodding, she said, "I think we've made a big enough gap. Let's give it a shot."

They hurriedly removed the towel and bar, dropping the rod to the ground with a loud clang. Ariana waved at Tate, who nodded again and moved over to the rather small opening. Taking a deep breath, she eased her head and shoulders out. She got hung up at her chest for a moment and had to do some wriggling to ease her upper body through the gap.

"Guess it's a good thing I've lost so much weight these past few days," Tate said as she managed to spill out the rest of the way. "There's no way these hips could normally do that."

Ariana quickly followed her out. Tate grabbed her arms and helped her to her feet. They glanced around the room. Approaching a table full of implements, Tate hefted a sharp tool that resembled an ice pick. Not wanting to be unarmed, Ariana grabbed a similar tool.

"Let's be careful when we leave this room," Tate cautioned. "We don't know where we are or what kind of dwelling this is. Metis might have guards out here."

Ariana nodded. She realized that she wasn't as afraid as she probably should be. She just felt resolved.

Tate grasped the door handle and gave it a pull. Then she frowned. "You have *got* to be kidding me."

"What?"

"It's locked."

"Cephalus, stop your tirade. It is me—Metis."

She kept her gaze trained on a spot in the distance in case she once again had to teleport out of harm's way. Despite the fact that she wasn't looking directly at Cephalus, she certainly saw him. The six-armed giant was impossible to miss. If his extra appendages and fifteen-foot bulk weren't enough to draw attention, his purple skin and writhing head of silver hair sure were. His black eyes had no irises and were little more than narrow slits as he turned in her direction.

As odd as she considered herself due to Tethys' miscalculations during the creation process, she thanked her good fortune that she hadn't ended up like Cephalus.

"I know it has been many centuries since you last saw me, and I no longer look the same," she said as the giant hefted his spiked club. "But our creator gave me the ability to assume multiple forms."

His nostrils flaring, the giant took two long strides in her direction with his club held high. She teleported to the spot she'd been focusing on and watched the club shatter a pillar next to where she'd been standing.

Shaking her head, she wondered if she'd miscalculated in coming here. But she needed Cephalus' help to monitor and coerce the two females so she could go after the final scroll piece. She would also need his strength to get the two pieces from Eirik. She had nowhere else to turn.

"I will bring you away from this place, Cephalus, if you will but listen."

That finally caught the giant's attention. This time when he approached, he kept the club lowered. His hair waved around his head in a rhythmic manner that caught the sunlight. It would have hypnotized her if she hadn't known to avoid gazing at it.

"You would take me from this place after so many centuries of exile?" he asked.

"Yes. And all that I ask in return is that you aid me in acquiring something."

"Acquiring what?"

Knowing he wouldn't deny her when she offered him something so precious, she explained about the Elder Scroll, the two females and Eirik. The giant didn't move a muscle throughout her monologue.

"You can teleport me while in that form?" he asked.

"Yes. I wish to go to the laboratory first and acquire the two females. They will lead us to the third scroll piece."

"I agree to your conditions," Cephalus said without hesitation. "Let us depart."

Metis didn't want to waste any more time. She nodded and approached him. "You may be too tall to stand easily in my laboratory, so we had best do this while you are sitting."

He obeyed, laying his club on his lap. Closing her eyes, Metis touched his arm and visualized the laboratory, describing it out loud to help the teleport succeed. In the next moment, they both appeared next to the table where she had sat with Eirik less than an hour ago.

"I smell human blood," Cephalus said, getting to his feet very quickly considering his size. He had to hunch down to avoid connecting with the ceiling. When he lifted his club, it hit the table and sent it flying.

"Holy light!"

Metis had just realized the cage was empty when the exclamation issued from near the door. She froze in confusion as Cephalus whirled toward the sound of the voice.

"No!" she cried, reaching for the arm that wielded the club. "Do not injure them, you fool!"

He swatted her aside with one of his arms even as he swung his weapon. He aimed for the Kynzesti, scenting the human part of her blood. Tate stayed her ground until the club was less than a foot from her. Then she leaped to the side.

The door splintered with a tremendous crack. Metis felt her plans sliding sideways.

"Tate, get through the door!"

The Lekwuesti produced something with a glow of lavender light. She ran up to Cephalus as he yanked on his club to disconnect it from what remained of the door. When he again brought the weapon up, she flung the contents in her hand at the giant's eyes.

He reared back with a roar. Metis belatedly tried to figure out where she could teleport to, but it was too late. Her last, panicked thought before Cephalus knocked her senseless was that the females were escaping the room, and they were almost surely going to die.

Chapter 8

"THEY HAVE ESCAPED THE CAGE," ZACHARIAH ANNOUNCED.
Ini-herit listened to the murmurs around him and imagined everyone was excited by this news. He nodded in acknowledgement, but his attention was elsewhere.

What was wrong with Clara Kate?

"Bloody hell. The damn door is locked."

This time, the responses around Ini-herit had a distinctly negative sound.

Uriel asked, "Do they see a key or other method of opening the door?"

"They're looking."

Ini-herit's thoughts again turned inward. Clara Kate really had looked pale. He'd noticed it a few miles before Quincy finally insisted that she land with him. He had been wondering how he could possibly convince her to let him touch her so that he could assess her condition and heal her. After seeing how she reacted when Quincy almost suggested the same thing, he knew she never would have agreed.

Her behavior made no sense to him. If she was unwell, she should allow him to heal her. She was visibly exhausted. His abilities would have renewed her energy and adjusted any imbalances she suffered.

Then she would still be with them.

Instead, she was somewhere else with only three other beings for protection. Eirik and his followers wouldn't hesitate to capture any of the Kynzesti, especially the daughter of *archigos* Gabriel and *kyria* Amber. Her stubbornness had placed her in danger.

Blinking, he realized he was obsessing…something he'd never done before.

"Get down!"

Zachariah's warning had all of them starting. Ini-herit realized the Mercesti was reacting to something he witnessed through his connection to Tate.

"The door is no longer an obstacle," Zachariah said. He looked at Tiege. "But we'd better hurry. Judging by the size of the six-armed giant Metis just teleported to their location, they don't have much time."

Metis was a dead being.

Eirik stood in the meadow with Friedrich and the five males he had selected to accompany him back to the laboratory. It hadn't taken him long to realize he had been double-crossed. Now, as the sky lightened for sunrise, he had to decide what to do.

"Perhaps she is merely late," Friedrich suggested.

"No," Eirik said, his rage carefully held in check. "She is going to attempt to recover the third scroll piece. I am certain of it."

"Should we just fly to the location where the females are being kept?"

Now, some of Eirik's anger seeped into his response. "I have no idea where it is."

He wanted to kill someone. Instead, he clenched his hands into fists hard enough to crack his knuckles. Looking toward the library, he weighed his options.

Even if Metis somehow managed to get the two females to cooperate with her to recover the third piece of the scroll, she would need the two other pieces to make it work. She'd have to seek him out. He realized she could conceivably kill a being he considered trustworthy and assume his form so she could get close enough to try and get the scroll pieces from him. He would have to be even more on guard.

"I may not know where the laboratory is," he said at last, "but the moment the Kynzesti awakens, she will connect with her avowed."

"Her avowed?"

Waving off the question, Eirik continued, "We must fly to the library and take care to avoid detection by the Waresti. When they take flight after the females, we will follow them from a distance."

Without waiting for a response, he extended his wings and took flight. He cleared the tops of the trees and easily spotted the library to the east. The sun was just starting to rise when he realized that the Estilorians who were trying to rescue the two females had already taken flight. Their luminescent wings glowed like daylight stars a number of miles away.

"We must follow them," he ordered.

"We will never catch them," Friedrich responded. "They will acquire the females, who will surely lead them to the item you seek."

"I will worry about that later." Frowning, Eirik asked, "Why are there red wings among all of the orange? Did the Waresti take prisoners?"

"No, sir. Did you not know that Derian and his followers fought against us in the battle yesterday?"

Eirik hadn't known. He had gone into the library with Metis, Deimos and the two females before the battle had really gotten underway. Now that he thought back to his experience in the library, however, he realized there had been more than one pair of red wings heading toward them in the library just before Metis teleported them out.

"Do you know those among Derian's followers?" he asked Friedrich.

"Not all of them."

Why had the Marked Ones, as Derian and his tattooed followers were known among the other Mercesti, joined with the Estilorians trying to free the females? Derian wasn't an ambitious male. He had been content to bow to Kanika's pathetic leadership. His vendetta to rescue Mercesti with strong or unique abilities who had been forced to convert by Grolkinei's commanders was just as pathetic. The only time Derian entered into a confrontation was in those rescue efforts. Since Grolkinei and his commanders had been defeated nearly two decades ago, the Marked Ones hadn't been seen much around the mainland.

He must have teamed up with Zachariah out of a foolish sense of loyalty. They were both former Gloresti, after all.

"Well, at least the tattoos most of them wear will help us identify them," he said at last. "Just one more challenge for us to overcome to achieve our goal."

"A challenge that may be less difficult than you expect," Friedrich replied. When Eirik looked at him, he added, "I happen to know that at least one of Derian's followers is less committed to his cause than he believes. I am certain if we make the right approach, we will have a way to infiltrate them."

* * *

Clara Kate didn't allow herself to weep for very long. She had made her bed—quite literally—and now she had to lie in it.

Not offering any explanations to Sophia or Alexius, who appeared shortly after Sophia did, she wiped her face dry, took the supplements that Quincy handed to her and then extended her wings.

"Please let me tell him when the time is right," she asked Quincy.

"Of course," he said. He reached out and gave her hand a squeeze. "We'll get through this, C.K."

She didn't reply. Lifting into the air, she waited for Alexius to take the lead, following mental instructions from his elder. Then they started flying as quickly as they could to make up the precious minutes they had lost.

We'll get through this.

Quincy's comment circled in her mind as her shock began to ease. He hadn't said, "Congratulations, C.K." or "I'm thrilled for you, C.K." None of the things beings said to her mother and aunts when they conceived. Why would he? She was eighteen, unwed, unavowed, and the baby's father had no idea he had even slept with her.

Her father was going to absolutely kill her.

"Tate and Ariana managed to escape the cage," Alexius related, turning her attention. "But the door to the room where they are being held is also locked."

Clara Kate focused on increasing her speed. When she drew parallel to Alexius, he realized what she was doing. Nodding, he also flew faster. Behind them, Quincy and Sophia sped up to stay close.

"Are you all right, Clara Kate?" Alexius asked.

Surprised, she responded with an automatic, "Sure."

His burnt orange gaze held hers for a long moment. Then he said, "It's just that I haven't seen that level of emotion from you since you were a child. I know I'm not the best at expressing such things, but I want you to know that I care about you. Seeing you so upset…it bothered me."

Well, wasn't this just the day for grand revelations?

Clara Kate almost lost her composure again over the concern shown for her by one of the least expected beings. Alexius had been a part of her life ever since she was born, traveling frequently to her homeland to help her and her cousins and siblings train. She'd never suspected that he felt this way.

"Thanks, Alexius," she said, giving him a small smile. "I've got a lot to work through right now. My head's a little all over the place."

"Will you let me know if there is anything I can do to help?"

"I will," she said, and she meant it.

"All right." This time, he smiled. It was such a rare expression for him that it made her do a double-take. His features went from almost fierce to charming. "I'll hold you to that."

Before she could reply, his gaze once again grew serious. "Apparently, something urgent is happening with Tate and Ariana. Something about Metis and a giant."

"How far are we from the others?" she asked.

"Less than ten minutes. If we press ourselves, we can probably catch up with them in five."

"Then let's go."

Chapter 9

"WHAT DID YOU THROW INTO THAT GIANT'S EYES?" TATE ASKED AS SHE ran up the steps in the empty chamber outside the laboratory door.

Lifting her skirts to keep up, Ariana panted, "A combination of hot chili oil and pepper. He'll be blind for at least a few minutes."

"Awesome."

Fortunately, the door at the top of the steps was unlocked. They found themselves in the dining room of a rather normal looking cottage. Metis enjoyed fine things, judging by the china lining the shelves of a display cabinet and the beautiful, glossy wood of her furniture. Ariana wondered how she acquired such items, then decided she was better off not knowing.

Their feet made no sound on the thick rugs covering the wood floors as they left that room and entered the living area. Tate dodged a coffee table as Ariana jumped over a footstool. They ran to another door. Opening it slowly, Tate eased her head outside and glanced around.

Ariana's heart thundered in her ears. Her breath left her in painful draws. Sweat dripped along her hairline and dampened her gown. She looked over her shoulder, expecting the roaring giant to pound his way through to them any second. His booming shouts and loud clatter as he fought to regain his vision echoed through the small cottage.

"What is this?" Tate asked, easing the door all of the way open and stepping outside.

Not wanting to be in the dwelling anymore, Ariana rushed outside with Tate and shoved the door closed behind her. As she clutched her weapon in one hand, she stared at the high wall of greenery standing before them. If they took three steps, they would hit the wall. There was a solid border to their right. They ran along the wall of greenery to where it opened up on the left. When they looked around the corner, they saw another hall-like stretch of two ivy-covered walls on either side.

Above them, the sky was lightening as the sun rose. Ariana tried to extend her wings so she could fly above the walls.

Tate glanced at her. "I can't extend my wings. Can you?"

"No. There must be some kind of enchantment in place prohibiting flight."

A loud boom sounded from just inside the cottage. Not having any other choice, they ran down the new hall of greenery. At the end of the long path, they reached a section where they could go either left or right.

"What in the world?" Tate said, glancing wildly from one side to the other. "This is some kind of maze!"

"A maze?" Ariana repeated. "Like a puzzle?"

"I guess. Crap." Tate put her right hand on the wall and started running. "I sure hope this maze isn't full of fun surprises."

"Why are you touching the wall?" Ariana asked as they reached the next bend.

"It's one possible way to solve a maze. My Aunt Olivia taught us about it. You hold your right or left hand against the wall and don't lift it. Eventually, you'll either reach the other end or you'll end up back at the beginning."

"Tate, this is not the time for jests."

"Unfortunately, I'm not joking. But we've got to try something. Sparky thinks he's close. As soon as they land, I'll draw on our connection and lead us out."

"Okay, okay."

They ran for a couple of minutes. The noise from the cottage grew fainter, which relieved Ariana.

She should have known better.

When they rounded the next bend, they came face-to-chest with several enormous clay figures. They looked like sculpted male Estilorians. The only thing that gave them away as something other than inanimate was their very lifelike red eyes, which glowed bright enough to light the area.

"Clay golems," Ariana gasped, backing up a step and holding up her pick. "They're incredibly strong. Our weapons won't have any effect on them."

She was suddenly grabbed from behind by a pair of clay arms and squeezed so hard she couldn't even scream. Her foot flew up as she left the ground, catching Tate's shoulder and sending her into the grip of one of the other golems.

"I don't think so," Tate said as her arm was wrenched behind her. Holding her palm out toward the four golems reaching for her, she produced a large ball of water. Then she used it to dissolve the fingers of the golem holding her.

Of course. Ariana used her power to produce buckets full of warm water. They started pouring of their own accord, dumping water onto the heads of all of the creatures. She slid from the grasp of the dissolving golem holding her, only to have another golem grip her ankle and drag her along the ground. She saw Tate slipping from one muddy grasp to the next as the water continued to damage her attackers.

Another hand grabbed Ariana by the hair, pulling her back to her feet. She gasped from the pain in her scalp and quickly generated more buckets. Within a few seconds, there were at least thirty buckets over their heads.

When she managed to escape the hold of the golems trying to stop her, she lurched closer to Tate. The Kynzesti was covered head to toe in mud. Figuring she looked much the same, she met Tate in the middle of the group and stood back-to-back with her. Tate continued to toss water as quick as she could produce it and Ariana filled the buckets again and again. The effort had her swaying with exhaustion.

A couple of minutes later, they stood in a large puddle of mud.

"Holy light," Tate said as they stepped through the mess to hurry on their way. "That was the creepiest thing I've ever seen. They didn't make a sound!"

Ariana couldn't argue.

"The stupid things have us looking like we bathed in mud," Tate added with a huff. "Sparky's never going to let me near him like this."

"I'll clean you—"

"You'll do no such thing," Tate interrupted as they edged around another corner. "You're seriously drained. You should take it easy. Well, outside of hauling your backside out of here."

Appreciating Tate's concern over her well-being, Ariana just nodded. When they reached the next bend, they both sniffed the air.

"Oh, no. Please tell me that's just me I'm smelling," Tate said in a whisper.

Bringing her hand to her nose, Ariana shook her head. "That is definitely not you."

"Damn."

That was when they heard the growling.

Metis pressed a cloth against her head as she stumbled out of her destroyed laboratory and hurried after Cephalus and the two females. Her head was a solid ball of pain, but she couldn't take the time to feel sorry for herself. She had to find the blasted females and save them from themselves.

What a mess this had turned into.

"Cephalus!" she shouted, hoping he was within earshot. "Do not harm the females!"

When she reached her cottage, she hurried through the open doorway. Seeing the swath of destruction, she came to a stop and gaped. Her voice was trapped in her throat. If it hadn't been, she would have screamed in fury.

"You damned brute of a giant!"

He was nowhere she could see. Wondering how long she had been dazed, she debated teleporting to somewhere within the maze in hopes of intercepting the females. But there was no way to predict where they'd end up. She had no choice but to do her best to follow their trail and pray that if Cephalus found them before she did that he was smart enough to keep them alive.

Her eyes on the ground, she headed right. Cephalus had practically obliterated the tracks of the females, but that only made it easier for her to follow them. When she reached the turn leading to the clay golems, she frowned. If the golems fulfilled their purpose, the females would be held captive until she arrived to give the command for their release. That meant they would be sitting targets for Cephalus when he reached them.

So she was once again surprised to the point of coming to a halt when she found nothing but a huge puddle of mud where her golems should be.

Issuing curses under her breath, she edged around the mud to avoid getting filthy and then started running. The obstacles facing the females now that they had defeated the golems were only more fearsome.

More deadly.

She heard thrashing ahead and eased to a more cautious pace. There were guardians of the maze with the ability to roam freely. Even she wasn't sure where they were at the moment.

"I am near you, females," growled Cephalus.

Relieved, Metis again hurried around the corner and spotted the giant. His club dragged on the ground, leaving a clear trail.

"And I scent something else, too," he continued as his feet thudded on the dirt path. "Something that will rend the flesh from your bones before I can accomplish it."

Her eyebrows lifting as she also caught the scent, Metis fought back a surge of anxiety. If the females had encountered Tethys' most precious creation, she was sure they were already dead.

Chapter 10

ALEXIUS HAD BEEN RIGHT. WITHIN FIVE MINUTES, CLARA KATE SAW THE outlines of the wings of her family and friends at the edge of the horizon.

"We should be to Tate and Ariana's location soon, if Zachariah's gauge is correct," he said.

"Good," she replied, giving him a smile. "Thanks."

He winked at her, an action that made her do a double-take. She'd never seen him wink at anyone. What did that signify?

Hoping she was giving the wink more import than he'd intended, she returned her gaze to the wings in the distance and focused on flying. She felt bad having such thoughts. Alexius was a wonderful being. But she was nowhere near a point where she could even consider entertaining the attentions of a male.

She was going to have a baby.

The thought kept spinning through her head, despite her efforts to try and push it back. She'd just witnessed her mother delivering her baby brother, Jack. Now she was going to deliver a baby of her own?

Shaking her head, she forced herself to think about one crisis at a time. Her gaze settled on the only set of silver wings among the group now less than one hundred yards ahead of them. Somehow, she had to tell Ini-herit that he was going to be a father. Just as importantly, she had to endure the fact that the news would be of absolutely no interest to him.

Oh, she was sure he'd be responsible in his own way. He'd stick with her through the pregnancy and possibly invite her to move in with him. He might even be willing to relocate to a spot within the Kynzesti homeland.

Because her father was likely to insist on it, he'd probably ask her to marry him. That would be the most he could offer her, considering an avowing required love.

She didn't want any of those things. She just wanted her Harry back.

He turned and caught her gaze when they approached. For the briefest moment, she thought she caught a glimpse of something cross his face. Relief? Concern? Some combination of each?

Surely not.

"Hey, C.K.," Tiege said, flying closer. "Are you okay?"

"Fine and dandy," she lied. "Quincy gave me a supplement and my energy is right back where it should be."

"Good."

"How are Tate and Ariana?" she asked.

"I don't know. Zachariah is focused on whatever they're doing. He hasn't spoken since they got away from the clay golems."

"Weird. I hope they're okay."

Her attention shifted as murmuring flowed from the front of the group and back to them. Moving to the outer edges of their flight pattern, she looked ahead to see what had captured everyone's interest.

At first, it looked like a very large, squared-off expanse of greenery. She would have mistaken it for a forest if the top of the green square wasn't so uniform in height. As they got closer, she realized that it wasn't just solid green. There was an unusual pattern etched into the square.

"Is that the maze?" she asked Tiege. "It sure looks like one."

"It has to be," he said. "I've never seen one like this, but Zachariah is leading us down there."

She nodded. Then a strange feeling washed over her...a sense that they shouldn't proceed.

"Stop," Uriel said, just as the word made its way to the tip of her tongue.

They all hovered and looked at the Waresti elder. He glanced at Ini-herit, the only other elder to have made the journey with the speed-enhancing potion.

"Do you sense that?"

Ini-herit nodded. "We cannot proceed in the air. We must land."

Clara Kate didn't hesitate to lower herself to the ground. She saw Zachariah wanting to argue, but he either knew better than to dispute the elders or he realized that agreeing was quicker. She guessed the latter, since he wasn't opposed to disagreeing with anyone.

"Draw your weapons," Zachariah said as he led them at a run to the exit of the maze. "I'm not sure what awaits us on this end, but judging by what Tate has conveyed, we'll need all the protection we can get."

Ariana hadn't ever heard of a creature like the one she and Tate faced after the golems. She guessed it was some kind of cursed, deformed canine. Saliva dripped from its long, black maw, sizzling when it hit the ground. Its eyes glowed like coals. Cracks in its scaly-looking black hide revealed more of the molten substance. Heat and stench radiated from it.

Standing almost as wide as the gap between the walls, it blocked their escape on either side. Leaves started smoking as it inhaled and its expanded ribcage came into contact with the shrubbery. So far, it was just sitting there growling at them, probably assessing the threat they posed. Neither of them dared to move. From somewhere not very far away, they heard the giant pounding his way closer.

"Well, this sucks," Tate said in a thin voice.

"Yeah," Ariana managed.

"What do you suppose the odds are that I could boost you up to the top of one of the walls?"

Giving a quick glance up, she answered, "Not good."

"Crap."

As the creature took a step closer, Ariana asked, "Do you think it eats meat?"

"Um…I hope not?"

"No, let's hope so."

She used her Lekwuesti abilities to generate a goat carcass. The moment it appeared in front of the creature, it leaped. Its powerful jaws opened. It sank its pointed teeth into the goat's flesh, ripping it and flinging pieces in their direction. Both females stepped back and emitted high-pitched squeals.

"Ohmygod," Tate said in one breath. "I didn't know you could create animals!"

"Not live ones."

"I don't care. Get me at least one more of those things so we can distract the beast and I'll be indebted to you for the rest of my existence."

"Not a problem."

Although it drained her energy to a dangerous level after the work with the golems, Ariana pulled forth her power and produced three more dead goats. The creature made a terrifying noise and pounced on them.

"Run," Tate said. "Jump over the thing if you have to. Go!"

Not pausing to think, Ariana grabbed her gown with her free hand and ran to the creature's left side. It had shifted enough to allow her to pass through. Even turning sideways and sucking in her breath, her back brushed against its side. Heat seared along her spine, but she couldn't worry about that. When she got past the beast and turned, she watched Tate spring up and over it, using its back as a launching pad.

"Don't stop!" Tate shouted.

Ariana ran. After a moment of blindly making turns, she vaguely realized that she was getting wet from behind. She dared to glance over her shoulder and saw Tate bringing forth water and throwing it at her.

"You were on fire," she explained as they stumbled to a stop.

"I was?" Ariana gasped. She tried to look over her shoulder to see what damage had been done.

"I saved your hair, but the gown is a loss." Tate reached out and patted her shoulder. "The good thing is that only the bottom was burned."

"Oh." Unable to stop herself from running her hand along her hair to make sure it was intact, Ariana said, "Consider us even, then."

Tate managed a small smile. "Sure."

Behind them, the sounds of vicious ravaging from the creature combined with loud shouting and pounding from the giant had them hurrying on.

"I think we've lost our bearings," Ariana said as they reached another bend.

"Yeah. But Sparky and the others are landing outside the maze. I can follow the pull to get us to them."

Ariana nodded and moved forward with Tate, her weapon at the ready. She wanted to feel relieved, but after what they'd already seen and endured in this maze, she couldn't help but worry about what else lay ahead.

"Does it feel colder to you?" Tate asked as they rounded another bend.

"Yes."

"Geez." Tate lifted her weapon. "We just can't catch a break."

They were prompted to advance as noise clamored behind them. Ariana even thought she heard Deimos' voice, something that made the hair stand up on the back of her neck. She fought the urge to whimper as she joined Tate in facing their next challenge.

As they made a left down the next turn of the maze, the cold grew more invasive. They could see their breath.

"What the—?" Tate began.

She stopped speaking and walking when they saw her. A tall, beautiful woman with black hair and blue lips. She was so pale that she almost appeared transparent. The cold oozed from her.

Ariana lifted her weapon with a hand that trembled from cold as well as fear, but Tate reached out and grabbed her.

"No. Drop your weapon."

Recent training had Ariana wanting to defend, but she obeyed. Both she and Tate tossed their weapons to the ground. When Tate lowered to her knees and bowed low in submission, Ariana did the same.

"Sparky's telling me that this is a spirit called a Yuki-onna," Tate whispered. "There isn't much known about them. They were originally thought to be evil, but he thinks she has empathy toward humans."

Trying not to focus on the fact that Tate was the only one of them with human blood, Ariana stayed in a bowed and submissive position. The spirit remained still, but didn't dissipate.

"Come on, Sparky," Tate murmured.

The temperature dropped at a sharp rate. Ariana started shaking in earnest as her body temperature lowered. Crystals formed on her hair and eyelashes. Her wet clothes froze to her skin. When she dared to glance up for a quick look, she realized the spirit hovered directly over them. Its vacant dark eyes shifted between her and Tate. It was then that Ariana noticed the bundle in her arms.

A child.

No wonder she had empathy for humans, Ariana thought. The spirit had surely been one if she could bear children. Why was she on this plane rather than the human one?

Sounds reached them from both directions, distracting her. Fierce growling, loud pounding and the drum of a male voice emerged from behind them. The noise of battle approached from the front. Ariana's limbs were numb. Not knowing what else to do, she remained bowed beside Tate and simply prayed.

"Any t-time n-now," Tate stuttered through chattering teeth. Her breath came out in white wisps.

Less than a minute later, Zachariah, Tiege and the others sprinted out from behind a wall. The spirit turned to face the new threat, causing the group to stagger to a halt. When Tate tried to move, probably wanting to protect her avowed and her brother, Ariana managed to touch her shoulder to stop her. She knew there was more human blood on the other side of the spirit than on theirs.

Ice formed on everyone's skin. They all lowered their weapons. Tiege, Sophia and Clara Kate rushed forth, likely having been coached to do so by Zachariah because they shared the only human blood in their group.

The spirit looked at Tiege, then Sophia. The cold continued building to a point that Ariana couldn't feel her body. Her vision blurred in and out of focus.

Then the ephemeral woman turned her attention to Clara Kate.

Hovering, it gazed intently at the eldest Kynzesti. Clara Kate didn't bow, but looked the spirit in the eyes. Its dark gaze moved from her face to her waist and remained focused there for several seconds.

Then, without any other warning, the Yuki-onna issued a tormented scream and vanished.

Chapter 11

WHEN THE YUKI-ONNA FOCUSED ITS ATTENTION ON CLARA KATE, Ini-herit moved up to just behind and beside her. He didn't know why. That strong sense of protectiveness continued to drive him and he didn't bother to resist it.

He watched the spirit move its gaze to Clara Kate's midsection. It didn't look away. Why did it find this area of Clara Kate's body of so much interest? Glancing again at the creature, he watched it clutch its phantom child closer to its chest before it shrieked and disappeared.

The piercing wail hadn't even faded before Zachariah surged forward and reached down for Tate. He lifted the Kynzesti as Tiege approached Ariana. Ini-herit realized both females were covered in ice, among other things. Despite the filth all over them, he could see their skin was almost blue. Not a good sign.

They all turned around and headed back the way they'd come, leaving Uriel and his Waresti to deal with Metis, her giant and any other creatures they might encounter. On the way into the maze, several of the Waresti split off from their group to address any threats that could possibly approach them from behind. Now, Ini-herit stepped over the remains of several dead creatures, none of which he could identify. Why its creators had felt the maze required such powerful guardians, he had no idea.

They emerged from the high hedges and hurried a brief distance away. Nothing unexpected followed them.

"Ariana lost consciousness," Tiege said.

Zachariah stopped and caught Ini-herit's gaze. "So did Tate."

Nodding, Ini-herit placed his hands on both Tate and Ariana. Closing his eyes, he focused on diagnosing and healing their injuries. They ranged in significance. Frostbite, extensive bruising, abraded skin, mild to moderate burns, reduced functioning of their cardiovascular and pulmonary systems, dehydration, exhaustion. One by one, he addressed each problem and applied his power until both females were once again in perfect condition.

Well, physically, anyway.

Opening his eyes and lowering his hands, he said, "They will be fine, but they require rest. I have induced a state of restorative sleep for them both. Sebastian should arrive soon with the others. He can assist Tate and Ariana with any cosmetic issues, such as their torn clothing and the dry clay. He can also provide them food. I believe it has been quite some time since they were fed."

"Thank you," Zachariah said at the same time Tiege issued, "Thanks, *archigos*."

He nodded. When he looked at Clara Kate, he realized she was staring at him. Not for the first time, he wished he could read what she conveyed through her deep blue-green eyes.

"We should get away from this place," Zachariah said. "Something could slip past Uriel and his warriors and we might not be prepared to meet it."

Ini-herit considered this. "I will stay here. I wish to remain available in case any of the Waresti need healing."

"I'll stay with you," Clara Kate offered. She drew her blessed butterfly swords. "Couldn't hurt to have extra hands around if needed."

Something about her offer had his brow wrinkling and an unusual sensation flooding his chest, but he merely said, "Of course."

"Very well," Zachariah said. "We'll move to the edge of whatever flight barrier is in place around this area and wait for the others to arrive."

Ini-herit watched as the Mercesti turned and started walking, followed closely by Tiege, Sophia and Quincy. When they were alone, he looked at Clara Kate. He realized her cheeks were pink.

"Are you all right?" he asked.

She blinked. "What?"

"You appear flushed."

Rolling her eyes, she looked at the exit of the maze and muttered, "No kidding."

"Do you require healing?"

"No, I don't require—" Cutting herself off, she shook her head and caught his gaze. "This is absolutely ridiculous. I'm flushed because of all of the inappropriate thoughts I have when I look at you, okay? Your tank top reveals quite a bit of skin and muscle. You're seriously cut and, well, *hot*. I was standing here wondering just where all of those silver markings extend on your form. So, there you go."

"Oh."

"Yeah."

After a moment, he said, "Your tank top reveals quite a bit of skin and muscle, as well." When she lifted an eyebrow, he added, "And it conforms to your breasts."

Her lips twitched. "You noticed that, did you?"

"Yes. As well as the fact that your combat pants sit low on your hips and display your rear end in a way that draws my eye."

Now, her entire face grew pink. "Seriously? You had those kinds of thoughts about me?"

"Yes."

"Do you have those kinds of thoughts about other females?"

Despite the mild tone to the question, he sensed its import. "No," he replied.

"Huh." She grinned. "What do you know?"

"What do I—?"

"No, no," she said with a shake of her head. "Look, I stuck with you right now so that I could discuss something with you. Something important."

"All right."

"Back on the human plane—" she began.

"Uriel is approaching," he interrupted.

Both of them turned to look at the maze's exit. The Waresti elder and a number of his warriors emerged. They looked grim, but none of them needed healing.

"We were unable to capture Metis or her giant," Uriel reported. "She teleported before we could get to her. She could be anywhere on the Estilorian plane by now."

"You imbecile," Metis snapped at Cephalus.

The two of them stood in the woods outside of the dwelling that once belonged to the former Mercesti leader, Kanika. It was the first place that sprang to Metis' mind when the Waresti bore down on them inside the maze. She had studied this landscape a great deal in recent weeks.

"I rescued you from the Isle of Gegenee so that you could join me in ascending to greatness," she continued as she paced. "This is how I am repaid?"

Having calmed down once he could no longer scent the two females who had injured him, the giant lifted his massive shoulders. "I cannot change the way things stand. I helped you assume a new form, did I not?"

"Just how is that supposed to help us get the scroll piece?"

As she issued the question, Metis lifted her arms, which were now those of a hulking Waresti male. She had managed to teleport the Waresti along with Cephalus out of the maze. Once they materialized in the woods, the giant injured the disoriented male enough that Metis was able to use his own sword to kill him. The decision to change forms had been panicked, prompted when she realized the Waresti intended to capture or harm her.

Now, she questioned whether it had been the right decision. Yes, most of the Waresti knew Deimos' form very well and would surely be looking for her everywhere on the plane. But at least in that form she could teleport if the need arose. As this Waresti, she could no longer draw on that ability. She really had to learn to make better decisions while under pressure if she was going to be an elder.

Oh, well. At least if she met up with Eirik in this new form, she would stand a good chance of defeating him. An innate knowledge of weaponry and battle strategy flowed through her now.

"Where have you teleported us?" Cephalus asked. "Perhaps we could return to the females and wrest them from their rescuers."

"We are miles from there." Frowning, she debated what to do. "I can no longer draw on Deimos' abilities, and you cannot fly. We will have to travel on foot."

"Where are we going to go?"

"I do not know."

Turning, she paced in the other direction. She found herself ducking beneath tree branches more often than she had in the past and realized this was the tallest form she'd ever assumed. It would take some getting used to.

"Well, you now resemble a Waresti," he said. "Unless things have changed since I freely roamed the plane, you can throw a rock and find Waresti scouts. Perhaps we could search for such a patrol and attempt to find out where the females will be taken. Then we can travel to them."

Weighing the idea, Metis nodded. "That has merit. Because we succeeded in parting the females from their guards this last time, I am certain it will be difficult to accomplish it again. However, even if we cannot find a way to lead them away from the others, we could follow them when they go in search of the next scroll piece. Surely once the piece has been found, we can develop a plan to acquire it."

"Very well," Cephalus said. "I am at your service. I will do what I can to balance things between us, sister."

"Oh, yes. You will."

Chapter 12

ZACHARIAH COULDN'T PUT TATE DOWN.

He considered it when everyone sat down to await the arrival of the others. She needed to rest, and she'd probably be more comfortable in a prone position. He even bent to lay her on the ground. But he couldn't.

His gaze settled on her face as he paced with her in his arms. Though her bruised cheeks were streaked with clay and blood, he focused on the markings around her eyes. The deep blue-green cinquefoils with red arrows running through them matched the marking on his right bicep. The markings, even more than their shared thoughts, brought home the reality of their avowing.

She was his.

His to protect. His to marvel over. His to love.

For the first few weeks after he paired with her for her protection, he waited for her to tell him that she didn't really love him. He waited for her to admit that her feelings were a result of their adventure together and hadn't lasted. He even devised a plan to leave with Nyx and once again remove himself from Estilorian society. Tate couldn't possibly love a Mercesti, he reasoned, nor did a being such as him deserve the heart of one as magnificent as her.

As though she knew his thoughts, however, Tate conveyed her love to him every chance she had. She whispered the words throughout the day, catching him off-guard more times than he could count—once right after he threw her to the ground during an intense training session. She made a point to touch him frequently, the purposeful physical contact doing more to unravel him than anything else could.

And she listened to him, even when what he had to say brought tears to her eyes. In the dark of night, as he lay on her bedroom floor in front of the door that no enemy would ever breech, he'd told her things he never thought he'd reveal to another being. Things that even *archigos* Malukali didn't know.

Not once did Tate judge him. All she did was share herself with him, fully and unequivocally. It was all he needed. So it didn't take much soul-searching for him to know why he didn't want to separate from her now.

Before she was kidnapped by Knorbis, Zachariah's role in her existence had been to see to her safety. He had failed. As a result, Tate had suffered.

He was still perplexed by the fact that she had agreed to avow with him, even if only in their dream state. He convinced himself shortly after her abduction that since he'd failed at the one thing he considered his strength, Tate's love would surely falter. Yet, despite his failure, she had joined herself to him in the most significant way an Estilorian could.

Now, he looked at her matted hair and blood-encrusted scalp, then down at her torn clothing, remembering the attack she'd endured. He'd pressed her so hard to learn to protect herself. For weeks, they had been up and training before everyone else, staying out later than everyone else. He made her change her wardrobe to be more efficient and offer less fabric for an opponent to grab. He made her wear muted colors so she blended more with the environment around her, presenting less of a target. He made her remove her usual hair adornments, knowing the colorful beads and feathers once led Eirik's followers right to her. She had done it all, despite his dictates being more stringent than any she'd ever faced.

But in the end, none of that had mattered. His training hadn't helped her against Knorbis' elixir and mental influence. It hadn't found her a way to refuse Eirik's blackmail demands. It hadn't aided her in facing her attackers on her own. No being would have stood a chance against so many Mercesti. It was a miracle they hadn't killed her.

She would never be in that position again.

He glanced up as movement caught his attention. The remaining elders had arrived. Before he took two steps toward the section of trees where everyone emerged, Sebastian broke apart from the others and approached him.

"Let's see what we're dealing with here," the elder said, his lavender eyes calm as he evaluated Tate's condition. He lifted one of the torn straps from her tank top and gave it a thoughtful study. "This is easily repaired—"

"I don't want it repaired," Zachariah interrupted. "You can burn the thing, as far as I'm concerned."

Sebastian caught his gaze. After a moment, he nodded. "I see. I'll take care of it."

He used his abilities to remove all of the filth from Tate's hair and skin. He changed her clothing with a wave of his hands and flash of lavender light. Then he waved his hand one more time, briefly making her hair glow. He nodded again, satisfied.

As the elder moved to attend to Ariana, Zachariah said, "Thank you, *archigos.*"

Then he stared at Tate's face, now free of anything to mar its perfection. His chest tightened as her faint lemony scent reached him.

Her eyelids fluttered. Seeing the movement, he carried her away from the others. She slowly blinked back to awareness, easing herself up so that she was supporting some of her weight.

"Sparky," she whispered, gazing at him as though she thought he might disappear.

Once they were alone, he stopped and lowered her to her feet. She left one hand on his shoulder and lowered the other to his waist. When part of her ensemble—a shimmery wrap—fell partway down her arm, she frowned in bewilderment and looked down. She studied her new flowing sundress comprised of vibrantly colored fabric. Poking her foot out, she spied a pair of impractical strappy sandals.

Then she reached up and touched her hair. Although she couldn't see it, she likely felt that it was back in its usual style, completely bedecked with sparkling beads and feathers. Sebastian had added a few red beads and a couple of small braids accented with glittery red ribbons.

"You should sleep some more," he said, tracing her lips with his thumb.

Both of her arms wrapped around his waist. *I don't want to sleep*, she thought.

Then you should eat. They starved—

"Food can wait," she interrupted. "You're what I need right now, Sparky."

He knew exactly what she meant. He wanted to bask in her, in the light she brought to his dark existence. He wanted to take her away from there and keep her from the evil threatening to steal that light.

She held his gaze for a long moment. Then she pulled him closer and kissed him.

It was as though she offered a delectable feast to a starving being. He couldn't resist the siren-like allure of her parted lips. Backing her against the trunk of a nearby tree, he devoured her, growling low in his throat as her tongue met his.

The kiss quickly turned possessive. Ravenous.

Their hands roamed, staking claim and igniting heat. The thoughts flowing between them escalated the feelings until Zachariah knew he was crossing into dangerous territory.

Somehow, he managed to tear himself away from her tantalizing mouth. He crushed her against him as they both fought for breath.

When they had calmed themselves, Tate reached up and ran a hand through his hair. Smiling, she said, "Thanks for asking *archigos* Sebastian to clean me up. Did you pick my outfit?"

"Don't be ridiculous."

"Uh-huh. And you gave him the go-head on the beads and feathers?"

"He couldn't be swayed."

Grinning, she said, "Liar."

She kissed him again. Although he knew he should resist, he indulged himself. But he didn't allow things to get too carried away this time. He pulled away from her after a moment.

Brushing a stray curl out of her eyes, he said, "I have a promise to keep."

She tilted her head in consideration. Then her eyes widened. "You really want to exchange vows with me in person?"

"That's what I promised when you agreed to avow with me in our dreams," he said. Then he hesitated. "Unless you've changed your mind."

"Of course I haven't changed my mind. I love you, Sparky. We can get the others and—"

"My vow is to you, Beautiful. Not everyone else."

She considered this, studying him in silence. Eventually, she smiled and said, "All right."

He was eternally grateful that she understood him. Many other females would have insisted on having an audience for this intimate, important moment. He held her gaze to convey his appreciation. Then he spoke the vow he had issued once before.

"I, Zachariah, wish to pledge myself to you, Tate, in every possible way. You are my world now, as well as my heart. Though it may take all eternity, I will strive to prove myself worthy of your love. I offer you this ring as a symbol of my love and my unbreakable commitment to you."

He lifted Tate's hand and kissed the ring she already wore. Her eyes filled with tears. Though her voice was strained with emotion, she spoke her vow.

"I, Tate, love you, Zachariah, more than anything in the world, and want to spend the rest of my existence with you. I offer you this ring as a symbol of my love and my unbreakable commitment to you."

She kissed his ring, then they linked their left hands and kissed to seal the vow. Once again, his pairing marking flared with pain, signifying the power of the exchange and their connection. Tate gasped against his mouth, telling him she experienced the same thing. Their vows were now unequivocally sealed.

She was—to borrow the words she spoke to him after their first pairing—stuck with him.

Once Sebastian and the others arrived, Clara Kate joined her family within the forest located a couple of minutes from the maze. Despite its terrifying properties, the maze fascinated her. How had it been created? And why? The power required to generate the anti-flight barrier had to be significant. Also, where had all of the creatures inhabiting the maze come from?

The Yuki-onna had particularly troubled her. Seeing the child in the pale female's arms left Clara Kate frozen and speechless. When the spirit's eyes moved to her waist, Clara Kate somehow knew it sensed her pregnancy. The look on its face had her fearing the spirit would attack her, trying to harm the baby.

Fierce maternal protectiveness rushed through her then. She may have only known about the pregnancy for a very short time, but she wasn't going to let anything happen to her unborn child.

That was when the spirit screamed and departed. Somehow, Clara Kate understood that the unknown woman hadn't saved her own child, causing her devastated spirit to linger.

Hopefully that mother was at peace now, Clara Kate thought as she sat propped up against a tree. She rubbed a hand over her own flat belly and thought about what lie ahead for her. What would it be like to feel a new life growing inside her? Would she have a son or a daughter? Would he or she look like her or Ini-herit?

Glancing up, she realized the male in question watched her from where he sat a few feet away. He tilted his head, his eyes moving to her waist. When she realized it, her hand stilled.

What would he say when she told him? She thought she'd been prepared to find out when she was about to confess outside of the maze. Now, she hesitated. Could she really handle this?

Her attention shifted to the edge of the forest where Sophia and Quincy emerged. The two had been gone for a while. Judging by her cousin's rosy cheeks and secretive smile, they'd been engaged in a romantic interlude. Clara Kate couldn't blame them, but she could admit to envying them. Quincy treated Sophia like a goddess, and despite what they currently faced, her cousin hadn't ever seemed so light of spirit.

A small commotion had Clara Kate looking around. She realized that the remainder of their group had arrived. She spotted Derian first. The large Mercesti male was hard to miss. He wore only a kilt and knee-high boots, and half of his face and upper body were covered in colorful tattoos. His dark hair was pulled back, reminding her of how Ini-herit often wore his hair on the human plane.

Derian's mate, Melanthe, stood by his side. The former Lekwuesti currently wore her golden-brown hair in a braid secured tightly to her head. Her gown flattered her, even if it was partially covered by leather armor. Much like Derian wore his lochaber axe strapped to his back, she wore a bo attached to a special holster. The pair had been at the front of the line in their recent battle, and their efforts—as well as those of their followers—had been noted by everyone involved.

As the new arrivals entered the forest, Clara Kate got to her feet. She saw Sebastian approach Tiege, who held Ariana. As the elder's power glowed, Clara Kate took the opportunity to move a little deeper into the forest for a couple minutes of privacy.

Once she saw to her personal needs, she took a moment in the rare solitude to center herself. She didn't have just herself to think about anymore, a thought that terrified her. She knew allowing herself time to rest was important.

Just as she started back to camp, she caught a glimpse of color through the trees. She paused out of curiosity and spotted Tate and Zachariah. She realized that Tate was awake and now clean and clothed in an outfit unlike anything she'd worn in weeks. Her hair was done in its usual style, as well. When she heard Tate asking Zachariah if he'd selected the wardrobe items, she inferred from her cousin's response that the Mercesti had.

The couple kissed, making Clara Kate turn her gaze, intending to give them privacy. But her heart ached for this kind of interaction. She found herself unable to walk away.

Thus, she witnessed their avowing. Her eyes filled over Zachariah's heartfelt vow. She wouldn't have dreamed him capable of such emotion. It made her so happy for Tate.

After the vows were exchanged, Clara Kate started to head back to the others. She noticed Ini-herit watching her from between two trees. Embarrassed over having been caught spying, she hurried closer to him and out of earshot of Tate and Zachariah.

"Do you need something?" she asked.

"I thought you might wish to continue our earlier conversation."

Thinking about the shared love she had just witnessed between Sophia and Quincy and then Tate and Zachariah, she couldn't find it in her to share her news with him. She knew how important it was. But her heart wasn't ready.

"Not right now. But soon," she said, and really hoped she wasn't lying to them both.

From a distance, Eirik watched the team of Estilorians that he, Friedrich and the other chosen Mercesti followed from the library. They entered a thick forest located within aerial sight of the maze outside of Metis' lair. Unable to see through the thick trees to be sure, he assumed the two females had been rescued.

"You said the Kynzesti was incapacitated," Friedrich said. "She would surely not be able to make it through the maze in the condition you described."

Although fury had his vision going in and out of focus, Eirik replied, "Nothing would surprise me at this point. Perhaps the Kynzesti's blood ties to Gabriel have given her exceptional abilities. She must be able to harness the strength and intelligence of the elders to have gotten this far without breaking."

"So you believe that she and the Lekwuesti managed to escape the confines of their cage and then avert each of the deadly creatures you described within the maze?"

"Whether or not I believe it, that certainly appears true," Eirik retorted. "No one is trying to enter the maze, which tells me that they have found the beings they expected to emerge from it."

Nodding, Friedrich said, "Very well. So we believe they have the two females who can lead us to the final piece of the artifact. How do we get them back?"

"We do not need the troublesome females," Eirik said after a moment. "We can follow this group to the artifact and wrest it from them after they go through the effort of recovering it. Then we will have all of the pieces we need."

"Did you not say that we will have to figure out how to imbue the artifact once we have all of the pieces?"

"We will, but that is not a concern. I am confident we will know what to do once we have it complete. With us working together, no one will be able to stop us."

PART II:

DISTURB

Disturb [dih-**sturb**]: To interrupt the quiet, rest, peace or order of; to interfere with or hinder.

Chapter 13

BECAUSE URIEL WAS BUSY STRATEGIZING AND ISSUING ORDERS SHORTLY after the rescue of Tate and Ariana, Ini-herit conveyed the situation to Gabriel using their mental connection as elders. He didn't want his friend worrying more than necessary.

I'm so glad everyone's okay, Gabriel thought once he had been caught up on everything. *It's been so hard, not being able to help. The strain has really taken a toll on all of us.*

Ini-herit sensed Gabriel's relief. Amber, Olivia and Skye had all given birth within the last week. For the safety of their newborns, both parents needed to stay within close contact of the babies for at least a month, preferably longer. For this reason, none of them had been able to join the search for the Elder Scroll.

We've all talked about it, Gabriel continued, *and we think it would be best for our kids—well, those with you—to travel to Central right away to pair with Lekwuesti.*

But the third scroll piece—

Isn't going anywhere, Gabriel interrupted. *Twice now, Tate has been separated from you and the others without the benefit of a paired Lekwuesti. This last time, Sophia was, too. We want our kids to have someone they can connect to for food, water and other things they need to survive, like all full Estilorians.*

Ini-herit considered this. Tate and Ariana were still targets, now by two villains. Recent events proved that Eirik and Metis would do anything possible to get the third scroll piece, and they intended to use Tate and Ariana to do it. Neither the Mercesti male nor the form-assuming female would hesitate to use one of the other Kynzesti to lure the two females back into their clutches, which put them all at risk.

Including Clara Kate.

Very well, he thought. *I will communicate with the others about this. We will head to Central as soon as possible.*

Thanks. How is Clara Kate?

The question made him wonder if he had conveyed his thought about her, but supposed it didn't matter. Thinking back to his conversation with Gabriel's daughter as they stood outside the maze, Ini-herit almost mentioned that she wanted to talk to him about their time on the human plane. Perhaps his friend had some insights into his daughter's mindset.

Then he thought better of it. There had to be a reason that Clara Kate was acting in such an unusual manner. Perhaps she didn't want her parents involved.

She seems all right, he thought at last. *She is unharmed and finally getting some rest.*

Good. It's hard having her away. Let her know we love her, okay?

Although he would impart the words without understanding their meaning, Ini-herit gave a mental nod of agreement. Once he disconnected from Gabriel, he went in search of Clara Kate, figuring he could pass along Gabriel's message. He found her hiding behind a tree, watching Tate and Zachariah.

The look on her face had him stopping rather than approaching her. While he might not have ever experienced it himself, he recognized the longing he saw in her expression as she witnessed her cousin and the Mercesti interact.

Was Clara Kate seeking from him the level of emotional commitment that existed between Tate and Zachariah? Although he couldn't hear the words they spoke, he certainly recognized the pairing of hands, pressing of lips against lips and the flash of light that resulted from an avowing. The act required powerful, unconditional love.

He knew he couldn't fulfill Clara Kate's obvious wish. As he followed her back to camp after she refused to tell him what was on her mind, he decided that it was in both of their best interests that she wasn't ready to ask him for something he couldn't possibly give her.

* * *

Tate wanted to spend some time with Tiege when she returned to the camp. Zachariah made sure she was seated and had something to eat before he moved a few feet away from the twins. He knew how important the sibling relationship was to Tate. Since he witnessed Ariana walking in the other direction, he imagined she knew it, too.

Sebastian prepared food for those who wanted to eat, so Zachariah took a handful of biscuits flavored with honey. They would give him energy without being too filling. Beside him, Ini-herit considered the food offerings and took a plum. They exchanged brief nods before they turned and approached Uriel, who stood with Harold, Alexius, Knorbis and Malukali.

"We should leave the area now that everyone has regained consciousness," Uriel said as Zachariah stopped walking and took a bite of a biscuit. "We can discuss our next steps in a more secure area. Metis could teleport back here whenever she wants and bring any number of other beings with her."

Derian and Clara Kate joined them. Zachariah belatedly realized that he hadn't noticed the return of the other Mercesti. He caught Derian's gaze and returned the other male's chin-lift of greeting.

Glancing beside him, he realized that Ini-herit was focused on Clara Kate where she stood on the opposite side of the small circle. Zachariah had noticed that Tate's cousin kept her distance from the Corgloresti elder. Beside her, Alexius caught her gaze and smiled. Seeing the look, Zachariah again looked at Ini-herit. Although the elder's expression didn't change, he did stop chewing the bite of plum in his mouth when he saw the exchange.

Interesting.

"Have all of your warriors checked in with you?" Malukali asked Uriel.

Frowning, he replied, "No. Caesar is missing. I have spread the word and would appreciate each of you doing the same. If anyone sees him, they had better approach him with caution."

There were nods around the circle.

"If Metis assumes Caesar's form, will she still retain the ability to teleport?" Derian asked.

"We can't be sure," Knorbis answered.

Looking over at Tate where she sat sharing a fruit tart with Tiege, Zachariah said, "It's best not to chance it. We should move somewhere Metis won't know so she can't visualize it."

"I intend to spearhead the search for Eirik," Harold said. "Ariana revealed that Metis transported him somewhere around the library, but he has somehow eluded us. So far, none of his followers that we have found knows where he is."

Derian looked at Zachariah. "We can aid the Waresti in the search, sir. There may be some among our allies on the mainland who have seen Eirik. Verrell, Oria and Alys are already working on recruiting some of them to our cause."

Derian, a former Gloresti, still looked to Zachariah as a commander. Zachariah had told him that the formal term of address was no longer appropriate since he now bore no rank, but the tattooed male hadn't stopped using it. After several attempts to dissuade him, Zachariah just gave up and accepted it.

"Very well," Zachariah said. "They will be more likely to speak with you, anyway." His gaze moved from Derian to Harold. "Should you find Eirik—"

"He's all yours," Harold assured him.

Nodding, he said, "Then let's move out."

A few minutes later, Clara Kate adjusted her cloak and extended her wings. Not too far from her, she heard Tate arguing with Zachariah, who held a flight harness.

"I'm perfectly capable of flying, Sparky. You don't have to carry me."

"Stop arguing. You can hear my thoughts now. You know you won't win this one."

Tate sighed. Then she grinned, flashing a dimple in her left cheek. "You know I'll only distract you with my thoughts while you're holding me, right?"

He shook his head as he secured her in the harness. "I'll endure it somehow."

That made Tate laugh. Clara Kate smiled over the exchange as Zachariah took flight with Tate securely in his arms. Her smile faded when Quincy approached. He held some items wrapped in a cloth.

After he looked around to make sure they stood alone, he said, "Take this food and store it in your pockets. You said you haven't felt hungry every day like a typical expectant mother, but your appetite might be suppressed. You've been a little, um…"

"Depressed. I get it." Clara Kate took the food, telling herself not to blame Quincy. It certainly wasn't his fault she was in this position. "Thanks, Quincy."

"Of course. I'd like you to drink this supplement, too," he said, handing her a small vial. "You normally only need it once daily, but you were particularly exhausted and dehydrated earlier. I'm concerned about anemia—"

Seeing a few of the Waresti glancing at them because everyone else had taken flight, Clara Kate took the vial, downed its contents and handed it back.

"Thanks again," she said, hoping she didn't sound too rude. "Are we good?"

"Sure. You'll let me know if you need anything?"

Nodding, she offered him a small smile. "We're all good, Quincy." Then she took flight, hurrying to catch up with the others as Quincy joined Sophia and they followed.

They didn't fly more than twenty minutes before finding a good location to camp for the night. The small island sat in a huge lake, giving scouts easy visibility of anyone approaching. Although there were a number of trees, most of the flat ground was covered in grass or sand, making a great foundation for the tents Sebastian created.

As the sun lowered in the sky, Clara Kate sat on one of the chairs Sebastian placed around a campfire. She fought the impulse to get up and move when Ini-herit sat beside her. Although she felt his gaze on her, she remained focused on the flames.

"What? I'm still hungry," Tate said from across the way. She held a stick covered in marshmallows over the fire as Zachariah stood beside her with his arms crossed.

"You're going to catch yourself on fire, you crazed female," Zachariah grumbled, taking the stick from her. "Sit down and rest."

"Okay, okay." She smoothed her dress and took a seat. "I like them dark, but not too—"

"I know how you like them, Beautiful."

Sophia wiggled her eyebrows from beside Tate and nudged her cousin. "He *is* still talking about the marshmallows, right?"

Tate giggled and Clara Kate snorted out a laugh. Quincy rolled his eyes from Sophia's other side as Tiege approached the fire with Ariana. Tate's brother lifted an eyebrow over the sight of Zachariah roasting marshmallows.

"Are you taking requests, bro?" he deadpanned as they took their seats.

"Don't press your luck," the Mercesti responded with a glower.

The other elders joined them. Knorbis and Malukali sat on Clara Kate's other side. She'd noticed that the couple gave Zachariah a wide berth. After Knorbis lured Tate and Ariana away in an attempt to save his wife, Zachariah had wanted to kill the elder. In the end, when Zachariah saw how badly Malukali had been tortured to gain Knorbis' compliance, he had acknowledged a level of understanding about the abduction…but he hadn't forgiven it.

"Have you mentioned Gabriel's request to everyone yet?" Malukali asked. She leaned forward to look at Ini-herit before asking the question.

Curious, Clara Kate also turned to look at him. His level silver gaze moved briefly to her, making her heart twist painfully. Then he looked back at the Orculesti elder and said, "No. They only just sat down."

"What does *archigos* Gabriel want?" Zachariah asked as he sat beside Tate and handed her one of the marshmallows. She mashed it between two graham crackers and a layer of chocolate.

"He has asked that we all travel to Central immediately so that the Kynzesti can pair with Lekwuesti," Ini-herit said.

Clara Kate's eyes widened over the eruption of sound after that statement. It seemed nearly everyone had something to say in response to her father's surprising request. Lifting her fingers to her lips, she let out a shrill whistle. Everyone quieted.

"Dad wouldn't want what happened to Tate and Sophia to happen to any of us," she said, understanding his rationale. "I think he's right. It'll only take a day or two."

"I can escort Ariana to acquire the last scroll piece while you're away," Uriel said as he walked up and stood near Ini-herit.

Ariana's face paled at the suggestion. Clara Kate figured she was remembering that she hadn't fared too well with a Waresti escort the last time they attempted to acquire a scroll piece. But the Lekwuesti didn't argue.

"If I'm going to Central, I want Ariana to come, too," Tiege said. "We'll all go after the scroll piece once we're done with the pairings."

Uriel exchanged glances with Ini-herit, Malukali and Knorbis. Sensing an argument brewing, Clara Kate said, "Our grandfather indicated that our fates are tied to the scroll. I think Tiege's right to want to keep everyone together."

There were nods around the fire. Zachariah, however, frowned. Clara Kate belatedly considered the protections in place around the main base that prohibited Mercesti entrance.

"Aunt Skye's powers aren't regenerated enough yet to teleport Zachariah to Central," she pointed out.

"I'll get him there," Tate said as she licked chocolate from her thumb. "Our connection allowed him to get into our homeland, and those protections are just as strong—if not stronger—than the ones around Central."

"That sounds good," Clara Kate agreed.

Tate tilted her head as she studied Zachariah. His frown hadn't eased. Leaning toward him, she kissed his cheek. "It'll be fine, Sparky. You'll see."

As everyone exchanged glances, Clara Kate could only hope her cousin was right.

Chapter 14

METIS HAD ONLY BEEN FREE TO ROAM THE MAINLAND FOR A SHORT TIME now. For most of her millennia of existence, she had lived under the care of her creator inside the laboratory and attached cottage. She hadn't known much at all about the world outside of the maze, which she hadn't been allowed to enter because the creatures inside it were too dangerous. If she hadn't come across some of Tethys' personal writings, in point of fact, Metis might still be living in ignorance.

Thank the darkness she had decided to disregard her creator's instructions to respect her privacy. On that fateful day, Metis discovered that the world was much, much larger and more interesting than she had been led to believe. It wasn't limited to just the space she shared with her creator and the small Gegenee Island she once visited when Tethys wanted to show off another of her "experiments."

There were far more beings on this plane than Metis had been told, as well. There were even many different classes, some of which contained human blood.

Metis now thought that her creator's stability began to diminish with the arrival of the daughters of Saraqael to the Estilorian plane. After all, Tethys once lost the heart of a human male she loved because she couldn't bear children. Then along came the progeny of a random Corgloresti and they started having enough babies to constitute an entire class. That must have been more than Tethys could handle.

Because Tethys had grown distracted and careless, she left her writing out one day when she went into the maze to feed the hellhound. Upon reading it, Metis also learned that Tethys didn't want to introduce her to the other

Estilorians. She considered Metis a potentially dangerous mistake, but one she couldn't bring herself to destroy.

Well, Metis had no compunction about destroying her creator.

That was when she discovered she could assume the forms of those she killed. When she realized she had changed into Tethys, she puzzled over it for several days. She finally concluded that because she had been created in an attempt to produce life, she had somehow inherited the ability to assume the lives of other Estilorians. The power of her ability made itself known when she made it safely through the maze because the creatures thought she was Tethys.

It was a talent she was still trying to master. Because she didn't assume the memories of her victims, she had trouble making others believe that she was the being whose form she assumed. When she killed Kanika, she'd had to fake memory loss to make it believable.

As she thrashed through the woods in the much larger form of the Waresti male with Cephalus right beside her, she tried to put herself into her victim's mindset. His class was dedicated to offense. He wouldn't likely be alone like she was. Most of the Waresti who had inhabited Kanika's home with her had worked in groups or pairs. When they did separate, it was for brief periods of time or unusual circumstances.

Glancing at Cephalus, she realized the giant presented the "unusual" reason she might need to explain her solitary situation. Now she just needed someone to explain it to.

She still wasn't sure what she would do when she came upon other Estilorians. Mercesti couldn't be trusted. Many of them followed Eirik and might know to look for her. Others might be in league with the male paired with the Kynzesti female. Although she knew little about Zachariah aside from what she heard Eirik spout about him, she knew enough to suspect he would hunt her down for having anything to do with the abduction of his avowed.

No, she had to find a way to enmesh herself into the world of non-Mercesti Estilorians if she wanted any chance of getting near the two females who could lead her to the final scroll piece. That might mean abducting someone who could teach her more about the other classes. It would also mean trying to grow more familiar with this hulking male form.

"I smell others," Cephalus said a couple of hours into their hike.

"Be still and silent, then," Metis hissed, slowing her own pace. "If you find a single being, only detain him."

She knew she moved too much like a female, but couldn't figure out how to adjust her body language to more naturally reflect a male's. Frowning, she eased through the forest ahead of Cephalus, keeping an eye out for patrolling Waresti. She briefly debated whether to remove her sword from its sheath and carry it, but she wasn't trained. Despite the innate knowledge of weaponry she absorbed when she assumed the Waresti form, she knew she might end up hurting herself before she harmed anyone else.

About a hundred yards ahead, she caught sight of some Waresti. Judging by the way they walked and shifted their gazes, they were patrolling a very small area. She wondered if it might be a Corgloresti transition point.

Tethys had documented the traditional process of Estilorian reproduction, which Metis tried to reproduce herself when creating Deimos. Metis knew that Corgloresti transitioned to the human plane from secret, protected locations on the Estilorian plane. The Waresti kept the area clear of possible predators.

Easing away from the sight of the patrols, Metis turned back in the direction of Cephalus. How could she possibly convince these soldiers that she was one of them? She didn't know their commanders well enough to say who ordered her to aid them. Could they possibly already know she had killed the Waresti whose form she now wore? What if they attempted to take her prisoner to confirm her identity?

The complexities of what she was trying to achieve had her head hurting. When she approached the place where she left Cephalus, her frustration made her want to scream. She didn't see the giant anywhere.

"Over here," he rumbled from deeper in the forest.

Hurrying forward, she passed between two trees and came to a halt. Cephalus stood above two prone forms. One was that of a female. The second was a Waresti male.

"They arrived shortly after you departed," Cephalus explained. "The female sought privacy and the male was keeping guard."

Metis noticed the Waresti had very few orange markings, which meant he was relatively young. She imagined Cephalus might not have been able to best a more seasoned warrior even with his enchanted, mesmerizing hair. Like other beings in his class, the Waresti male was quite large and muscular.

Bending down, Metis opened one of the female's eyes. She realized the second being was an Orculesti.

"A mind reader," she murmured.

Remaining in a squat, Metis considered what to do. It would be safer to assume a new form, just in case the Waresti were aware of what she had done in the maze. The question was, which form should she assume?

As a Waresti, she could roam freely across the plane without much question. She would be in a form strong enough to subdue or defeat Eirik when they inevitably met again. It would take only a bit more training and education to confidently blend in with the rest of the Estilorians, which meant she could once again gain access to the Kynzesti and Lekwuesti and the final scroll piece.

The Orculesti, on the other hand, had the ability to read thoughts. Some even had the ability to influence the minds of others. Eirik had a strong mind, which meant it was unlikely an ordinary Orculesti would have much influence on him. If he was skilled in masking his thoughts, it would also be hard to read him.

Any mind reading ability, however, would surely be more helpful than mere strength, Metis reasoned. Plus, she had recently realized that she much preferred forms in her base gender. The question was, how old and powerful was the Orculesti in front of her?

When the female made a noise indicating that she was regaining consciousness, Metis decided she didn't have much choice. Although she risked her own existence if this Estilorian was too powerful for her to assume her form, time had grown short. Pulling her sword from its sheath, she ended the Orculesti's life. Then she used her power to absorb the female's essence.

It was a mighty struggle, telling her that the female was powerful. Pain from the initial transformation flashed through her. Used to it by now, she let it pass. After she worked through that, however, a void of darkness threatened her. She knew she was having difficulty absorbing the Orculesti's abilities.

The sounds of thousands of voices clamored in her head, causing her to cry out. A red haze filled her mind. She battled against it, using the same strong will that had gotten her this far.

Eventually, she centered herself enough to focus on her breathing and slowly brought herself back to awareness. When she did, she spotted

Cephalus on the ground. The giant was dead, a fact that confused her.

That was when she realized she was surrounded by Waresti. And all of them were armed.

Chapter 15

"WHY IS IT YOU WISH TO AID US?" EIRIK ASKED THE MERCESTI STANDING in front of him and Friedrich.

"Derian is not a leader," the being replied. "When he stood against Grolkinei, I thought he intended to seek a position of power among the Mercesti himself—that his supposed support of Kanika was a ruse. I have since learned that he wishes to avoid the so-called 'burden' of leadership."

Friedrich asked, "Why do you not take over as leader of the Marked Ones, then?"

Sniffing, the being replied, "The fact that he is a converted Gloresti seems to cause the others to respect him more than others."

"Then Zachariah's reappearance must not thrill you," Eirik observed, watching the expression of Derian's follower.

"If I thought he would be any stronger a leader than Derian, I might not have minded," the being admitted. "But he is obsessed with the Kynzesti female, much like Derian focuses so much on Melanthe."

"One would think their lingering Gloresti traits would make them effective leaders," Friedrich observed. He shrugged when Eirik looked at him. "It seems logical."

"That depends upon to whom they apply their Gloresti loyalty, does it not?" the being rejoined. "So far, nothing has been done to unite the Mercesti class and bring us back as equals with the other classes. We remain loathed and feared…outcasts."

"Is that the limit of your ambition?" Eirik asked. "Equality?"

The other being frowned. "What else is there?"

"Superiority."

"Bah. Grolkinei spouted such propaganda for centuries. He sought a Mercesti class that ruled over both planes. You know how far that got him."

Eirik's temper reared, but he held it in check. "Have you learned what it is we seek?"

"No," the being responded with a frown. "The shapeshifting Kynzesti was vague when discussing it, and I have learned nothing new since rescuing the other Kynzesti and Lekwuesti. The elders are keeping nearly everyone in the dark."

Nodding, Eirik asked, "What if I told you that we have a way to fulfill your wish?"

"Equality?"

"To begin, certainly."

The being gave him a skeptical look. "You have my interest. What is it you seek?"

"The last piece of an artifact that will allow us to institute a class structure equal to the others…an elder included."

"But—that is impossible."

"Not only is it possible, but well within reach," Eirik said. "The Kynzesti and Lekwuesti you just rescued have the abilities to find it, which is why I was holding them prisoner. They refused to help me of their own volition, so I had to resort to dramatic action."

He caught Friedrich's arched eyebrow out of the corner of his eye, but ignored it.

"What do you need me to do?"

"Do you know where the two females are right now?"

"They are on their way to the main base. The elders want to pair them with Lekwuesti as soon as possible."

Eirik considered this. "They will surely resume the hunt for the final piece of the artifact once the Lekwuesti pairings are done. I need you to keep us informed so that we can acquire it."

"We also need you to do what you can to keep the Waresti and Mercesti searching for us off our trail," Friedrich added.

"And what will I get out of this?"

"A class you can respect, for one," Eirik said. "I will also consider you for a role of great responsibility once our new class structure is in place, if you prove worthy."

The being was silent for a long moment, moving a considering gaze between them. "Very well. I can accept that."

Eirik's posture eased. "Perfect. So glad we can count on you."

And if it proved he couldn't, the traitor's death at the end of his krises was always an option.

Clara Kate hovered with the others over a grouping of yellow platforms floating in the ocean water. The platforms were the only way to get to Central, which floated far above the ocean in an area humans referred to as the Bermuda Triangle. Like everyone else, she turned her gaze to Zachariah, who currently carried Tate.

"I see them," he said in answer to everyone's unspoken question. "Now we have to see if I can actually land on them."

"Here goes nothing," Tate said. Her smile told Clara Kate that she wasn't concerned.

It turned out her cousin was right. Zachariah flew to one of the platforms and stood on it without issue. Although he released Tate from the flight harness, she continued to hold onto him.

"Better safe than sorry," she said. "I've heard that physical contact helps when trying to extend your abilities to another being."

Zachariah's gaze moved sharply to Tiege, who landed next to them on the platform along with Ariana. Tate's twin raised his eyebrows and lifted his hands in a show of innocence. "Don't look at me."

Shaking his head, Zachariah sat on the platform, pulling Tate down onto his lap. Clara Kate imagined he didn't really mind the close contact. She settled onto a second platform with Sophia and Quincy, and winced when she saw Ini-herit flying closer. Then Alexius swooped up and landed on the platform before Ini-herit reached them.

Uncertain whether or not to be relieved, she gave Alexius a smile in greeting and watched Ini-herit as he gazed at the Waresti. Was that annoyance she saw on his face? He turned and flew to a platform with Malukali, Knorbis and Sebastian before she could tell.

Then the platform lifted from the water. Not expecting the sudden acceleration, she gasped and grabbed Alexius, who reached out to steady her.

"Geez," she said, embarrassed over her reaction. "Seat belts might be a good idea."

"I've said that for years," Quincy agreed with a grin.

Sophia frowned, looking down at the water. "The platform with Zachariah hasn't taken off yet."

They all looked over the edge. Clara Kate's concern grew as the group on the water got smaller and smaller.

"Kiss Tate!" Quincy called down.

Clara Kate raised an eyebrow over the suggestion, but she knew that of all of them, Quincy had the most insight into the unexplainable. His unsurpassed faith was what allowed him to do things like deliver the Kynzesti. The line on the Elder Scroll that supposedly pertained to him—*One most pure in blood and soul*—suited him perfectly.

Zachariah must have agreed, as he did what the Corgloresti suggested. Within seconds, the platform lifted into the air.

"Are they going to have to make out the entire trip to Central?" Sophia asked.

The idea made Clara Kate laugh. "I'll bet Tiege would *love* that."

"I'm sure Zachariah would love it more," Alexius added, making Clara Kate laugh harder. The Waresti didn't really understand sarcasm.

She didn't realize that he had kept his arm over her shoulders until she glanced over and saw Ini-herit staring in their direction. His eyes were focused on her and Alexius. It wasn't the first time she had seen this kind of reaction from him when other males touched her, she realized. Even though she couldn't read his expression, something about the intensity of his silver gaze told her that he didn't like it.

Was it possible he was beginning to experience emotion?

"Did *archigos* Ini-herit mention that it's almost time for the annual masquerade ball at Central?" Alexius asked.

Blinking over the change in subject, Clara Kate said, "Masquerade? No."

"It is?" Sophia asked. "Is that the ball my mom told us about? The one that started after Grolkinei was defeated?"

"Yes," Quincy said. "There was an effort made after the big battle to help the classes blend. As a way to celebrate and to try to involve the Mercesti, the first ball was held on the mainland. Kanika attended, but few other Mercesti did. The daughters weren't willing to give up on the idea, though. It's been held every year around this time. They made it a masquerade to help blur class distinctions and encourage everyone to mingle more."

"But now it's at Central," Clara Kate said. "So it didn't really work."

"No," Alexius agreed. "It didn't. The Mercesti never attended, so it was moved to Central a few years ago because the other classes didn't want to give up on the tradition. The elders insist on continuing it. I think they hope that it will one day fulfill its ultimate goal."

"When is it scheduled this year?" Sophia asked.

"Originally, it was going to take place next week," Alexius responded. "However, the elders have requested that it be moved up to tomorrow so that you can all attend."

"Really?" Sophia considered this, then shrugged. "Well, a ball could be fun."

"Actually, I wondered if you would allow me to escort you, C.K.," Alexius said.

Clara Kate looked blankly at the Waresti. Had he just asked her out on a date? She was pregnant and in love with another male...a male who barely reacted to her presence. What in the world could she say?

"Sure," she replied. "That'd be great."

"A ball? That seems like a strange event to host right now considering everything that's going on," Tiege said as their platform hurled through the sky.

Ariana nodded and gave his hand a squeeze. "I thought so, too. But it's a very important event among Estilorians. I've gone every year since it started. We so rarely venture outside of our individual class homelands, so this ball gives us something to look forward to."

"Hmm."

His gaze was trained on the horizon. She understood that he was trying to avoid looking at Tate and Zachariah, who were very, well, *intent* on each other at the moment. They weren't only kissing, she had realized after sneaking a few peeks over her shoulder after she and Tiege turned around to give them some semblance of privacy. She'd seen them just gazing into each other's eyes, possibly sharing thoughts. Another time, she'd seen Zachariah whispering something into Tate's ear. Whatever it was they were doing, it was keeping them moving and on course for Central, so she wasn't about to interrupt them.

Instead, she trained her gaze on Tiege's strong profile. Like his twin's, his hair was fairly curly. His was solid brown rather than having multiple colors, however, and he wore it short enough that the few loose curls that fell across his forehead didn't quite reach his deep blue-green eyes. Being a male, the marking that indicated he had a second power decorated his right pectoral muscle as opposed to around his eyes. He'd shown it to her once when she asked about it. She remembered it was a triangle with a horizontal line across the top third of it.

"Tiege, I started to talk to you earlier about the coming pairings with Lekwuesti," she said after a moment. "I've been intending to talk to you about this for a while, but I haven't had the courage."

Now, his gaze moved to hers. She thought he could possibly see right into her soul with his insight. Her hand tightened its grip on his as she allowed her feelings to enter her gaze.

"Please don't say that you want to be my paired Lekwuesti," he said quietly.

Her heart sank. He didn't want her?

Was it because she was such a coward and had nearly cost Tate her life? She supposed she couldn't really blame him. He was beautiful and perfect. He deserved the very best in everything.

But who knew rejection would be so painful?

Unable to come up with anything better to say, she loosened her grip on his hand and murmured, "Okay."

"Ariana, it isn't that I don't want—" Tiege began.

"Central, straight ahead," Sebastian called out from the platform not very far away. "Prepare for docking."

"We'll finish this conversation later, okay?" Tiege said, squeezing her hand. "I promise."

She didn't reply. The fact of the matter was that if she wasn't good enough to be his paired Lekwuesti, there really wasn't anything more to say.

Chapter 16

"WELCOME TO OUR HOME BASE," SAID THE LEKWUESTI COMMANDER, Caoilinn.

Clara Kate joined the others in thanking the commander as they stepped off the platforms into Central's landing bay. They'd met the beautiful, red-haired female several times when she ventured to the Kynzesti homeland for various gatherings, but Clara Kate didn't know her very well. She'd met a handful of the class commanders over the years. Only the Waresti commanders had spent any significant amount of time with the Kynzesti, and that had been for training purposes.

"It will be my pleasure to show you all to your accommodations," Caoilinn continued. "We are thrilled you have made the trip, regardless of the reason."

Falling into step beside Quincy and Sophia as they all followed Caoilinn through the enormous tunnel comprising the landing bay, Clara Kate looked around and tried to absorb everything. She'd been told about the huge floating city with its tall, colorful buildings and an underbelly that looked like ripped up chunks of earth, but seeing it herself was really something else.

"As *archigos* Sebastian may have mentioned," Caoilinn said as they walked, "we have moved the date of our annual masquerade ball to coincide with your visit. It seemed like a fun way to introduce you to many Estilorians at once."

"It's an unnecessary distraction," Zachariah countered.

Tate smacked him on the arm and gave him a warning look. He quirked an eyebrow.

"Well, we hope you will all enjoy the event," Caoilinn said, though Clara

Kate noted she avoided looking Zachariah in the eye. "I will have several Lekwuesti here in the morning to prepare all of you."

"Will one of them be Penelope?" Sophia asked.

Giving Sophia a curious glance, Caoilinn replied, "She isn't one of the Lekwuesti I've selected for this, no."

"Oh, okay." Sophia looked disappointed. "Will she be at the ball?"

"I believe so."

It was an odd interaction, Clara Kate thought. There had to be a reason for it, though. Sophia didn't ask random questions.

It took them nearly fifteen minutes of walking, transitioning in specially-powered tubes and climbing stairs before they reached their destination. Clara Kate wondered why they hadn't seen a single other being during the trek, then guessed the elders had wanted them escorted through private passages. This was much like it was for her mother and her aunts the first time they came to Central, she thought. She and her cousins had grown up listening to stories about their parents' experiences shortly after they transitioned to this plane.

When they finally reached the corridor housing their rooms, she noted that it looked much like a hallway in a plush hotel on the human plane. Thick rugs lined gleaming wood floors. Gilded mirrors sat at both ends of the hall. High windows stretched along the left side of the corridor, while intricately carved wooden doors lined the right.

"We've found that when your parents stay here, adjoining rooms work best," Sebastian said, now stepping forward and joining his commander. "These rooms all have doors that join them from the inside. That way you don't have to venture into the hallway if you wish to communicate with each other."

"Thanks, *archigos*," Clara Kate said on everyone's behalf.

Nodding, Sebastian looked at Ariana. "Although you have your own rooms here at the base, Ariana, we thought you would be more comfortable staying here with your companions."

"I do appreciate that, *archigos*," Ariana said softly.

Clara Kate wondered over the Lekwuesti's sad and withdrawn demeanor, as she had seemed better before they arrived at Central. Then she glanced at Tiege. He was shifting his weight from foot to foot and running a hand through his hair as though anxious about something.

Sebastian opened the door to the first bedroom. Clara Kate caught a glimpse of dark wood and creamy linens before her attention was turned by the Lekwuesti elder's next words.

"Ini-herit will also stay with your group. Since we believe your fates are tied together, we think it's best that you have as much time as possible to connect right now. He will also be able to communicate with me should any of you need something." Waving toward the open door, he said, "This will be your room, Ini-herit."

"Thank you, Sebastian."

"Of course. Clara Kate, as the eldest Kynzesti, you will have the room next to this one. It is equally appointed to see to your every comfort."

Wonderful. She'd now be rooming next to the male who already caused her unhealthy obsessions. Smiling to mask the thought, she just said, "Thanks."

"Quincy, your room is next to Clara Kate's, and Sophia will be next to you, followed by Tiege, then Ariana, then Zachariah, with Tate's room at the end of the hall."

"My room won't be needed," Zachariah said. "I sleep where Tate sleeps."

Caoilinn's eyebrows lowered in a frown. "You can leave the connecting door open—"

Zachariah cut her off with a single look.

Sebastian placed a hand on Caoilinn's arm and said, "Of course. I will ensure suitable sleeping arrangements are made so that you don't have to lie on the floor." Turning his calm lavender gaze to the rest of them, he said, "Each room has an attached bath, which has been stocked with your preferred toiletries. You will find an assortment of refreshments in each of your rooms, as well. I took the liberty of generating sleepwear and one spare set of clothing for you. As Caoilinn mentioned, several Lekwuesti will be here in the morning to aid you in preparing for the ball."

"I can't wait!" Tate said, bouncing on the balls of her feet. "We never have a chance to dress up."

Clara Kate smiled over her cousin's enthusiasm. It was true. Maybe it would be a fun experience.

"We'll leave you all to enjoy some rest this afternoon," Sebastian concluded. "Please don't hesitate to tell Ini-herit if you need anything."

As everyone thanked the elder and moved to their rooms, Alexius approached Clara Kate. "I will come and pick you up here to escort you tomorrow evening," he said. "If you need me in the meantime, you can always send a message through *archigos* Ini-herit. *Archigos* Uriel will ensure I receive it."

"Sure thing," she replied, highly conscious of Ini-herit's gaze on them from where he stood a few feet away. "Thanks, Alexius. Have a great night."

He smiled. "I will. I'm looking forward to tomorrow."

"Me, too," she said.

When he walked away, she caught Ini-herit's eye. He had just heard her making plans with another male. She longed for a reaction from him—any reaction. But nothing flickered in his placid silver gaze.

It was really incredible, she thought, opening the door to her room as tears stung her eyes, how much pain could be inflicted with no emotion at all.

Metis didn't have to feign disorientation as she returned to her senses and noted all of the Waresti surrounding her. She realized she had assumed the female Orculesti's form as well as her abilities because a number of voices now ran through her head.

Where did the giant come from?

Is this the giant archigos *Uriel warned us about? If so, where is Caesar?*

The giant must have killed Raymond.

What is that dark pile? It looks like blood mixed with sand. Are those...remains?

Was Jocelyn harmed?

"What happened?" she asked, staggering to her feet. Then, wanting to add credibility to her role, she added, "Where is Raymond?"

"He has fallen," replied a Waresti with fiery red hair and a number of orange markings lining his skin. "It appears he was attacked by this giant, which took all of us to defeat."

"Did you not perceive anything?" asked another male.

"I—I do not remember," she said, careful to maintain her confused state. "Is this the giant we were warned about?"

More thoughts circulated. She did what she could to interpret them as they rushed through her mind, rubbing her temples as she concentrated. After a brief moment, she picked up a thought that caught her attention.

At least the Kynzesti are safe at Central for now.

Metis realized that the females she needed were at the Estilorian stronghold. That made things decidedly more difficult.

Why is she just standing there?

Realizing she was acting strangely and drawing attention, Metis glanced at the body of Raymond. She wondered how the Orculesti would react. Hoping it was the right response, she widened her eyes and put a hand to her throat.

"Holy light!" she exclaimed. "The giant did that?"

"Yes. There is also a weapon here that does not belong to him."

Caesar's sword.

The stray thought had her realizing that the male whose form she had recently assumed was Caesar, and they wondered how his sword had come to be there.

"I am trying to remember what happened," she said haltingly. "This beast came out of nowhere, wielding multiple weapons."

Perhaps he killed the being acting as Caesar, one Waresti thought. Metis hoped he voiced the idea to the others. Having them believe that she was dead would make the rest of her plans come together more easily.

"I—I believe I was shoved and hit my head on a tree," she said, rubbing a nonexistent pain at the base of her skull. "I am not sure."

She is clearly not well. I have never heard Jocelyn speak so formally.

"Are you in pain?" the red-haired Waresti asked. "Do you need to travel back to the main base for treatment?"

Metis considered this. Would she, in the Orculesti's form, be able to travel to the location considered off-limits to Mercesti? She had killed numerous beings for reasons other than defense, which typically converted Estilorians into Mercesti. But she wasn't in a Mercesti form now.

Well, there was only one way to find out.

"I believe I do need to return to the base," she said at last, infusing her voice with as much weariness as she could muster. "How soon can we depart?"

Chapter 17

A FTER PASSING AN UNEVENTFUL EVENING IN THEIR ROOMS, DURING which time Clara Kate showered, ate an unwanted snack and went to bed, the group gathered down in Ini-herit's room to meet the Lekwuesti who would be assisting them before the ball. Like hers, Ini-herit's bedroom was very spacious and contained not only a bed large enough to sleep four adults, but a seating area with a sofa, loveseat and two cushioned chairs. She deliberately sat in a chair facing away from the bed so she didn't humiliate herself with fantasies involving Ini-herit and that particular piece of furniture.

"Clara Kate, Sophia, Tate and Tiege, I would like to introduce you to four of our most talented Lekwuesti," Caoilinn said once they were all together. "Sun-Mae, Yasmina, Ellsbeth and Gregory."

Clara Kate glanced at the Lekwuesti and offered them a smile. Sun-Mae was quite delicate-looking with petite features, flawless ivory skin and long, dark hair. She wore a deep purple kimono-style garment decorated with embroidered flowers. In contrast, Yasmina stood nearly a head taller, several inches broader, and had dark skin and short hair. Her outfit was a practical tank and floor-length skirt, but she wore an abundance of complementing jewelry. Ellsbeth's ginger-colored hair matched the freckles dusting her cheeks and nose. The clingy dress she wore revealed more skin than Clara Kate was used to seeing among Estilorians. She noticed the only male, Gregory, glancing her way more than seemed usual and figured the outfit had something to do with that.

"They will each have an assistant when the time comes to outfit you," Caoilinn said. "For now, I thought it best to acquaint you so we can decide who will work with each of you."

When Clara Kate got to her feet, she noted that none of the Lekwuesti smiled. She supposed she should have expected the lack of expression, but she had thought that her mother and aunts had helped most of the Estilorians at Central re-learn human emotions. Maybe these Lekwuesti were older beings who hadn't yet grasped them.

She also realized that they kept sliding glances in Zachariah's direction. It must be unsettling to have the first ever Mercesti within the vicinity, she supposed. Still, the looks seemed unwelcoming. She hoped that was only because of their lack of expressions.

"Hi," she said, approaching the quartet. "I'm Clara Kate." She glanced at her cousins, who all rose from their seats and joined her. "This here is Sophia, and the twins are Tate and Tiege. It's so nice to meet you. We really appreciate your help."

"We look forward to assisting you, daughter of *kyria* Amber and *archigos* Gabriel," Yasmina said with a formal bow. "I would appreciate the opportunity to work with you."

"Sure—"

"As the only male in the group," interrupted Gregory, "I shall assist you, Tiege."

At the same time, Sun-Mae and Ellsbeth said, "I would like to work with you, Sophia."

In the clamor that followed, Clara Kate struggled to understand who was saying what. All she managed to piece together was that the three females were all debating who would work with her and who would work with Sophia. When she glanced at Tate and saw her hurt expression, Clara Kate suddenly understood. They didn't want to work with Tate because she was paired with Zachariah.

Indignation surged through Clara Kate. These beings had no right judging Tate or Zachariah. He'd made it to Central, hadn't he? Why wasn't that enough to prove the strength of his character? She opened her mouth, prepared to defend her family.

Ariana beat her to it.

The Lekwuesti stepped forward, her lavender eyes casting darts of anger at her peers. All conversation silenced at the look. Then she turned her back on them and addressed Caoilinn.

"Commander, I would like to request your permission to work with Tate," she said. "We've been through a lot together. And, well…" She trailed off and turned to face Tate. "I was actually hoping you might be willing to pair with me."

Tate's eyes widened. "Really?" A slow smile spread across her face. "You'd like to be my paired Lekwuesti?"

Clara Kate glanced at Tiege, whose expression was strangely unreadable. She sensed there was still something unresolved between him and Ariana. The two hadn't interacted with each other since they arrived at Central. When she shifted her gaze and noticed Ini-herit studying her, she realized she had plenty of unresolved issues of her own to handle.

"Yes," Ariana confirmed. "It would be an honor to pair with the daughter of *adelfi* Skye and *adelfos* Caleb…the niece of *archigos* Gabriel and *kyria* Amber, and the avowed of the Mercesti, Zachariah, who has saved my life more than once."

When Clara Kate saw the other Lekwuesti exchanging uncertain looks, she barely contained a smile. She knew very well why Ariana had gone through the trouble of listing all of the important people connected to Tate. She was subtly reminding her peers just who they were insulting with their behavior. Since Tate's eyes filled and she hurried to pull Ariana into a tight hug, Clara Kate figured her cousin understood, too.

"As it appears Tate welcomes this idea," Caoilinn said, "I will discuss it with *archigos* Sebastian. Should he also approve, we will guide you both through the pairing once we travel to the Lekwuesti homeland. For now, I certainly approve of you working with Tate before the ball."

Ariana smiled. "Thank you."

"I'm wondering if you have a few other Lekwuesti we could meet, commander," Clara Kate said. "Tiege, Sophia and I are rather…particular about the company we keep."

"Of course," Caoilinn said, not batting an eye. "I apologize for any—"

"You have nothing to apologize for," Clara Kate interrupted. "You've treated all of us with courtesy and respect. That's all we ask."

Bowing her head in acknowledgment, Caoilinn used her power to open the bedroom door and indicated that the four Lekwuesti leave the room immediately. They did so with a combination of huffs, lifted chins and snide looks, which earned them an earful from their commander as she closed the door behind them.

Clara Kate glanced at her family. One corner of her mouth lifted. She held out her fist. Sophia, Quincy, Tiege and Tate all tapped it. When Clara Kate looked at her, Ariana grinned and did the same. Then Zachariah surprised her by unfolding his crossed arms and touching his fist to hers. That prompted a giggle from Tate and the first smile of the day from Tiege.

She started to lower her fist, but realized Ini-herit had stepped closer. His gaze was focused on her hand. Her breath caught. Did he possibly remember that they used to exchange fist bumps on the human plane?

His gaze moved to hers. "You share your father's sense of loyalty," he said.

Lowering her hand and ignoring the pain in her chest when she realized he didn't intend to touch her, she murmured, "Yeah."

Even when that loyalty was to a completely lost cause.

"You'll be the most spectacular being at the ball," Ariana declared.

"If you do say so yourself, right?" Tate said with a grin.

Returning the smile, Ariana stepped back to eye her handiwork with Tate's hair. The mass of colorful curls had been a challenge to tame even with her Lekwuesti abilities, but they were now all arranged into a beautiful up-do, secured with gleaming jeweled pins. A few select curls tumbled free, making the look less formal and more like Tate.

Because she and Tate had decided on a deep garnet red for her ball gown and jewelry, her cosmetics were designed to complement the look. Ariana was convinced Tate's lush lips had been made to wear the dramatic shade of lip color she'd created. Her deep blue-green eyes were a brilliant, seductive contrast to the smoky eye shadow Ariana applied. Even though Tate would be wearing a half-mask, Ariana hadn't wanted to overlook even the smallest detail.

"Perfect," she said with a nod.

"Everything really is perfect, Ariana," Tate said, catching her gaze in the mirror. They were using Tate's bathroom to prepare her. "Thanks again for asking to pair with me."

Blushing, Ariana shrugged. "It really is an honor for me. I wasn't just saying that."

"I know. I can see the truth, remember?"

"Oh, right." She shrugged again, fighting her embarrassment. "Well, I appreciate you agreeing to the pairing."

Reaching out, Tate took Ariana's hand. "You know why Tiege refused to pair with you, don't you?"

Frowning, Ariana shifted her gaze to the ground. "No. He has yet to explain himself." She didn't add that she had deliberately kept her door closed to him since they arrived at Central, not wanting to deal with her confusion and heartache when she was still so exhausted.

"Ariana, Tiege seeks more from you than just that kind of pairing."

Blinking at that, Ariana again looked up. "What?"

"Look, I understand that to you, pairing with someone as their lifelong Lekwuesti is the most significant bond you think you can offer another being. By asking Tiege to pair with you, you were trying to convey how much he means to you. Right?"

"Yes," she murmured.

"Well, he wants more than that with you, though he's apparently terrible at conveying it."

Finally, Ariana understood. Tiege didn't want her for her abilities. He wanted her heart.

When her eyes filled with tears, Tate reached out and pulled her into a hug. "None of that, or I'll start crying and ruin the amazing job you did with my makeup."

Ariana sniffed and let out a watery laugh. "I know. You're right. Thank you for helping me understand."

"Sure thing. It's what sisters do."

Sisters. That had Ariana waving a hand in front of her face to try and keep the tears back. She didn't know how her heart could feel so full when just a minute ago she swore it would never heal.

"Okay, we need to decide on your shoes before I size your gown," she said in an effort to turn her attention from her emotions. "With your long legs, you don't need much of a heel."

After a moment of consideration, she used her power to create a pair of dancing slippers with low heels. Giving them a careful study, she decided that the shoes were a bit too ordinary to suit Tate's usual style. With another surge of her power, she added three-inch heels and deep red ribbons that laced up ballet-style around Tate's calves and tied in little bows behind the middle of her thighs. The effect they had on Tate's legs was exactly right, Ariana thought.

"Why don't you walk around in those for a minute or two and make sure they'll be comfortable enough to wear all evening?" she suggested, waving toward the open door.

"Sure," Tate agreed with a shrug.

Following Tate into the bedroom, Ariana assessed the other female's stride with a Lekwuesti's eye. Although the shoes wouldn't be visible under the long ball gown once Tate was dressed, they were an important part of the ensemble. As she watched Tate stroll in a slow circle and perform a few dance steps without any hitches, she decided the shoes would work well.

"Ariana, would you give us a minute?"

Belatedly, she remembered that Zachariah stood just outside the bathroom door. His gaze had latched onto Tate, who now paused in the middle of a dance maneuver and glanced at him over a bare shoulder. Dressed in only a lacy red bustier, matching panties and the heels, she had definitely caught the Mercesti's attention. The look in his eyes was downright predatory.

"Um, sure," Ariana said.

She went back into the bathroom and closed the door. Unable to fight her curiosity, she got as close to the door as she could without actually pressing her ear against it. She thought she heard a gasp and a muted thud, but then nothing.

A minute later, the door opened. Tate stumbled in, her cheeks flushed and her eyes glazed. Concerned, Ariana reached out to steady her.

"Oh, dear." She frowned as she second-guessed herself. "These shoes just won't do."

"Lekwuesti," Zachariah said from somewhere in the bedroom, "if you do nothing else in the course of this bloody day, don't change those shoes."

Chapter 18

INI-HERIT OPENED THE DOOR TO HIS BEDROOM WHEN HE SENSED MALUKALI and Knorbis on the other side of it. He had been dressed for the ball for more than an hour and as he spotted the other two elders, he realized they were also already wearing their formal wear. Malukali's green gown complemented her eyes, as did the emerald jewelry she wore at her throat and in her dark hair. Knorbis wore a black tuxedo with a coordinating green vest. It was a similar style to the tuxedo Ini-herit wore. The clothes weren't Ini-herit's usual style, but he thought they might appeal to Clara Kate.

The desire to draw her attention was new for him, but much like his instinct to watch over her, he didn't fight it. The unusual thoughts he'd been having lately were the very reason he had asked the two other elders to visit.

"Thank you for coming," he told them as he closed the door.

He directed them to the seating area. The couple took the loveseat as he sat in an adjoining chair. Although they could all communicate through thought, he didn't want the other elders to know about this conversation. Malukali conveyed an understanding of that through her quiet gaze.

"Of course," she said. "What can we do for you?"

Now that they were here, he wasn't sure what to tell them. Not having an understanding of the thoughts and compulsions that had struck him in recent weeks, he found it hard to put them into words.

Eventually, he asked, "Did the Orculesti who paired with me and my Gloresti—or Clara Kate and her Gloresti—convey anything to you about our relationship while we were on the human plane?"

"Clara Kate didn't have an Orculesti paired with her," Malukali explained. "The minds of the Kynzesti are very difficult to read, even for me, so it was seen as a waste of effort. Hermes, the Orculesti paired with you and your Gloresti, hasn't discussed anything that he might have intercepted."

Ini-herit didn't know whether or not to be grateful for that. "So the only one who knows what took place between me and Clara Kate on the human plane is Clara Kate?"

"Yes."

He considered this. "As you know, you unlocked a memory of mine from the human plane when you were seeking information about the map to the scroll piece. I would like you to try to uncover more."

The couple exchanged a look. When Malukali again turned her gaze to him, he knew enough to interpret sympathy. "Ini-herit, that memory didn't help you reconnect with your human self. It held no context for you. Anything we uncover at this point—"

"Please," he interrupted. "I...something is different. There have been things..." He stopped himself, unable to vocalize what he had experienced when he realized Clara Kate would be attending the ball with Alexius. "I do not know for certain, but I think I could possibly be experiencing feelings."

Now, Malukali's eyebrows rose. She glanced again at Knorbis. After a moment, they both nodded.

"Very well," she said. They got to their feet and approached him in the chair. "If you suspect there is something to be uncovered, we will make another attempt. Perhaps if you focus on Clara Kate, it will help our efforts."

That wouldn't be a problem. He'd been thinking about her almost constantly for months now. As the energy of the two elders glowed, he closed his eyes and thought of the female who loved him.

"So, what'd'ya say, hon? Is it a date?"

Over the top of his menu, Ini-herit watched Clara Kate interact with Brent Douglas, the captain of the high school football team and the dream date of every girl in Coweta County. Even though Clara Kate had only lived in the area for a few weeks, Brent had zeroed in on her the moment she walked in the front doors of Newnan High. He'd been rather relentless in his pursuit, a fact that irritated Ini-herit more than he wanted to admit.

Not that he couldn't understand the other guy's interest, he mused as he studied Clara Kate. In her simple white sundress and summery sandals, she outshined every other female in the restaurant. She wore a barrette with some kind of flower on it that gave her a refreshing, innocent quality that most girls their age lacked.

It wasn't just her appearance that drew attention, either. She had a quick, contagious smile and a friendly nature. In the time they'd lived together at Mrs. B's, he'd discovered that she was unfailingly polite and earnest. She'd made a lot of friends in a short amount of time and it was clear she really cared for everyone she allowed into her circle. It wasn't about being popular to her.

No, it wasn't a shocker that Brent was asking her out. But Ini-herit didn't have to like it, did he?

"Oh, um, it's really nice of you to ask, Brent," Clara Kate said.

Ini-herit saw her glance at their table, which she'd been walking back to after a visit to the bathroom. Was that a hint of desperation he saw in her eyes? He frowned as he tried to decide whether or not to intervene.

"Great. When can I pick you up?" Brent asked. He reached out, probably to brush away the single wave of hair that had escaped Clara Kate's barrette.

When she jerked back and once again glanced in his direction, Ini-herit made his decision. He knew panic when he saw it.

"Hey, Angel," he said as he approached, keeping his tone casual. He saw her brow quirk at the new nickname, but thought it was a nice touch. It sure suited her with her white dress and everything. Swinging an arm over her shoulders, he asked, "What's taking so long? I'm hungry."

"Sorry, Harry," she replied, understanding what he was doing. The gratitude he saw in her lovely eyes told him he'd made the right move. "I was just chatting with Brent."

"Oh, yeah?" He turned a politely curious gaze to the large, blond male. His confused expression almost made Ini-herit smile. "What's up, Brent?"

"Well..." He frowned. "Clara Kate, what's going on? When did you and Harry hook up?"

She shrugged and looked at Ini-herit, who said, "We weren't advertising it or anything."

Brent's broad brow remained furrowed. "Is this some kind of joke?"

"Only if you consider this a joke."

Then right there in the middle of the restaurant, he pulled Clara Kate close and did something he'd been contemplating for a while now. He kissed her.

He wondered for half a second whether she'd shove him away. He knew she wasn't the kind of girl who gave out kisses like candy. The appearance of innocence wasn't a façade for her. So when her hand moved to the back of his head and she met him halfway, he was a little surprised.

And more than a little thrilled.

She didn't wear much makeup—didn't need to—and it was nice to enjoy the feel of her soft, unpainted lips against his. He realized that she was letting him lead the way, so he reached up and gently stroked her jaw. Taking the hint, she parted her lips for him.

Then he was lost in the taste of her…the essence of her. Sweet spring days. Brilliant blue skies filled with white, billowing clouds. Colorful gardens bathed in sunlight.

She accepted the bold stroke of his tongue, countered it with a timid but eager brush of her own. He knew then that she'd never been kissed before, and the knowledge touched his heart like nothing else possibly could.

When they parted, he looked into her eyes for a long moment. He knew immediately that she felt the same.

"Okay," Brent said beside them. "You're not joking."

Holding Ini-herit's gaze, Clara Kate whispered, "No. We're not."

Surfacing from the memory, Ini-herit blinked to regain his focus. While Malukali and Knorbis moved to sit again on the loveseat, he fought to hold onto the emotions that the memory evoked. Maybe they didn't have much meaning to him now, but he liked how they'd made him feel while he was experiencing them.

It was no use, though. He felt nothing.

"I'm sorry," Malukali said quietly. "I've never had anything like this happen before. It's as though your memories from the human plane belong to another being."

"We extracted the memory easily enough," Knorbis added with a thoughtful frown. "But we couldn't connect it with the emotions you felt at the time. It's almost as if you've locked the emotions down."

Malukali sighed. "We don't appear to have the key," she concluded.

Ini-herit listened to them and absorbed the words. Though they weren't what he had hoped to hear, their conclusions were no different from his own. He supposed it was a small consolation that a being who couldn't experience emotion couldn't be disappointed.

Chapter 19

ON THE RIDE TO CENTRAL, METIS CONSIDERED HOW TO PROCEED. THE fact that she was successfully en-route to the Estilorian main base had her feeling what could only be described as *exhilarated*. It was a real first.

She feigned exhaustion and lay down on the intriguing platform as they rose into the sky. While she pretended to sleep, she did everything she could to listen in on the thoughts of the Waresti traveling with her. The leader of the small group had only spared three of them for this trip, as the others needed to stay back at the Corgloresti transition point.

The less protection she had, the better, she thought.

In reading their minds, she learned a lot about Waresti procedure. They really did focus on their tasks with the sole purpose of seeing them through. Even though they were on an enchanted platform that couldn't be accessed by their primary enemies, all of them remained diligent and attentive for the duration of their travels. She wondered if a stray Mercesti could possibly fly by and spot them.

In any case, she also picked up a few more tidbits. Their typical procedure when an Orculesti suffered any kind of trauma that impacted his or her thoughts was to bring that Orculesti to *archigos* Malukali for assessment. That knowledge didn't please Metis. She had recently overseen the torture of the Orculesti elder, and was fairly certain her thought signature would be recognized by the perceptive female. If Malukali somehow didn't recognize her, Metis imagined her perceptive husband would. He wasn't likely to forget anything about the being who had hurt his wife and blackmailed him.

Fortunately, there was some kind of gala that very evening. The Waresti were wavering on whether or not to interrupt the festivities and the elders over this situation, or just have Metis rest until after the event and tell them then. This was exactly the chink in the security she needed.

She sensed when they were slowing down and pretended to blink back to awareness. Stretching, she caught the eye of the closest warrior and did what she could to raise the corners of her mouth.

"I feel surprisingly better after resting," she said. "Perhaps I spoke too soon when I asked to come back here. I hate to think we have come all this way for no reason."

Using her new abilities, she sensed the mild sense of relief that flowed among the Waresti as they gave her a scan with their perceptive eyes and then drew their own conclusions that she was faring better. One of them—she gleaned from their thoughts that his name was Patrick—still thought she was speaking strangely and she wondered what she was doing wrong. She pulled the word "contractions" from his thoughts, but didn't know what he meant.

"I am still a bit out of sorts," she said, rubbing her temple, "but *archigos* Malukali can surely assist me after the ball."

"Do you feel you can wait that long?" the male called Carl asked.

"Certainly. It will only be a few hours, correct?"

Patrick frowned. She sensed his continued doubt about her speech pattern and decided to test another of her abilities on him.

"I would appreciate it if you would escort me to my accommodations," she said, exerting her mind control toward him.

"Of course, Jocelyn," he said.

Unfortunately, she couldn't tell if he was responding to her efforts to influence him or acting of his own accord. Keeping her frustration contained, she nodded and made another attempt to lift the corners of her mouth. It seemed to appease him.

Her first glimpse of the main base had her staring. They docked at a huge floating island topped with numerous tall buildings. Eight smaller islands spiraled up and out from that one. The array of colors and stylings of each island had her undeniably intrigued. Tethys hadn't known much at all about the base that had become known as Central in recent years. Thus, Metis was going to have to learn as she went along.

"You're probably too weary to fly," said Carl. "We'll escort you to the platform leading to the Orculesti homeland."

If she stays here, we could attend the ball, another of them thought.

"I hate to be any more trouble than I already have," she said. "Is there somewhere here that I could stay for tonight? This would keep me closer to *archigos* Malukali for whenever she is free, as well."

There was a brief flurry of thought, but eventually, they all nodded. "We can ask a ranking Lekwuesti to identify a room for your use," Patrick said.

"Thank you," Metis murmured, containing her satisfaction and offering another demure smile. "That would be just perfect."

Clara Kate stood in front of the full-length mirror in her room and studied her appearance. Paulina, the Lekwuesti who assisted her in preparing for the ball, had requested her input in the design of her ball gown. Not having any experience with such things, Clara Kate gave her what ideas she could.

Was it just a coincidence that she looked like the human version of an angel? Or had she consciously guided the Lekwuesti in this direction? It was a toss-up.

She'd told Paulina that she typically wore pastels and wasn't particularly fond of clothing that clung to every part of her body. She also said that she wasn't used to anything elaborate and wouldn't be comfortable in something too flashy or ornate.

As a result, she now wore a white, floor-length gown with a soft silver overlay to make it glimmer. Since her date was a Waresti, she also wore a broach of orange and deep blue-green gems between her breasts, which the high-waisted gown displayed in what she thought was a flattering way. Accenting the long sleeves, flowing panels of sheer white fabric had been secured to her shoulders and wrists with delicate straps. Whenever she raised her arms, the panels gave her the appearance of wings.

The circlet on top of her head also added to the angelic image, she realized now. That had been Paulina's suggestion since Clara Kate didn't want to wear any other jewelry. Her hair otherwise looked much like it usually did. Even her makeup was about as basic as it could get.

One element of her ensemble seemed less than angelic to her mind, though. The intricate white mask covering the top part of her face gave her an element of mystery that she supposed was the point of an event like this.

A knock sounded at the door. Since Paulina and her assistant had left to get themselves ready for the ball, Clara Kate strode across the room to answer the door herself. Her shoe caught on the edge of her rug. She barely stopped herself from falling. Flushing over her clumsiness and briefly touching her waist, she fixed the bunched rug with her toe and hurried the rest of the way to the door.

Sebastian had created peepholes, so she saw Alexius standing in the hall. She realized that he wore a nicely-tailored tuxedo and a black half-mask. The combination suited him.

Her gaze moved to the door that connected her room to Ini-herit's. She couldn't help but remember the one time he'd taken her to a school dance on the human plane. It had been so much simpler and more thrilling than this.

Taking a deep breath and shaking off the memory, she opened the door. When Alexius saw her, his mouth fell open. The reaction contributed to her lingering blush.

"You look amazing," he greeted her as a smile touched his lips.

"Thanks," she said. "You do, too."

He just stood there for a moment, staring at her. Then he seemed to jog himself and pulled his right hand out from behind his back. She realized that he carried something.

"Your mother and your aunts contributed their knowledge of modern human traditions during the planning of the first ball," he explained. "Now it's a tradition for a male to bring his date a floral token."

She realized that he held a small corsage of white flowers. The sight of it once again prompted her to think of her high school dance with Ini-herit. To mask the discomfiting thought, she smiled.

"That's so sweet of you, Alexius," she said. "Thank you."

While he was securing the corsage to her wrist, the door to Ini-herit's bedroom opened. She told herself not to look over. Alexius deserved her attention right then.

Still, when she heard Ini-herit step into the hall followed by a period of silence, curiosity got the better of her. She lifted her wrist to smell the flowers in the corsage and glanced a few feet down the hall. Ini-herit stared back at her. Although she half-expected him to turn and walk away without a word, he surprised her. His lips moved on a murmured word.

"What did you say?" she asked. Her heart thudded into her throat. Had she understood him correctly?

"Angel," he repeated more loudly. "You are dressed like an angel."

"Yes," she said, taking a single step closer to him even though it made her feel guilty to turn her back on Alexius.

"That is a clever play on one of the human myths about our kind."

She forced herself to ask, "Is that the only significance my costume holds for you?"

Once again, silence fell in the hallway. Behind her, doors opened as her family made their appearances so they could all go down to the ball together. Ini-herit gazed at her from behind his black and silver half-mask without any kind of reaction. She knew she wouldn't receive the answer she sought.

"Are you ready to go to the ball, C.K.?" Alexius asked.

Hoping her mask helped hide her tears, Clara Kate nodded. When Alexius offered her his arm, she took it. Then she walked past Ini-herit without looking at him again, determined to enjoy the ball with a male who actually wanted to be with her.

Chapter 20

INI-HERIT WALKED WITH THE OTHERS FROM THEIR ROOMS TO THE ballroom. He had never been to the space before, as it had been created after he transitioned to the human plane. Alexius took the lead and guided them through the halls with a confident stride.

Seeing Clara Kate dressed as she was, holding the arm of another male, had Ini-herit recalling the memory of her in the restaurant with the human male, Brent. For the briefest moment, when he emerged from his bedroom and first saw her in the hallway, he even experienced a flash of the emotion he'd felt as a human. The feeling caught him off-guard. He'd stood there trying to recapture it, but realized when Clara Kate finally looked at him that he wasn't going to succeed.

There had been many things he'd wanted to tell her when she asked him whether her ensemble held any significance to him. He considered telling her about the memory Malukali and Knorbis recovered. He also thought about mentioning the twinge he'd felt when he spied her in her costume.

Then he'd noticed Alexius looking between the two of them. Although Ini-herit wasn't entirely sure what he read in the other male's expression, he knew that it held more emotion than he could possibly give Clara Kate.

She deserved better than Ini-herit could give her. So he hadn't said a thing.

Seeing her tears made him rethink his decision, but by then it was too late. Everyone else had emerged from their rooms and they all headed out in a bustle of conversation and activity.

He noticed as they walked that the other females in their group had all dressed in very different gowns. Whereas Clara Kate's gown resembled something from the late nineteenth century on the human plane, Sophia's silver and deep blue-green garb was medieval in style, as though from a fairy tale. Ariana had opted to wear a Renaissance-era gown in shades of rose and violet. Tate's satin gown was the most contemporary, having a sleeveless, form-fitting bodice and full, floor-length skirt. The dark red garb was sure to garner attention. Red was a color rarely worn by non-Mercesti.

Ini-herit realized that Zachariah had chosen not to wear a mask. The Mercesti had donned a tuxedo, but that was apparently the extent of his attempt to blend in. Even his blond hair looked as untamed as usual. With his intent gaze moving constantly from one shadowed corner to the next, Zachariah made it clear he wasn't comfortable with their location.

"The plan is for all of the Kynzesti to be announced into the ballroom once most of the guests have arrived," Alexius explained as they walked. He looked down at Clara Kate. "*Archigos* Sebastian felt this would be the best way to introduce you to everyone at once."

"I would prefer to avoid that direct attention," Zachariah said.

Alexius glanced at him. Ini-herit knew that both Alexius and Harold had maintained strong relationships with Zachariah when he had been the Gloresti second commander. Both Waresti had accepted Zachariah without judgment after discovering his conversion to Mercesti. The look exchanged now between the two males had a distinct sense of camaraderie. After a moment, Alexius nodded and turned to Ini-herit.

"Would you please convey this to *archigos* Sebastian? We believe it would be better to just enter the ball with everyone else and blend in with the crowd."

"Of course," Ini-herit replied.

As he sent the thought out, he considered Zachariah's possible reasoning for the change in plans. In his mind, it made more sense to introduce the Kynzesti at one time. There would be a great many beings present at this event. Making many separate introductions seemed inefficient.

Oh, well. He might not understand their reasoning, but he saw no reason to argue.

When they arrived at the grand ballroom, it was filling up with beings. Alexius led them through the main entrance, which was marked by two enormous wooden doors. Several Waresti currently stood guard. They bowed to Alexius and Ini-herit as the group entered the room.

It was larger than any other social gathering space at Central, Ini-herit realized. His gaze lifted to the high ceiling, which was currently enchanted to look like the night sky. Thousands of stars winked down on them. Candles glowed from long, linen-covered tables lining every side of the room, highlighting an impressive spread of food and drink that scented the air with mouth-watering aromas. On the other end of the room, a group of instruments played themselves, guided by a Lekwuesti's power. Bright music filled the air, blending with the hum of conversation as Estilorians from different classes caught up with each other. The dance floor was already occupied by a number of beings.

"We had better identify a meeting point," Alexius said to Zachariah. "Somewhere we should all gather at an established time."

The Mercesti nodded. "The base of the clock would work well," he said.

They all glanced over to the right side of the room, where a large clock, supported by an ornate, black, wrought-iron base, stood almost as high as the ceiling and at least fifteen feet wide. It was impossible to miss.

"We should meet there hourly," Zachariah suggested.

No one argued with him. With the parameters of their evening now established, the group broke off into smaller pairings. Ini-herit only then considered the fact that he was the only one without a companion. His instincts had him wanting to follow Clara Kate as she moved away, but for some reason, the idea of spending an evening watching her interact with Alexius made him—

What, exactly? He didn't even know what the odd sensation in his chest meant. But as he watched Clara Kate disappear into the crowd and he then turned to begin his version of socializing, he knew he didn't wish to continue experiencing it.

In truth, he'd rather feel nothing at all.

"I have been to every one of these balls," Ariana said as she and Tiege moved away from the others. "The Lekwuesti, especially, enjoy the diversity among the costumes and the elaborate décor."

"Do they change the setup every year?" Tiege asked as his gaze moved around the room.

She sensed he wasn't really curious about the décor and she couldn't blame him. Although she had hoped to experience her usual enthusiasm while attending the masquerade, she felt only a sense of obligation. How could she revel in an event like this when there was so much more in the balance?

A few months ago, her existence would have revolved around clothing, music, food and hospitality. Were it not for her recent experiences, she would likely even now be standing with a group of her friends, including her best friend, Tisha. She might be judging the costumes of the attendees, pointing out things she liked and disliked about each of them. She would likely sample the food and offer similar judgments, thinking her opinion was of such importance. Perhaps she might have even accepted an offer or two to dance.

Now, Tisha was dead. Now, Ariana knew what it meant to live outside of any level of comfort…to live within the confines of abuse and torture. She was no longer an innocent and naïve young female who couldn't see beyond the surface.

"The theme changes," she said at last, her grip on Tiege's arm tightening as she spotted a group of familiar faces. "It appears they've gone with 'Victorian Romance' this year."

Tiege touched her hand on his arm and looked down at her. They stopped walking as he got a good look at her face. "Are you all right?" Before she could reply, he said, "Ariana, I'm sorry I didn't do a better job of explaining myself before. I've wanted to talk to you for weeks, but something has always come up."

"Ariana, is that you?"

She recognized the voice of Elena, a fellow Lekwuesti. Knowing that a response would cause a lengthy delay, she ignored her.

Tiege continued, "I think it's great that you're going to pair with Tate. Thank you for offering that to her. I never thought about how her pairing with Zachariah might impact her potential relationships with other Estilorians."

"Ariana?"

Again, she ignored the greeting, this one from a Lekwuesti named Bridget. She chose instead to focus on Tiege, whose gaze was shadowed by his black half-mask.

"I love you," he said. "I love you more than I know how to express. I don't want you obligated to serve me in any way. When the time is right, I want to avow with you. I want to marry you."

Tears filled her eyes. How had she ever gotten so lucky?

"Ariana. That *is* you."

This time, there was no avoiding Elena and Bridget or the group of other female Lekwuesti approaching with them. Turning with a polite smile, Ariana said, "Hello."

"I figured you might not have heard me over the music," Elena said, her gaze moving to Tiege. "Hello. I'm Elena. This is Bridget."

"It's a pleasure to meet you," he responded. "I'm Tiege."

"Ah. The son of *adelfi* Skye and *adelfos* Caleb," Elena said.

Bridget ran her eyes over him and added, "The twin brother of the female who paired with the Mercesti."

Ariana was sure Tiege heard the frost in the tones of the other females. She felt him stiffen. Then Elena quirked an eyebrow and looked back at Ariana.

"Are you together, then?" she asked, lifting her chin as she spoke.

Irritated by the other Lekwuesti's behavior, Ariana replied, "Yes. Tiege is my fiancé."

When he turned to look at her, she met his gaze and smiled. They both heard the indrawn breaths from the group beside them.

"Really?" he asked.

"Yes," she said, feeling more joy than she had ever thought possible. "I love you, Tiege."

When he leaned in to kiss her, she met him halfway. She knew better than to make a scene in the middle of the ball, but she took a moment to enjoy the feel of his lips against hers. He made her feel like the most important female on the plane and knew that was because he believed it to be true.

"I suppose that your pairing is rather fitting," Elena said when they parted. When Ariana glanced at her, she added, "No respectable female would want to be associated with someone so closely connected to the Mercesti. And no other male would want a female who had been kept by the Mercesti for as long as you. You are clearly damaged—"

"You should stop talking now," Tiege interrupted, his voice soft. When his gaze met Elena's, she took a step back. "Neither of us wants to hear what you have to say. Your words are crafted by ignorance and stupidity. And I've decided it isn't a pleasure to meet you, after all."

"Well, I—"

Tiege took Ariana's elbow and pulled her away as Elena sputtered behind them. Not sure whether to laugh or worry, Ariana did neither. She nodded at a few beings who spotted her and tried to greet her. Just as she was about to ask Tiege to stop so she could catch her breath, he whirled her around and pulled her against him. Then, to her surprise, he guided her into a dance.

"I hope you aren't upset that I interrupted your conversation," he said after a moment.

She felt the tense muscles in his arm. "Of course I'm not upset. Are you okay?"

"No. I'm seriously pissed off."

Blinking, she said, "Oh."

"I should have expected this," he said. Ariana realized his gaze moved among the crowd, so she also began looking around. There were many eyes on them. "We know Zachariah. We understand what was done to him to cause him to convert. Most of the beings here don't. They're judging Zachariah and Tate. It seems they're judging us, too."

She didn't know what to say. Dancing without much thought as the music continued, she looked over to where Tate danced with Zachariah on the other side of the dance floor. There was a three-foot circle around them as beings shifted away. The couple, their focus on each other, didn't appear to care.

Well, if the other Estilorians wanted to judge, so be it. Ariana was determined to enjoy her dance with Tiege. In her mind, this was the beginning of their future together. No one would take it away from her.

Zachariah was only too aware of the attention he drew as the sole Mercesti in attendance. He was a curiosity, a being who left Central fifty years ago and converted to something most Estilorians abhorred. He caught the gazes of many beings who once knew him as the Gloresti second commander. Nearly all of them failed to hide their disgust.

That, he could have handled. He'd been prepared for it. With his murderous past, he could hardly fault them for their holier-than-thou attitudes.

But what he couldn't deal with was the treatment of his avowed.

The behavior of the four Lekwuesti initially assigned to work with Tate and her family had blindsided him. Up until then, it hadn't occurred to him that Tate would be treated differently because of him. He'd been trained to respect all of the elders and those of importance to them. Tate fell within that category as Gabriel's niece. In his mind, she and her kin deserved the upmost respect.

That obviously wasn't the case in the minds of other Estilorians. Tate hadn't let him dwell on it, though. When his temper threatened to get the better of him and he envisioned physically tossing the offensive Lekwuesti out of Central, she calmed him with her thoughts. He knew she was happy with her pairing with Ariana, so he supposed it had all worked out in the end.

Now, however, he had to deal with the crowd in the ballroom. Rude looks were one thing. The hungry stares of most of the males in the room when they looked at Tate were quite another.

He knew what caused the reactions. His avowed was naturally beautiful. Add in Ariana's cosmetic enhancements, a great deal of well-toned skin bared to the soft candlelight, and the unique color of her gown, and there was no denying she was the most stunning being in the room. Her effortless grace as they moved along the dance floor also drew attention.

She had removed her mask when she realized he wasn't wearing one. She asked him about it before they left their room, wondering why he didn't want to wear it. His answer was simple: he was tired of hiding who he was.

Now, he caught her gaze as they completed another turn. With the colorful markings curving around her magnificent eyes, she didn't need a mask. She devastated his senses enough as it was. Her bright smile and obvious adoration for him only added to the impact she made.

It was the many other males in the room who also appeared to notice this that had Zachariah on edge. When they first entered the ballroom, he spotted a number of the Gloresti who had been selected to pair with Tate for her protection before he showed up. They stood on the side of the dance floor staring at Zachariah and Tate. He kept part of his attention on them as they danced.

So he noticed when they stepped onto the dance floor with the intent to engage him. Judging by their expressions as they moved their gazes from him to Tate, Zachariah was pretty damn sure they weren't all going to make it out of there alive.

Chapter 21

"IS THERE ANYONE IN PARTICULAR YOU WOULD LIKE TO MEET?" ALEXIUS asked.

Clara Kate considered the question as she allowed him to guide her through the crowd. She deliberately ignored the sensation of Ini-herit's gaze on her back as they walked away from him. Her focus had to be on Alexius right now.

"No one in particular," she said. "Is there anyone you think I should meet?"

"Why don't we start with the class lieutenants? You haven't met very many of them."

"Sure. I'd like that."

They made their way around the room. She met more than just lieutenants, though Alexius did tend to steer her to those in higher level positions. After the initial reception they received from the Lekwuesti the day before, she understood why. The older and more trusted Estilorians would know better than to treat any of the Kynzesti or their extended family with anything less than respect.

As they mingled, Clara Kate kept a careful eye on her family and friends. They had been through too much in the past few months to let down their guards. On top of that, a powerful sense of "wrong" had settled in the back of her mind. It was a feeling she'd never experienced before. Her skin tingled with the need to act.

Chalking it up to the unfamiliar environment and the many masked faces around her, she continued strolling through the ballroom with one hand on Alexius' arm. Even as she greeted the Lekwuesti lieutenant, Hinto, she watched out of the corner of her eye as Sophia and Quincy chatted with a blonde Lekwuesti female. Sophia handed something to her.

"That's Penelope," Alexius explained.

"Ah," Clara Kate replied.

She understood now. During her recent attempt to rescue Tate and Ariana, Sophia had met with the unusual Scultresti, Hoygul. In the course of her negotiations to get the map to the ancient library, Sophia had offered to bring a message to Hoygul's one true love, Penelope. Sophia was now fulfilling her end of the bargain. Judging by Penelope's expression, it was a welcome gift.

Clara Kate's gaze moved to Ariana and Tiege, who conversed with a group of Lekwuesti before they moved to the dance floor. When she saw Tiege's expression and the looks on the faces of the Lekwuesti females behind him, the tingle she felt turned into something more.

All of her senses heightened. She could focus on an individual and hear what they said, even if they were across the room. Every movement registered in her brain as though in slow motion. Something powerful coursed through her, starting in her chest and surging out until it energized her fingertips.

The strangest part of all was that it felt natural.

As Alexius greeted a fellow Waresti, Clara Kate shifted her gaze to Tate and Zachariah. They danced on the other side of the floor and appeared to have slipped into their own little world. She registered the subtle movement of Zachariah's eyes, however. His attention was definitely split.

That was when she noticed the Gloresti males gathered in a corner. She recognized the blond one standing in front. Maddock. He had nearly paired with Tate for her protection before Zachariah came on the scene a couple of months ago. Now, his narrowed gaze rested on the couple dancing less than fifteen feet away.

"He has a lot of nerve," said one of the other Gloresti. She heard him in her altered state as though he stood next to her.

"He surely feared we would show the Kynzesti what a mistake she made by picking him," said another.

The power pulsing in her chest had Clara Kate asking, "Alexius, have you heard anything negative around Central about Zachariah over the past few weeks?"

Alexius frowned. Her instincts flared.

"I'll take that as a yes. Let's walk that way." She lifted her chin to indicate the group. "I'd like to say hello to the Gloresti who visited my homeland."

He didn't question her. Instead, he used his size to help them progress through the crowd. Clara Kate lost sight of Tate and Zachariah for a minute. When she once again spotted them, she realized they were standing by the Gloresti. For some reason, the males had stepped further onto the dance floor, making the confrontation inevitable. The glares issuing from her father's followers heightened the sensation coursing through her.

"I'm amazed that you showed up here, Mercesti," Maddock said, not even bothering to address his former commander by name. "It seems senseless to present yourself to everyone after falling so far from grace. It isn't as though you're welcome here."

"I'm not seeking a welcome, nor am I seeking a conversation," Zachariah replied in neutral tones. "Step back to your little corner and leave us be."

"Hey," Tate added brightly, "maybe if you all stop glowering and acting like jealous asses, someone might even ask you to dance."

Clara Kate once again lost sight of them. They were less than twenty feet away, but there was a crowd gathering around the spectacle. Alexius had to use more force to allow them passage.

"Jealous?" Maddock sputtered. "Of *him*? A murderer and defiler of innocents?"

Anger joined the building power flowing through Clara Kate over the harsh and untrue words. She barely resisted shoving bodies out of her way in an effort to progress more quickly. Her instincts were raging, telling her to *move.*

"What are you implying?" Zachariah asked in a dangerous voice.

"You know what I'm implying. Just look at her, dressed in this—"

"Don't ever touch her again."

The words were spoken in such a controlled voice that Clara Kate knew Zachariah was close to giving Maddock the thorough beating he deserved. Finally, Alexius got them through the crowd. The music stopped playing as Clara Kate hurried to Zachariah's side. He had pushed Tate behind him, but Tate kept stepping to his side to face the Gloresti with him.

"What if I do?" Maddock taunted, moving close enough to Zachariah that mere inches separated them. "What are you going to do? Kill me like you did those who followed you fifty years ago?"

There were gasps from the crowd. The other Gloresti with Maddock had moved closer to support their friend. Clara Kate knew their menacing stances and close proximity had Zachariah's protective instincts at their height.

"Get back," she warned the Gloresti as Tiege and Ariana also approached. Her skin all but sizzled with energy.

"You're certainly giving the idea remarkable appeal," Zachariah said in response to Maddock's challenge.

"Just try and lay a hand on me, Mercesti," Maddock snarled. "Then when I kill you, it will be in self-defense."

That did it.

Clara Kate stepped forward. "I said *get back*!"

She felt the power propel out of her, a blast of energy that had all of the Gloresti staggering back several feet. More gasps issued from the crowd. She registered the exchanged glances among the Gloresti as well as Sophia and Quincy's approach in a fraction of a second. In the next fraction, she sensed Ini-herit and the other elders nearby, though she didn't see them. As she positioned herself in front of Zachariah, the rest of her family created a circle around him.

"You should be ashamed of yourselves," she said, focusing on Maddock. The words came from her, but they felt as though they came from a part of herself she'd never known existed. "My father would never stand for you treating his nephew this way."

Several of the Gloresti lost their arrogant and angry expressions as they absorbed her words.

"Zachariah is avowed to Tate, which makes him family. He's the nephew of the Gloresti elder. *Your* elder. And he's also now a cousin to me...the Kynzesti elder."

She'd never referred to herself that way, but as this foreign part of herself spoke the words, she recognized the truth in them. It settled over her like a comfortable cloak. As her gaze moved from one offending Gloresti to the next, she watched them avert their eyes.

"We all deserve your respect," she said. "Each and every one of us. Do you understand me?"

After a moment, Maddock murmured, "Yes."

"Yes, what?"

"Yes, *archigos*."

As soon as he realized what was happening, Ini-herit connected with Gabriel so his friend could observe his firstborn daughter assume her powers as an elder. All of the elders had known this was a possibility, but even those who suspected Clara Kate would naturally grow into the role of the Kynzesti elder hadn't believed it would happen so soon.

But he'd felt the elder connection blossom not long after she walked away with Alexius. There had been no question in his mind what was taking place. Although millennia had passed since the last time an elder assumed power, the feeling was impossible to forget. He received thoughts from the other elders confirming they were all experiencing the same thing. It was like there was another being resonating with each of their abilities, both drawing on their strength and contributing to it.

Cyclical. Synchronous.

Still, when Clara Kate physically moved the Gloresti back with one command, Ini-herit sensed the surprise of the other elders. Only Gabriel had ever been able to do that.

Hearing the Gloresti refer to Clara Kate as *archigos* had another round of murmurs filling the room. Ini-herit took that opportunity to approach her. Jabari, Sebastian, Zayna, Malukali, Knorbis and Uriel also stepped through the crowd.

"I believe that's enough unscheduled entertainment for the evening," Jabari said.

As the eldest Estilorian in both age and appearance, as well as the Elphresti elder, his words commanded immediate obedience. The music once again cued up. The crowd dispersed, though curious glances were thrown over shoulders as couples resumed dancing. Ini-herit noticed that Clara Kate and her family remained in their protective stances, surrounding Zachariah. When he looked at the Mercesti, he couldn't read his expression.

Maddock and the Gloresti started edging away. Jabari raised a hand. They froze.

"Commander Hitoshi is on his way and would like a word with each of you," he said. "You will adjourn to the parlor room off the central corridor. Commander Caoilinn will show you the way."

The Lekwuesti commander appeared at Sebastian's side. "At your service, *archigos.*"

Each of the Gloresti mumbled an apology to no one in particular as they followed Caoilinn out of the ballroom. Only when they were gone did those around Zachariah move from their positions. Clara Kate blinked as though trying to clear her head. When she swayed, Ini-herit moved forward.

Quincy was faster. "I've got you," he said as he took her elbow and helped keep her steady. His gaze flickered briefly to Ini-herit, but Ini-herit couldn't read the look in his eyes.

"What was that all about?" Alexius asked, reaching out and taking Clara Kate's other arm.

"We should discuss it as a group," Jabari said, his dark face breaking into a wide smile. "But the short answer is that Clara Kate has just assumed the role of the Kynzesti elder."

Chapter 22

THEY LEFT THE BALLROOM AFTER JABARI'S ANNOUNCEMENT. THEY HAD not even gotten to enjoy one hour of the masquerade. Although Clara Kate felt a little bad about that, she knew they had bigger things to address at the moment.

"How do you feel?" Tate asked as they walked.

"I feel…different," Clara Kate said. "I can't really explain it."

She kept expecting the flow of power to subside. It had come on rather abruptly, after all. Now that the danger to her family had been removed, shouldn't she return to normal?

Alexius gave her several sideways glances as they walked. She knew the hold she had on his arm was rather tight, but she didn't feel quite steady yet. The intensity of what had rushed through her when she confronted Maddock and his followers left her drained, despite the sensation still spiraling in her chest.

Sebastian led them outside of the building containing the grand ballroom. They walked across a plaza to another building, this one a soft purple in color and so high that Clara Kate couldn't even see the top. Once inside, they took a series of air tubes until they reached yet another hallway with two high, wide doors at the end. Clara Kate realized as they got closer that they were gold and contained intricate lavender etchings. When Sebastian paused outside the doors and pressed his hands against them, the etchings glowed. Locks snicked open.

Turning, he said, "We would like to speak with just Clara Kate first." His gaze swept over her family. "Then we'll invite you in to discuss this. You will find seating inside the rooms attached to this one. Those are commander

Caoilinn's quarters."

Since his gaze settled on Zachariah, the Mercesti nodded. Clara Kate released Alexius' arm, giving him a reassuring smile when he caught her gaze. Then she turned and walked into Sebastian's quarters. Although her knees felt like they didn't want to support her, she drew upon her energy to at least get her to one of the chairs forming a circle on the far right side of the room. It took her a moment to realize that there were ten chairs, one in each class color. She puzzled over the red Mercesti chair. That class hadn't had an elder since just after the separation of the planes. Did the elders think that would change?

Taking the deep blue-green seat, she caught Sebastian's gaze. "How did you know?"

He sat across the circle in the lavender chair. "How did we know that there would be a Kynzesti elder? It was a simple deduction based upon the evolution of our kind. We have suspected since your birth and the births of the other Kynzesti that an elder would emerge. Each class requires governance that extends beyond the bonds of parenthood."

She blinked. No one had ever mentioned this to her.

"We never suspected it would happen while you were still so young," Knorbis explained. "Our assumption of power took place over centuries of being."

"Oh." She gripped the arms of the chair as she continued wrestling with the powerful sensation. Now that all of the elders sat in the circle, the surge in feeling had her wanting to jump out of her chair. "Why do you think this is happening now?" she asked.

Belatedly, she considered the pregnancy. Her gaze darted to Ini-herit, who sat next to Sebastian. He looked back at her without expression, though he did tilt his head as though in question.

"It could be because you have such powerful parents," Jabari replied. "Your father is the Gloresti elder and your mother is the most skilled fighter on the plane. It was when she was your age that your mother assumed her abilities."

That was true, Clara Kate thought. It brought to mind the line of the Elder Scroll supposedly pertaining to her: *One conceived of age and might.*

"Whatever the reason, there are steps that must be taken now that you have come into your powers," Malukali explained.

"Each class requires a hierarchy of leadership," Uriel said. "In the past, each elder selected a commander, second commander and lieutenant as the core group to govern the class. Second lieutenants on down the hierarchy were then selected jointly by this core. This process, like our development as elders, took place over a period of time."

Clara Kate nodded. "I understand. But I don't need time. My core is sitting in the next room."

Jabari smiled. "We reasoned you would say as much. We'll firm up those details with your cousins in a moment. Right now, we need to discuss what it means to have assumed the powers and abilities of an elder."

"Will I always feel like this?" she asked, pressing a hand to her chest.

"Yes," Jabari said. "What you need to understand is that you are now connected to all of us. Right now, that connection is physical. If you are in danger, we will sense it. You'll also sense when one of us is threatened. This is quite instinctive and will require no thought on your part."

Malukali added, "Once we travel back to your homeland and see your father, we'll all perform the proper ritual to connect you to our thoughts, as well."

That had Clara Kate biting her lip. Her hand lowered from her chest and passed briefly over her abdomen. Joined in thought with all of the elders? That meant that her thoughts could possibly be intercepted by her father or Ini-herit.

Though she wasn't sure she was ready, she knew the time to tell Ini-herit about their baby would have to come sooner rather than later.

It took Metis longer than she anticipated to slip away from the Estilorians who were caring for her. What was it with these creatures and their cloying concern? Was it too much to ask for some time to herself?

The Waresti had escorted her through so many tubes and tunnels that she lost her sense of direction. This place was even more challenging to navigate than Tethys' maze. Eventually, they reached a tall, wide room with many beings walking from various directions and continuing on their way. She gleaned from one of the Waresti's thoughts that this was the main hall. It joined multiple buildings and served as a central point of access.

They approached a collection of waist-high colored lights bouncing above the floor. One of the Waresti walked over to the lavender ball of light and took it into his hand. Then he tossed it into the air.

It sparkled and cast lavender light, bobbing well above their heads. Metis understood from the thoughts of her companions that this was meant to call the attention of the "ranking Lekwuesti in residence." Sure enough, within three minutes, a female with billowing blonde curls and lavender eyes approached with swift strides. When she got close enough, she extended her hand and called the ball of light back to her. Then she replaced it among the other lights.

"Greetings, warriors. I'm Dara. What can I do for you?"

"Dara, Jocelyn here has had an unsettling experience on the mainland," Patrick explained. "She requests a room here at the main base so that she can discuss her experience with *archigos* Malukali after the ball."

"Of course," Dara replied. "Please come with me."

It took another hour to get Metis settled in her accommodations. The Waresti left after she assured them she was fine and thanked them for their concern. The Lekwuesti, however, had apparently made it her mission to drive Metis out of her mind with all of her questions and comments.

Had her experience interrupted her connection to her Lekwuesti? Was she in need of healing? Did she wish to speak to *archigos* Malukali the moment the ball ended, or tomorrow morning? Were there any special requests regarding food, clothing or accommodations?

"I require nothing else," Metis finally snapped, unable to endure the other female's presence for a moment longer. "Except rest."

"My apologies," Dara said. *Ungrateful wretch*, she thought.

Catching the thought, Metis almost used her powers of mind control to have the female stab herself with a fork. Then she thought better of it, not wanting to draw undue attention to herself.

"No, I apologize," she said, not having to feign the weariness in her voice. "I fear my experience today has me acting out of sorts. While I do appreciate all of your efforts, I would like to rest now. I do hope you understand."

Compassion radiated from the Lekwuesti. "Certainly, Jocelyn. I'll leave you to your rest. We'll come and get you in the morning to meet with *archigos* Malukali."

"Thank you."

Metis thought about asking the female for information about the ball, having learned by listening in on the thoughts of those around her that Tate and Ariana would be in attendance. Then she realized how foolish it would be to attempt to get both females while they were so thoroughly surrounded, so she withheld the question. Pacing in her room once Dara left, she considered what to do.

She had no idea where the Kynzesti and their companions were staying. After scanning the thoughts of the Waresti and Lekwuesti earlier and discovering that they didn't know, either, she had attempted to listen in on other beings as she walked to her accommodations. It was quite difficult, though. Nothing she managed to pick up helped her at all.

Deciding it wasn't doing her any good to remain in the room, she strode to the door and opened it, taking care to check outside to make sure it was unguarded. Not seeing anyone, she closed the door behind her and hurried down the hall.

It took her another half-hour to find out where the ball was being held, and twenty minutes more to find someone she could follow to the main ballroom. Once she got close enough to the event's location, she eased behind a pillar of a nearby building and started listening. At one point, she had the uncomfortable feeling that another being was doing to her mind what she did to others, almost like the thoughts of another touched hers. The sensation was over as quick as she felt it, though, so she dismissed it.

She didn't have to stand there long to pick up many thoughts of unease, excitement, curiosity and other reactions that told her something notable was occurring inside the ballroom. Most of the thoughts were jumbled, but she easily picked up the name Zachariah. Then another: Clara Kate.

Blinking as the flood of thoughts intensified, she brought her hands to the sides of her head to try and block them. She briefly squeezed her eyes shut. When she opened them, she spied all of the elders in attendance and the group of individuals she sought exiting the ballroom. She had no choice but to follow.

Unfortunately, she couldn't read any of them except Ariana, who was talking to the male Kynzesti beside her. Her thoughts were focused on the male.

Frowning, Metis pressed her luck and did a more thorough scan of the Lekwuesti's thoughts. She shouldn't have done it. Within seconds, both Malukali and Knorbis glanced over their shoulders, probably having sensed the use of mental powers on one in their care. The couple then looked at the

Waresti elder in silent warning, and Metis knew she had to perform a strategic retreat.

As she hurried away, she clung to the scraps she had managed to glean from the Lekwuesti's thoughts.

Clara Kate's abilities…

… enable us…

…use the Elder Scroll.

What she concluded was that the key to using the Elder Scroll lay not in Ariana or Tate, but in the eldest Kynzesti. Metis realized that Eirik had been focusing on the wrong target in his ultimate quest. She was determined not to make the same mistake.

Chapter 23

WHEN THEY RETURNED TO THEIR ROOMS, ZACHARIAH ENTERED FIRST. HE conducted a sweep of the bedroom as well as the bathroom, then proceeded to check the empty bedroom beside theirs. Only when he determined there were no threats did he tell Tate to enter.

She walked into the room, casting a light as she did. He sometimes forgot that the others couldn't see in the dark. It made him all too aware of his base nature.

Tate didn't seem to notice. She hummed as she moved around the room, performing a couple of turns that mimicked their dancing. When she twirled close to him, she grabbed his hand in an attempt to urge him to join her. Rather than resist, he moved in line with her and continued dancing.

"What is that you're humming?" he asked.

"I have no idea," she said with a smile. "Just one of the songs we heard tonight."

He quirked an eyebrow. She couldn't carry a tune to save her life.

When she laughed, he realized he had conveyed the thought to her. Fortunately, she already knew this about herself and wasn't offended. Her eyes sparkled as she caught his gaze. He glanced at her lips and considered kissing the smile from her lovely face.

"Are you okay with the fact that Clara Kate named me the Kynzesti second commander?"

Coming to a stop at the abrupt question, he lowered his arms and frowned. "Of course. It's an honor for you."

She reached up and fiddled with his tie, not meeting his eyes. "I know. It's just, well, that was once your role with the Gloresti."

"I'm aware of that. It doesn't diminish the achievement for you."

Now she met his gaze. He recognized the worry there. "Okay, Sparky," she said.

She gave him a small smile that he knew was meant to reassure. He watched her step away, watched the smile fall from her face when she turned from him. His eyes moved to the symbol marking her right shoulder blade. He wondered if she could ever know how significant that mark would always be to him.

"Tate," he said. She looked back at him. He rarely used her name when addressing her. "The fact that you would ask me just reinforces why I love you so much."

Her eyes widened. When her lips parted, a knock sounded at the door.

"Tate?" came Ariana's voice through the door. "Would you like my assistance changing into your nightclothes?"

Zachariah continued to hold Tate's gaze. He could tell by the moisture gathering in her eyes that her voice had failed her.

"We'll be all right," he called out.

"Okay. Good night."

Not bothering to respond to the Lekwuesti, he pulled Tate closer. She pressed her cheek against his chest. He rested his chin on top of her head and wrapped his arms around her, inhaling her scent. When she continued to hold him, he trailed his fingers along the nape of her neck and along her shoulder. Then he traced her marking. She shivered.

"I wish we'd had more time to dance," she said after a while. Her voice was muffled against his jacket.

Knowing he was the reason the ball was cut short for her and the others, he briefly closed his eyes. "I'm sorry."

"You should be," she said. She lifted her head, prompting him to open his eyes to look at her. "You kept me from getting the other Estilorians to do the Chicken Dance."

Blinking, he repeated, "'The Chicken Dance?'"

"Yeah." Now, she grinned. The guilt that had gripped him eased at the look in her eye. "Haven't you heard of it? Okay…just picture *archigos* Iniherit doing this."

She stepped a few feet away from him and started humming again. Then she moved her fingers in what he assumed was the manner of a chicken beak moving up and down, followed by an exaggerated flapping of her arms and jutting of her chin. She looked…absurd.

While she was in an awkward squat halfway to the floor, she froze. He realized she had stopped humming. Her deep blue-green eyes rested on his face.

"What?" he asked.

She slowly rose back to her full height. Her expression ranged from disbelieving to ecstatic. "You—you're smiling."

"I am?"

Now, a wide smile spread across her face. "You sure are. And—wow. It's totally sexy hot."

"Is it?" When she got close enough, he reached out and grabbed her around the waist, pulling her against him. "I'll tell you what, Beautiful. If you let me see you in only those shoes and what you're wearing beneath this gown again, I'll give you all the sexy smiles you want."

Ini-herit showered and changed into his sleep tank and pants when he returned to his room after meeting with Clara Kate and the others. As he tied his damp hair back, he considered what this new development meant—not only to all Estilorians, but to him.

There would be no more avoiding contact with Clara Kate. Although he knew his presence caused her pain, he was now a permanent part of her existence. She would require extensive training on the use of her new power. Each of the elders would work with her on discovering and developing her burgeoning abilities. As her power grew, so would theirs. He and the other elders would work with her one-on-one to ensure she had a well-rounded grasp of each of their innate abilities.

He realized that he looked forward to that time alone with her. It wasn't a feeling he'd ever experienced before, so he wasn't sure what to make of it. In light of the other unusual feelings he'd had regarding Clara Kate, he had to take this as a positive sign.

There have been an unusual number of thought intrusions at Central this evening.

The thought flashed through his mind as he pulled back the cover on his bed. Malukali rarely expressed such concerns as this one, so it captured his attention as she warned all of the elders at once.

I'll continue to monitor this, as will Knorbis, she continued. *It could be a result of the masquerade. With so many beings trying to catch the attention of one another, there will naturally be unusual fluctuations in the use of mental abilities. But I want to explore this further to make sure it isn't something more concerning.*

Ini-herit appreciated Malukali's caution. These large events did tend to produce more reactions from their classes than usual, he mused as he climbed into bed. There was a sense bordering on urgency among those who rarely ventured from their class homelands to interact socially with the other classes. Although he didn't really understand the reasoning behind this human-like ritual, he acknowledged its influence on Estilorian society, especially the younger generations.

Glancing at the door that separated his room from Clara Kate's, he considered knocking and telling her this news. Since she wasn't yet connected to the other elders, she wouldn't know about Malukali's observations.

After a moment, he decided not to alarm her. Malukali hadn't implied that they were at risk. From what he understood, the Kynzesti were resistant to thought intrusion. Besides, Clara Kate preferred that he keep as far from her as possible. Closing his eyes, he decided he could at least fulfill this wish since he had failed her on so many others.

Clara Kate went to bed feeling exhausted, but she couldn't sleep. Her body still buzzed with the elder energy that now permanently flowed through her. While it didn't feel unnatural, it was still something to which she had to become adjusted.

After more than two hours of lying in bed without falling asleep, she tried taking a warm bath in her luxurious tub in an effort to relax. Despite the wonderfully scented bubbles, it didn't help. When she returned to bed, her mind continued to spin over how dramatically her life had changed in the span of only days.

She was now an elder. As the Kynzesti class grew, she would work with her cousins to shape it. Someday, they might even have a reserved homeland here at Central. They would learn more about their skills and elemental abilities and integrate them with those of the other classes, using them for the betterment of all.

No pressure, though, Clara Kate mused, rolling onto her side.

Regardless of her new elder status, she couldn't help but wonder what others would think about her pregnancy. How could her class—or any other class, for that matter—respect her in light of her circumstances? Her mother and aunts had given birth at her age, sure. But they had been married and avowed, too. In fact, if it hadn't been for their pregnancies, they might not have actually succeeded in fulfilling the Great Foretelling. Hard to question something like that, she thought.

The fact that her pregnancy had also resulted from a connection based on love wouldn't likely earn her any points on the respect scale. She had chosen to have unprotected sex with Harry. Period.

No, she knew she'd instead have to earn her dues through her future actions. It was fortunate that her first decision as elder was such a no-brainer. Establishing her core leaders within the class hadn't taken much thought at all. She and her cousins were as close as siblings. She knew their strengths and she knew there was no one else she trusted more.

The position of class commander involved direct support of the elder. It was a position for an unfailingly trustworthy and dedicated being, a description that applied to each of her cousins. Additionally, commanders had to make significant decisions in the elder's absence, which required sound judgment and reasoning ability. Outside of her recent misjudgment concerning Quincy's feelings for her, Sophia was the most balanced decision-maker Clara Kate knew. She had the ability to weigh all of the factors in a situation before forming a conclusion, a valuable trait that would make her an excellent commander.

The second commander supported both the elder and the commander. The position often entailed real-world training of the younger class members, such as when Zachariah led the group of young Gloresti to the mainland fifty years earlier. Beings in this role were valued for input gathered through regular interaction with their class and others, since elders often traveled from Central and commanders were usually left in control at their class homelands. She decided that Tate and Tiege would be co-second commanders. They had both learned a great deal in their recent adventures and would certainly learn more in time. They would then use that experience to train future Kynzesti.

As for her first lieutenant, Clara Kate chose her brother, Joshua. Like most lieutenants, he would work largely within the homeland to train their class. He had inherited their mother's fighting skills and their father's patience, a combination that would make him invaluable in this role.

With that decided and her cousins notably excited about their new roles and titles, Clara Kate was left with little to dwell on besides Ini-herit.

Placing a hand on her still-flat stomach, she thought again about the baby. She hadn't ever dreamed of being a mother at such a young age. She hadn't even thought she would fall in love until she was older and had more experience in relationships. But the feelings she had for Ini-herit developed so naturally on the human plane that she hadn't even questioned them. It was like the two of them had been made for each other. Although she knew that most people didn't meet someone and decide within a few months that they were meant to be life-long mates, she also knew that it hadn't taken half that time for her to fall hopelessly in love.

Her parents had a relationship like that. Maybe because she had their love as a model, she understood how significant it was when she found it. She couldn't explain it. It just…was.

That didn't excuse her poor judgment in seducing Harry. She had really let her hormones get the best of her. It had been a decision far outside of her character. But that had really been the point, hadn't it?

Now she had to pay the price. She supposed she would take some solace out of the fact that she wouldn't be the first elder with a child. Of course, that thought made her think of her dad.

Wincing as she thought of the disappointment she was bound to produce when she told her parents that she was pregnant, she once again rolled over and tried a different position to get more comfortable. Unfortunately, it didn't help. She couldn't escape the mental image of telling her parents that they were going to be grandparents. She had *so* screwed up.

Before that even happened, though, she had to tell Ini-herit. She couldn't decide what image was worse: the one with her parents going apoplectic or the one where Ini-herit didn't react at all.

Maybe one of her abilities as an elder was to reverse time.

Issuing a frustrated sigh, she flopped onto her back and pulled the pillow over her head. Then, because the pillow was there and she felt like doing it, she screamed into the muffling fabric as loud as she could.

The uncontrolled action helped. Finally, the constant barrage of thoughts and images stopped flooding her mind. A hazy fatigue settled over her. Her grainy eyes grew heavy.

Allowing the pillow to fall to the floor, she slept.

Outside Clara Kate's door, Metis waited. She was rather proud of herself for managing to follow this group from the ballroom to the offices of the Lekwuesti elder and then on to the rooms being used by the Kynzesti. It had required focusing her energy on Ariana's thoughts, as those were the ones she could most easily access.

Once she found the corridor leading to the rooms she needed, she listened at the doors with her ears as well as her mind to reason out which room belonged to Clara Kate. Because she identified the thought signatures and voices of Ariana, Zachariah and the Corgloresti named Quincy, and because she knew they were paired with the other Kynzesti, she soon deduced that Clara Kate was in one of the first two rooms. It didn't take long for her to pick up a feminine sigh from the second room. She confirmed her assumption when she heard a male clear his throat in the first room. That would be *archigos* Ini-herit.

With that determined, Metis had to backtrack and explore the building so that she knew how to escape with Clara Kate. She would have to abduct the Kynzesti while everyone else slept. That meant she had to navigate this unfamiliar territory without being seen. It also meant she required some supplies.

After more than two hours of walking hallways and accessing transportation tubes that used some kind of mystifying energy to move a being from one location to another, she finally had her plan mapped out. She spent another hour finding supplies, holding onto a few and stashing the rest along her anticipated route. Then she returned to Clara Kate's room, barely avoiding detection by a Waresti male patrolling the hallways. When he had finished his surveillance of the corridor she needed and then moved on, she moved silently to Clara Kate's door.

She had already determined that she couldn't infiltrate the minds of the elders when they were at their fullest strength. But she had learned during her recent time with *archigos* Malukali that if an elder was debilitated, her mind was more malleable. Using this knowledge, Metis stood outside Clara Kate's door and waited until the Kynzesti elder fell asleep.

Fortunately, it happened before the Waresti returned. Her mind suddenly connected with Clara Kate's. She knew from the unusual tenor of the Kynzesti's thoughts that she had accessed her subconscious.

Not wanting Clara Kate to awaken and reinstate the thought barrier, Metis carefully implanted thoughts in the Kynzesti's mind. This was going to be the most difficult part of her plan. She had to convince Clara Kate to leave her room on her own two feet. After that, the Kynzesti was all hers.

Chapter 24

"CLARA KATE, WE MUST HURRY."

Blinking to try and clear the fog from her brain, Clara Kate sat up in bed and looked to the door leading out to the hallway. Ini-herit stood there watching her. She didn't understand why he hadn't come through the adjoining door.

"I was out in the hallway conversing with Zachariah," he said, making her think she had spoken out loud. "There is no time to waste. Come with me."

Although she still didn't understand what was going on, she reacted to the apparent importance of what he conveyed. Climbing out of bed, she walked to the door. She moved much slower than usual. It felt as though it took her an eternity to cross the room. Once she did, she realized that the door was closed.

"What…?" She shook her head in confusion. Where had Ini-herit gone?

"Join me in the hallway, Clara Kate."

Ini-herit spoke from outside her door. He must have pulled the door closed, though for what reason, she couldn't fathom. When she grasped the handle, she realized it was locked. Why had he turned the lock when he closed it?

"Hurry."

How could he not have any sense of urgency in his tone even now? she asked herself, turning the lock with an irritated frown. It took her three tries to accomplish it. Her hand didn't seem to want to cooperate any more than her legs did. Finally, the door opened.

Ini-herit stood in the hallway. His expression didn't change when she emerged, but why would it? He did reach for her arm and began pulling her down the hallway, an action that surprised her.

"Where are we going?" she asked. The words felt thick as they left her mouth. They were barely audible.

"We must get you to safety."

Ini-herit's lips hadn't moved, she realized then. Had he been speaking to her through her thoughts this entire time? How was that possible?

Once again, she shook her head. It felt like someone had wrapped her brain in gauze and packed it back inside her skull. Her vision blurred in and out of focus. For a moment, it almost looked like Ini-herit lost a foot of height, but she guessed it had been a trick of her eye since he was his old self once she blinked.

"Why aren't we getting the others to safety, too?" she thought to ask. She started to turn to look behind her, but the path they were on tilted with the movement. "Whoa."

Grabbing her arm in a painful grip to stabilize her, Ini-herit said, "The others have already been brought to safety. You were the most difficult to rouse."

They had? Her cousins wouldn't leave her behind. Something must be terribly wrong for them to have done so. Her gaze moved along the passages as they walked. Every shadow now seemed ominous and threatening.

"What's wrong, Harry? Why—?"

"No more talking."

She blinked again. That hadn't been a tone Ini-herit had ever used before. He sounded impatient.

"Talking puts us in danger of discovery," he said in a low voice, once again reading her thoughts. "I do not want you to come to harm."

An unexpected feeling of hope stirred in her chest as they entered a transport tube. Ini-herit was concerned for her safety and didn't want her to come to harm. Could that mean that he was beginning to remember emotions?

No. He was probably concerned for her because she was now a fellow elder and the elders all looked out for each other.

"My intentions toward you are more than just that of an elder," he said.

Her breath caught. Did he really mean that? Then another thought right on top of that one: this wasn't right. He shouldn't be able to read her thoughts.

Her head throbbed like someone stuck it with a hot poker. She gasped and brought her hand up in an attempt to ward the feeling off. What in the world?

"Very well," Ini-herit said. "We will do this the hard way."

Something's wrong.

Malukali's thought brought Ini-herit out of a dream-filled sleep. The images in the dream had been dark and violent, making her interruption welcome.

A Lekwuesti named Dara came to me a short while ago, Malukali explained. *She said that Jocelyn, a talented Orculesti, was brought to Central earlier today after experiencing some trauma on the mainland. Dara intended to wait until morning to ask me to meet with Jocelyn and assess her mental condition, but when she went to check on Jocelyn after the ball, she was gone from her room.*

Ini-herit got to his feet. He sensed that what Malukali was about to impart was important. Clara Kate needed to be kept informed.

He knocked on her door even as Malukali continued, *When I tried to connect with Jocelyn's thoughts, I picked up an unusual thought pattern. I think Metis has gotten into Central.*

The news had Ini-herit reaching for Clara Kate's door handle. Propriety had no place in the face of something so urgent. As he pushed the door open, he cast a ball of light and looked over at her bed. Finding it empty, he strode over to the bathroom. The room was dark until the ball of light bounced in behind him.

Realizing Clara Kate wasn't there, he hurried to the door that adjoined her room to Quincy's. Once again, he ignored manners and simply opened the door.

Quincy sat up in bed, squinting as the ball of light followed Ini-herit into the room. As sleep left Quincy's gaze, he looked to the open door between his room and Sophia's. The expression on his face told Ini-herit that he had alarmed him.

Can you identify where Metis is? Uriel asked. The thought was directed to Malukali, though he sent it out to all of the elders.

"Clara Kate is not in her room," Ini-herit said to Quincy. "We must see if she went to someone else's room for the night."

Not so far, Malukali replied. *I'm trying, but whatever she does to assume a new form makes her mind blend with that of the being she kills. Rather like with the Kynzesti, my abilities aren't properly attuned to her.*

"What's going on?" Sophia asked, walking over from her room. She rubbed the sleep from her eyes and glanced at Quincy as he got out of his bed. Her eyes widened in concern as she received the thought he projected. "Where would she go?"

Ini-herit walked past her to the door leading to Tiege's room and said, "Malukali has discovered an unusual thought signature that she believes belongs to Metis. She is here."

"At Central?" Quincy asked. He and Sophia followed Ini-herit. "Holy light!"

Clara Kate is not in her room, Ini-herit broadcasted. When he walked into Tiege's room and saw only the male sleeping in his bed, he continued on to Ariana's door and left the explanations to Quincy and Sophia. *I am checking in the rooms of her family in case she moved for some reason. If she is not in one of these rooms, we can assume Metis succeeded in abducting her.*

A series of projected emotions rushed through him as the others processed this. He might have been imagining it, but the feelings seemed more intense than usual. It was almost as though the fear and worry they conveyed belonged to him.

We will ensure all platforms are secured, Uriel replied. *The Waresti patrolling the hallways near your rooms didn't see anything unusual, but we'll investigate.*

By the time Ini-herit walked through Ariana's door, Zachariah stood in the doorway on the other side of the room. The Mercesti was fully clothed and held his tomahawk. He appeared to know something was wrong.

Coming to a stop in the middle of the room, Ini-herit closed his eyes. It was surprisingly difficult to send out the thought.

Clara Kate is gone.

The responses ranged from Uriel's immediate focus on locking down Central to Gabriel's well-founded fear for his daughter. When Ini-herit again opened his eyes, he spotted Clara Kate's family standing around him. They exchanged looks as Quincy explained what was happening.

"We have to find her," Sophia said. Her cousins nodded. "Follow me."

With a flash of light, she shifted into a bloodhound. Then she took off at a run, leaving her clothing behind. Quincy grabbed the garments off the floor and followed her through the adjoining doors as Tate ran to get her blessed nunchucks. Ini-herit jogged after Sophia, watching Tiege grab his blessed kamas and toss a sheathed dagger to Ariana.

Once they were in Clara Kate's room, Sophia approached the pillow on the ground and spent a few seconds breathing in her cousin's scent. Then she let out a sharp bark and headed for the door. Zachariah opened it for her. They spilled out into the hallway in pursuit.

Ini-herit sent out a stream of thoughts to keep the other elders informed of their progress. As they darted down another hallway, he spotted Alexius and a team of Waresti racing through an adjoining corridor. Ini-herit might not have particularly cared for the sight of Clara Kate on the second commander's arm earlier, but he was glad to see the other male searching for her now.

It didn't matter who found Clara Kate. All that mattered was saving her life.

Chapter 25

METIS HAD HOPED THAT HER MENTAL ABILITIES WOULD ALLOW HER TO lead the Kynzesti to the exit platform that she had found without any issues. When she succeeded in implanting her own thoughts into Clara Kate's mind through her dreams, she believed she would get her wish. Unfortunately, while the female Orculesti, Jocelyn, had clearly been powerful, Metis hadn't been able to maintain her control over the Kynzesti.

It was a good thing she had secured a leaded bud vase during her travels through the Estilorian main base. Knocking Clara Kate unconscious became her only option. She waited as long as she dared so that she was close to one of the places where she left supplies.

Leaving the female where she fell, Metis hurried to the small nook she had used for storage. Propped against the wall was a lightweight plank with two lavender energy rails on the bottom and a thin rope at one end. She discovered it outside the main hall where the Waresti had brought her earlier and used it to transport her supplies.

Now, she lifted it and ran back to Clara Kate. It didn't take her long to haul the female's limp form onto the plank. The rails allowed her to move silently across any surface, so she didn't worry about being too cautious as she tugged the plank by the rope and continued along the route she had established. She had to stop twice to avoid stepping into sight of Waresti patrols. The second time, she was nearly seen and had to use her mental abilities to turn the guard's attention.

Outside of that incident, she focused on keeping her thoughts contained, knowing that there was a possibility the Orculesti elder might seek her out. One of the Waresti who had escorted her to Central might mention Jocelyn to the elder, or someone could check on the Kynzesti female and find her missing. Any number of things could lead to her discovery. She would do what she could to minimize that risk.

Sweat dripped from her temples by the time she succeeded in hauling Clara Kate to the room housing the platform she intended to use. As it had been when she first found it, the room was empty and the platform unattended.

She stopped next to a large crate filled with a couple of other items she found during her earlier explorations. Bringing the plank alongside the crate, she reached in and pulled out a long length of milky-colored rope. Then she used the rope to strap Clara Kate's body to the plank, working quickly in the darkness. In the event the Kynzesti woke up, she wouldn't be able to fly or use her elemental ability. A rag worked well enough as a gag.

Voices had Metis tensing and ducking down. She made sure Clara Kate wasn't visible and peered over the edge of the crate.

A small group of Waresti entered the far side of the room, their swords drawn. Several balls of light followed them. Metis scanned their minds and realized that she hadn't managed to avoid detection by the Orculesti elder, after all. The warriors had been sent to secure the platform so no one could leave.

Knowing it would be foolish to linger, Metis took advantage of the noise the Waresti made as they issued and fulfilled orders. She made sure the dagger she had stolen was still secured around her waist, then grasped the plank's rope and hurried away from the crate. Escaping the room from the direction she had come, she used the dark shadows to conceal them from view. She didn't detect any suspicion from the Waresti as she rose to her full height and hurried with the Kynzesti down a narrow tunnel.

That had been close, she mused. She supposed it wasn't much of a surprise, though, in light of the many protections in place around the Kynzesti. It was a good thing she had developed a secondary plan. There was more than one way out of this air fortress.

Ini-herit hadn't ever experienced the strange sensation that now clung like a band around his chest. The longer it took them to find Clara Kate, the tighter the band got. It was similar to a physical pain.

"What's that?" Tate asked.

They gathered around Sophia when she stopped to investigate a spot on the rug lining the hallway that apparently led to Clara Kate. She issued a soft whine and then moved on to an object a few feet away. Ini-herit identified the small, dark red patch as blood. The feeling in his chest intensified.

"There is blood on this object," Zachariah said, lifting the cylindrical vase Sophia sniffed. His gaze moved to Ini-herit. "This isn't a lethal weapon unless applied to the right spot on the skull. Judging from the amount of blood on the ground, Clara Kate is merely unconscious."

Ini-herit nodded. It was safe to assume Clara Kate was the one who had been incapacitated. If she had escaped Metis, she would have returned to them. They also knew if Metis killed Clara Kate that she would attempt to assume her form, which would leave evidence behind. He couldn't help but wonder why Metis hadn't already done so.

Sophia took off again, distracting him from his thoughts. They sprinted until they reached a narrow corridor. Though the tunnel itself was dark, he saw light flickering at the end of it. It would be a tight fit, but none of them stopped for a second to worry about that.

Because he was armed and could see in the dark, Zachariah entered the tunnel behind Sophia. Ini-herit went in after him. As they emerged, they were greeted by the Waresti guarding the platform.

"Have you seen anyone come through here?" Zachariah asked.

"No, sir," one of them replied. "No one passed this way."

Since Sophia investigated a wooden box near the tunnel, Ini-herit approached it. He noticed more smears of blood on the ground as Sophia gave another whine. When she turned and ran back into the passageway, they all followed her. They were trying to maintain some stealth, so Ini-herit fought the urge to cast a light as they ran. The darkness made him feel unexplainably powerless.

After another few minutes, Sophia's pace slowed. Ini-herit had never been in this part of Central, so deep in its bowels. It looked uninhabited. Sophia growled low in her throat as she approached a rock wall. Everyone with weapons raised them.

"Sophia thinks they're on the other side of this rock," Quincy said.

"That's not a rock," Tate replied. "It's an illusion. They're on the other side."

Where does this opening lead, Sebastian? Ini-herit thought.

Outside, Sebastian said. *It's one of the holes crafted as part of Central's natural cooling system. If Metis wanted to leave without accessing the platforms, she found the right place.*

Metis wasn't sure why there was a disguised room leading directly outside and she really didn't care. All that mattered was that it was about to serve her great purpose.

She had discovered the small chamber a couple of hours earlier when she watched a Waresti emerge from it. He must have been conducting a patrol, as his weapon was drawn and his gaze alert. If she hadn't been walking in complete darkness and taking care to remain among the shadows as she explored, she would likely have been caught. As it was, the Waresti paused and stared intently in her direction, so she used her abilities to make him believe he was seeing nothing but shadows.

Now, she retied the unusual rope she had used to secure the Kynzesti. It took precious time to unwind the rope from the unconscious female, but Metis knew the extra weight of the plank would hinder her ability to fly. It would have been easier to cut the Kynzesti free of the plank, but Metis needed to reuse the entire length of rope to properly secure her.

Although she worked quickly, she cursed the extra time it took to wrap the rope back around the Kynzesti's wrists and upper body. Considering Clara Kate's formidable abilities, though, Metis knew this was the wisest course. She had just finished tying the last knot when Clara Kate shifted and moaned.

"Good," Metis said. "It would be best for you to be conscious for this part." She pressed the tip of her dagger against the Kynzesti's neck, making her draw in a sharp breath. "Get to your feet. Now."

Clara Kate must have decided that it wasn't worth arguing, as she slowly rocked until she got to her knees. Impatient, Metis grabbed a handful of the other female's hair and urged her up with a hard tug. The Kynzesti's cry of pain was muffled by the gag. Metis ignored her.

"I have fastened the ropes around you so that you cannot use your abilities or extend your wings," Metis said. "There are loops for me to carry you. As long as you cooperate—"

The Kynzesti interrupted her with a hard lurch to the left. The dagger sliced her throat, but she didn't seem to notice. Metis followed her, her lips curling on a snarl.

"I will kill you, Kynzesti," she hissed, grabbing one of the loops she had made. "Come with me now."

Although she knew her abilities weren't powerful enough to affect an elder despite that elder's young age, Metis sent a direct wave of thought to the Kynzesti's mind. When the female sagged and the fight seemed to leave her, Metis wasn't sure if it was because of her powerful suggestion or the steady flow of blood pouring from her neck wound.

"Stay up," she snapped, using her greater height to aid her in keeping the Kynzesti upright. She put her dagger back in its sheath and took two more steps toward the edge of the stone floor leading to the pinkening sky beyond.

Then growling filled the room. Glancing over her shoulder, she saw the Kynzesti's family standing at the small opening to the chamber.

"It's over, Metis," Zachariah said.

Clara Kate jerked in Metis' grasp. Her head turned in the direction of her would-be rescuers and her body once again coiled as though regaining the strength to fight. Metis knew she had to act.

Turning, she yanked the rope around Clara Kate, sending them both falling from Central with nothing to break their fall but the roiling ocean many feet below.

Chapter 26

CLARA KATE COULD BARELY THINK. BETWEEN THE PAIN IN HER HEAD AND neck and whatever Metis was doing to try and influence her thoughts, she felt as though she was watching events unfold from outside her own body.

For a moment, when she heard Zachariah's voice and turned to see her family, some of her instincts and training returned to her. Her legs were free, she reasoned in the back of her mind. There was surely something she could do to escape. She glanced at Ini-herit. For the first time, she was sure she saw something stir in his gaze.

Then Metis pulled her. She expected to hit the floor. When she realized they were instead free-falling, terror seized her. Thanks to the gag, her screams came out as little more than muted mewling.

She felt tugging on the ropes that bound her and looked over her shoulder. Metis had extended her luminescent wings and was trying to stop their rapid descent. It wasn't working.

Above them, Clara Kate saw a streak of gold rapidly closing the distance between them and the dwindling image of Central. The further they got from the stronghold, the stronger the enchantments around it became. Soon, it would be gone from her sight and memory.

Issuing a curse, Metis maintained her hold on the rope and withdrew her dagger. She started hacking at the rope. Was she trying to free her?

The blade had no effect on the rope. Clara Kate knew by looking at the milky length wrapped around her that it was a special binding created by the Lekwuesti. It couldn't be cut by metal. Metis must not know that. Since Clara Kate couldn't communicate with the Orculesti through her thoughts, there was nothing she could do.

Metis gave up, letting go of the rope and using her wings to stop herself. Clara Kate watched her grow smaller and waited for the blast of pain that would mark her death as she hit the water.

Then the gold streak reached her. Sophia continued her dive in the form of the harpy eagle until she was able to clutch the rope in her talons. Clara Kate knew the bird would be no more successful in stopping her descent than Metis was.

Let me go! she thought.

No, Sophia returned, making Clara Kate realize they could now share thoughts like other elders and their core leaders. Sophia caught her gaze. *Trust me,* archigos.

Although she was the elder, Clara Kate had no choice but to obey.

Ini-herit knew he would dream of the seemingly eternal fall from Central for centuries to come.

When he walked into the cooling chamber and saw Clara Kate in Metis' grasp, he froze. His mind transposed the image of her in her white nightgown with the white sundress she wore in his memory from the human plane. The innocent image was now violated by the large red stain running from a cut on Clara Kate's neck down to her waist.

She didn't seem to realize how seriously she was injured. Her deep blue-green eyes moved to him, appearing hollow in her pale face. He had to get to her and heal her. She was going to bleed out.

But he didn't have time. Metis moved so quickly that she took all of them off-guard. Well, almost all of them.

Sophia surged forward as Metis jumped, her animal instincts prompting her into action. She reached the edge of the floor shortly after Clara Kate's feet disappeared. Then she leaped off the edge.

Ini-herit and the others followed as quickly as they could. He knew as he jumped that the head-start Metis got was probably enough to keep them from reaching Clara Kate before she hit the water. Still, he mimicked those around him by keeping his wings extinguished and streamlining his body as much as possible in a headfirst dive.

He tried to use his power to generate a protective landing barrier. He had done it once for Clara Kate's mother, Amber, when she was flight training.

But he'd been able to draw on Gabriel's elder power and fear for his avowed at the time, and he couldn't do so now. His efforts were unsuccessful.

Wind burned his eyes as he watched Metis extend her wings. Because she held Clara Kate, she didn't slow much. It was enough to allow them to gain some ground on her. Sophia surged closer to her cousin.

A couple of seconds later, Metis released Clara Kate and locked her wings. They all flew past her, not expecting the maneuver. Ini-herit saw the others briefly exchange looks, but none of them pursued her. Clara Kate had to be their priority.

The water was so close. Ini-herit fought the instinct to extend his wings to stop himself. They watched as Sophia reached Clara Kate and took the rope. He realized she wasn't going to succeed in slowing their fall. Her bird form was far too light. With mere yards to go before impact, all hope seemed lost.

Then Sophia wasn't an eagle. She shifted into a golden kragen. The creature's powerful wings tipped, the thick leather catching a current and lifting them into the air.

Everyone immediately angled their bodies to slow the airflow around them and then extended their wings. Ini-herit's boot clipped a wave as he managed to pull up just in time. Quincy extended his wings a fraction earlier than everyone else, probably interpreting his avowed's thoughts and realizing she wouldn't crash. He soared after Sophia.

On Ini-herit's right, he saw Zachariah grab the less experienced Tate around the waist and twist her sideways to keep her from striking the water. They skimmed the waves with him on his back and her on top of him.

Just as Ini-herit wondered about Tiege and Ariana, a splash of lavender caught his eye. He watched as the Lekwuesti disconnected from a parachute that she must have generated to slow their fall. Tiege had been holding onto her and now extended his wings, carrying her as the fabric vanished in a flash of lavender light.

"Sophia," Ini-herit called out. "Bring Clara Kate to me."

The wind stole his words. He hurried in pursuit of the kragen. Sophia instinctively headed in the direction from which they had come. He understood her reasoning, but he needed to heal Clara Kate.

He got closer to Sophia. Central reappeared in the distance. His gaze moved to Clara Kate, who dangled like a child's doll from the kragen's claws. Her eyes were closed. Something wet and warm hit his cheek as he got less than fifteen feet from her. When he reached up to wipe it away, his fingers came away red. Her blood, he realized. The inexplicable band around his chest tightened even more.

"Sophia!"

This time, his shout reached her. She turned her serpentine neck to glance at him.

"Let me heal her."

She slowed. He didn't pause when he reached Clara Kate's side. Instead, he wrapped his hands around her neck and brought forth the full power of his healing abilities.

First, he closed the artery that Metis had opened. Then he sealed the wound. His attention moved to her head injury next. He healed the small skull fracture, the bruising on her brain and the broken skin. Then he focused on increasing her circulation to more quickly replenish her blood loss. He realized his efforts weren't as effective as they should be. It was almost as though she had another injury requiring additional blood.

Before he could continue his examination, they reached Central. Sophia pulled Clara Kate from his grasp as she landed. The contact with the cold stone floor seemed to rouse Clara Kate. Her eyelids fluttered open. She still looked pale.

Ini-herit realized the other elders had made it to the room. They quickly gathered around Clara Kate, but he wanted to continue his assessment of her condition. Something wasn't right.

Sebastian used his power to dissolve Clara Kate's bindings with a single touch. Ini-herit approached her, removing her gag and pulling her to her feet. She held his gaze the entire time. He couldn't read whatever it was she tried to convey through her eyes, but he realized that the band in his chest eased the longer she studied him. For a brief moment, he wanted it to remain. In its place waited an emotionless void.

"Thank you for healing me," she said in a quiet voice.

"Of course," he said. "Seeing to the welfare of a fellow elder is my highest priority."

Again, he couldn't read her expression, but he knew it wasn't a positive reaction to his matter-of-fact statement. She crossed her arms over her chest and narrowed her gaze.

"Is that the only reason you came after me?" she asked.

He couldn't answer her. His mind told him that this was the only reason he possibly had to pursue her with such ferocity, but another part of himself—a very small part—whispered of something more. All he could do was hold her gaze and hope she somehow understood.

"Oh, the hell with it," she said, throwing her hands up in the air.

That small part of him shattered at the words. But then she stepped closer, grabbed him behind the neck and dragged him down to touch her lips to his.

A surge of energy exploded at the contact, followed by a series of exclamations by the witnesses in the room. Rather than pull away from Clara Kate over the unexpected reaction, Ini-herit drew her against him. When her lips parted beneath his, he claimed her in a way that was both familiar and foreign. Her taste filled him, provoking another powerful flash.

He was in Mrs. B's home in Newnan. He heard his guardian speaking to someone at the front door and got up from doing his homework at the dining room table to see who had come to visit. As he heard the sweet, feminine voice of the stranger, a picture formed in his mind of what she would look like.

Then he saw her. Every imagined image paled in comparison. When she smiled shyly at him, her beauty hit him like a physical blow.

Time moved forward. He sat with her outside the school's cafeteria, laughing at something she said. The sunlight shone on her upswept hair and her sparkling eyes. He felt himself falling hard for her and didn't bother trying to stop it. Only when he realized that there were many other guys looking at her the same way did his good humor fade.

That image shifted to prom. As they danced to a slow song, he held her close, enjoying the feel of her arms around him and breathing in her wonderful scent. When she tipped her face up to catch his gaze, his throat constricted. How could he have possibly earned her love?

Another whirlwind of time and he sat with her in Mrs. B's tree house. They spoke of things that should be impossible, but somehow felt all too true. She talked to him in her calm manner until he couldn't help but accept what she said. Then she gave herself to him in a way he hadn't expected...a way he would cherish forever.

That vow bled seamlessly to his next as they stood together at the transition point. Once he assumed his true form, he would make her his forever.

Then nothing.

Chapter 27

CLARA KATE WASN'T SURE WHAT POSSESSED HER TO KISS INI-HERIT. Normally, just the knowledge that so many people stood around them would have been enough to deter her. But as she held his gaze, she saw just the slightest flicker of expression as he considered how to answer her question about why he risked his life to save hers. It was enough to give her hope, and hope sliced right through her inhibitions.

She felt the snap of power all the way to her toes as their lips touched. After that, her every thought centered on the wonder and amazement that rushed through her when he kissed her. When he didn't deepen the kiss at first, she boldly parted her lips. That was all the encouragement he needed.

Her arms encircled his neck as he kissed her. He explored her with his tongue as though this was a new experience and he wanted to savor every second. But his hands moved along her body in a way that told her he remembered what pleased her most. A vibrant current flowed between them as the kiss continued, intensifying to an alarming level. Drawing on that, she instinctively funneled all of her love to him, sensing the current might help her convey how she felt in a way he could finally understand.

The energy crested. Clara Kate was so overwhelmed by a blast of emotions that tears filled her eyes. She couldn't breathe. She couldn't think. She needed Ini-herit.

She needed Harry.

Without warning, the kiss ended. Ini-herit's lips left hers and he fell to the ground. She looked at him in numb confusion. His eyes were closed. He wasn't moving. It looked as though she had robbed him of every essence of life.

"No!" she cried, falling to her knees beside him. "Harry!"

Ignoring everyone else as they moved forward, she wrapped her arms around him and pressed her ear to his chest. Hot tears spilled from her eyes as she listened for his heartbeat. His skin felt far too cold against the side of her face. An eternity without him in it stretched before her, bleak and unbearable.

"Please don't leave me," she whispered.

Then he stirred. Issuing a low moan, he brought a hand to his head. Clara Kate lifted her head and struggled to look at this face through her blurred vision. She couldn't keep her tears in check.

He slowly opened his eyes, blinking a couple of times as if acclimating to the lighting in the room. She sat back so he could sit up, but he just lay there for a long moment.

"Ini-herit?" she asked, wondering what to do.

Finally, he sat up and looked at her. She reached up to wipe more tears from her gaze so she could focus on him. Then she gasped.

His eyes were no longer silver, but gray.

"Please don't cry, Angel," he said.

Soft exclamations filled the air around them as everyone heard his human southern accent. The sound of Harry's voice struck Clara Kate right in the heart. In direct opposition to his order, she burst into hysterical sobs.

He reached for her. She was too overcome to fight him as he pulled her onto his lap and hugged her tightly to his chest. His voice was husky as he said, "I'm so sorry that I didn't keep my promises to you, love. I didn't realize how much I had to overcome to retain my human awareness. When I think of all you've gone through these past months, thinking that I no longer loved you—God, you're killing me, Angel. Please don't cry."

But she couldn't stop. His words were a wish she had harbored in her heart for so long that their power overwhelmed her. All she could do was cling to him and weep.

"You helped me remember," he said. He took an unsteady breath. For some reason, that gave her the strength she needed to regain some of her control. "All of these months, you've endured the pain of being near me. I can't even imagine how it must have been, hearing me tell you that I didn't remember you after I promised—"

He stopped talking. She knew he was close to losing his composure.

Taking a deep breath, she eased away from his chest and did what she could to wipe her face dry. She vaguely realized that they were now alone and silently thanked her family for giving her this moment with him.

"I love you, Harry," she said. "Even if you suck at keeping promises."

His lips parted in surprise. Then he laughed, long and deep. The sight and sound brought a smile to her face and a fresh round of tears to her eyes.

"Lord, I needed that," he said when his laughter faded. He cupped the side of her face, using his thumb to wipe away a tear. "I love you, too, Angel, more than I could ever possibly tell you. Now that I remember everything, I'll spend the rest of my existence making these past months up to you."

She started to reply, but he distracted her by leaning down and kissing her. Every other thought faded away. She sighed against his mouth, pleasure streaking through her with each stroke of his tongue. When his hands began roaming, caressing any bare skin they could find, she reciprocated. In the back of her mind, she registered the subtle differences between Harry's Estilorian form and his human one. Before, he'd been fit and toned. Now, he was muscular and sublime.

After a couple of minutes, she broke off the kiss. Her heart thundered in her ears as she struggled to catch her breath. She knew her cheeks were flushed. The intimate thoughts that ran through her mind as she felt Harry's touch were far from proper.

"Um, Harry…how do you think the whole 'sharing thoughts with my dad' thing is going to go?"

He quirked an eyebrow. "Well, up until you said that, fine. Now I'm having a hard time not broadcasting to him."

Her blush deepened. "Sorry. We'll have to figure something out. See, there's something I have to tell—"

"Hey, can we come back in yet?" Tate shouted from outside the room. "We'd like to meet the 'new and improved' Ini-herit."

Sighing, Clara Kate caught his gaze and said, "I guess we can't tell them we're never leaving this place, can we?"

"We could," he answered, a grin flashing across his sinfully gorgeous face, "but I'd prefer never leaving somewhere with a bed."

Oh, how she hoped he was keeping such thoughts from her father! Blushing with the intensity of a thousand suns, she shoved at his shoulder and shook her head in mock censure. He got to his feet, bringing her with him.

When they both stood, he wrapped an arm around her waist and anchored her against his side. Then he kissed the top of her head and nodded.

"Come on back," she called out to her family, her eyes on Ini-herit's.

The others filtered into the room. Clara Kate recognized the curiosity in most of their gazes. Even the elders looked intrigued.

While everyone else hesitated a few feet away, Tate walked right up and flung her arms around them. Clara Kate's heart swelled over the sincerely joyous gesture. She returned the hug with a big smile.

"I'm so happy for you!" her cousin exclaimed, her embrace tight and full of enthusiasm. When she pulled back, she gave Ini-herit a cheerful wink. "I knew you'd come around eventually. No one can outlast C.K.'s stubbornness."

"Hey," Clara Kate said, but she grinned as Ini-herit squeezed her shoulder. "Show more respect for your elder."

Tate responded with a dimpled smile and a shrug.

"Thanks, Tate," Ini-herit replied. "I appreciate the vote of confidence."

"I wonder how long it'll take me to get used to you smiling," Knorbis said.

That started a loud conversation that flowed around Clara Kate like happy chaos. She barely registered the words as everyone approached and shared their variations of congratulations. At some point, Sebastian used his power to clean the blood from her clothes and skin. Several times, tears of elation pricked her eyes and she had to force them back. It all felt like an impossible dream.

"Congrats, you two," Sophia said as she approached with Quincy. The hum of conversation continued behind them.

"Thanks, Soph," Clara Kate said. She reached out and hugged her cousin. "And thanks for saving my life, while I'm at it."

"Oh, sure," Sophia replied, returning the hug. "What kind of commander would I be if I let my elder die on my first day on the job?"

Laughing, Clara Kate pulled back from the embrace. "Well, you certainly confirmed today that I made the right choice. All of you confirmed it."

"It's strange, though," Sophia mused. "I heard your thoughts so distinctly when we were falling. Now, I can't really hear you at all."

"Your connection is still growing," Ini-herit explained. "It'll get stronger over time. For now, you'll experience it more when there's a need."

Sophia nodded. Quincy put his arm over her shoulders and smiled at his elder.

"It's great to see this new side of you, *archigos*," he said. "I know this change will make everything easier for both of you, especially with the baby and all."

All conversation ceased. Clara Kate struggled not to flush with guilt as everyone glanced in her direction. When she glanced at Ini-herit, she realized that he just looked confused. Beside them, Quincy paled.

"Oh, no," he said. "I'm so sorry, C.K. I assumed…"

"It's okay, Quincy," she assured him. Then she took Ini-herit's hands and turned to face him. For the first time, her pregnancy filled her with something besides shame and fear. "What Quincy is saying, Harry, is what I've been unable to until now. The thing is…you're going to be a father."

Metis knew better than to return to the main base. She couldn't risk getting captured, and all of the entrances would certainly be secured by now. The knowledge had fury scalding the back of her throat. Battling the urge to scream, she wished that she could dispose of these emotions that had come to her as a result of her new form.

It was so much better to feel nothing.

She had come so close to achieving her goal. Although she didn't know why Clara Kate was a key to acquiring the Elder Scroll, the fact that everyone risked their lives to rescue her told her that she had been on the right track.

Now she had to figure out how she was going to find Clara Kate again. Although the elders knew Metis' current form and would take measures to ensure every one of their followers did, too, she decided that she needed to retain her Orculesti abilities. She hadn't been in this form long enough to hope she could still read and influence thoughts if she changed forms. Even if she could, it wouldn't be at the same level. No, she couldn't afford to lose this particular power.

She would have to find knowledgeable Waresti on the mainland and attune herself to their thoughts. The Kynzesti would return to the mainland eventually, if for no other reason than to stop Eirik on his quest.

When they did, she would be ready. The Elder Scroll would be hers.

PART III:

ELDER

Elder [*n.* **el**-der]: A person of greater age and/or higher rank than oneself; an influential member of a tribe or community, often a chief or ruler.

Chapter 28

THEY FLEW TO THE LEKWUESTI HOMELAND FOR THE PAIRING CEREMONIES a couple of hours after Clara Kate's announcement. Ini-herit insisted on carrying her. Although he'd done a second round of healing on her as soon as his brain cleared enough for him to do so, he knew she was exhausted. She slept even now.

He indulged himself by reaching around her to touch the taut skin of her abdomen. She had worn the uncharacteristic belly-baring top and low-waisted, floor-length skirt for just this reason. The skin-to-skin contact allowed him to use his abilities to listen to the heartbeat of his future son or daughter. The strong pulse of it brought a ridiculous grin to his face.

Dear Lord, he was going to be a father.

He was sure his expression had been rather comical when she told him. Because he was still filtering different parts of his human and Estilorian selves, he'd experienced two different reactions.

His millennia-old self nodded in acknowledgement of the news. They'd had sex, she had conceived. Got it.

His eighteen-year-old human self wavered between absolute elation and immobilizing fear. He had no doubt that her father was going to choke the life out of him.

In the end, even the knowledge that he probably wouldn't live to see his child's birth hadn't stopped the smile from spreading across his face. He had wanted to touch her abdomen right then, but she wasn't about to let him lift her nightdress in front of everyone. Instead, they had enjoyed another round of congratulations as he once again used his healing abilities on her.

When they were alone in their rooms, she bared her midsection so he could connect with the baby for the first time. It was a moment he wouldn't ever forget. He just stood there for several minutes without speaking.

"Are you excited, Harry?" she asked in an uncertain voice.

She must have seen the emotion in his eyes when he caught her gaze. Rather than wait for a response, she leaned up and kissed him. Love for her filled him with such potency that he almost couldn't bear it.

He thought again of the past few months from her perspective. He tried to imagine how he would have felt if he awoke on this plane after experiencing everything they had on the human plane and then learned that she had no memory of it. Then he added the pregnancy to the equation. He knew it would have slain him.

But his angel had borne it. Though he didn't know how, she had. He was convinced she was the strongest being on either plane.

And the sexiest. They hadn't even been alone in their rooms for ten minutes before he pinned her against the wall, showing her how much he loved her…craved her. He wanted her to know everything he held in his heart for her. He interspersed words of love with the kisses he rained on her.

This time, when her eyes filled with tears, they didn't cause him such alarm. He understood.

Before they left for the Lekwuesti homeland, he sat in his bedroom and connected with Gabriel. There was no doubt that this was a conversation he should be having face-to-face with his best friend. Unfortunately, circumstances prevented it. He'd have to make due and just be grateful the other elders had kept the details to themselves so he could do this.

Gabriel?

Ini-herit?

Yeah…um, I know I sound different. I'm sure you sensed it earlier. Something's happened.

Is Clara Kate all right?

That was a tough question. Not knowing what else to say, he conveyed, *Sure. She's, well, thrilled. She helped me remember my human existence.*

Ah. That explains a lot, Gabriel responded. His happiness for both of them was clear in the thought.

Yeah. Well, I wanted to let you know a couple of things. I'm sorry we can't do this in person. The situation is complicated.

I understand.

Cool. The first thing I want to discuss with you is how much I love Clara Kate. I told her when we were on the human plane that I wanted to avow with her, and that hasn't changed.

I see.

I'd also like to ask you for her hand in marriage.

There was a long pause. Ini-herit's leg bounced up and down and he had to consciously stop himself from doing it.

You've only known each other for, what, a few months?

Five months, three weeks and two days. Our love is certain, regardless of time. If you reach deeply enough into my thoughts, you'll know I'm telling the truth.

I get that, and I know that Olivia and Skye knew their hearts in an equally short amount of time. But what's the rush? You both have centuries ahead of you.

Swallowing hard, he thought, *Yeah...about that. I have some other big news for you.*

What's that?

You're going to be a grandfather.

All in all, the conversation hadn't been as bad as he feared. Yes, there had been a moment when he thought Gabriel might somehow reach through his thoughts and strangle him. But in the end, his friend had deferred to his base nature, which was patient and understanding. He knew Ini-herit and Clara Kate had acted out of love and that they hadn't expected the consequences. Gabriel also confessed he was relieved to know that the Kynzesti could bear children, though he hoped the rest of them decided to wait until they were older to do so.

Ini-herit received his friend's blessing to avow with Clara Kate whenever she was ready, and Gabriel said there would be a wedding the moment they returned to the Kynzesti homeland. He figured it would give Amber, Olivia and Skye something to focus on besides the continued danger their firstborn children faced. Ini-herit vowed to protect Clara Kate and their unborn child, a fact that went a long way to smooth things over.

As the Lekwuesti homeland came into sight, he leaned down to kiss the side of Clara Kate's neck. She smelled so fresh and sweet. He could breathe in her scent all day and be content. When his lips caressed her soft skin, she sighed and murmured something in her sleep.

"Wake up, Angel," he said near her ear. "We're about to arrive at our destination."

She blinked awake, reaching up to rub the fatigue from her eyes and yawning. Wishing she had more time to rest, he landed on the platform that had been reserved for them and began unfastening the flight harness that secured her in front of him. Commander Caoilinn stood waiting for them. She stared at him longer than usual.

"It's the eyes, right?" he guessed. When she blinked and her lips parted, he added, "And the new accent. But, hey, I still have my pairing markings."

The Lekwuesti commander quickly regrouped, giving him a genuine smile. "Well, this is exciting news. I'm thrilled to see you so happy, *archigos.*"

"Thanks. Me, too."

Clara Kate took his hand and entwined her fingers with his, gifting him with a smile. Once everyone landed, Sebastian and Caoilinn led them along the paths leading to the place where the pairings would take place. The Lekwuesti homeland looked much like a human suburb, comprised of many dwellings of various sizes, most bearing thatched or clay tile roofs and brightly painted exteriors. There were also large gathering places such as parks and café-style buildings, seeing as the Lekwuesti was a social class. They were led to just such a space, a three-story stone building with numerous glass windows and colorful awnings.

Once inside, they took a transport tube to the second floor. A large, round auditorium had been created there. Ini-herit spotted at least a hundred Lekwuesti in the space.

Sebastian stopped him and Clara Kate before they entered the room. "Clara Kate, as we explained to you before, I'll soon be paired with you just like I am the other elders. As soon as we perform the necessary ceremony and join in thought, I'll see to your hospitality needs." He smiled. "I'm looking forward to producing your maternity wardrobe."

She flushed and glanced briefly at Ini-herit, who grinned. "Thanks, Sebastian," she said.

"Absolutely. My point in mentioning this is if you'd like to take this time to rest while your cousins are paired, I've arranged for some accommodations just down the hall."

Ini-herit sensed her relief in the set of her shoulders and answered for her. "That would be great, Sebastian. I'll go with her."

"Excellent." Sebastian sent him the thought of the room's location, as well as another thought that had Ini-herit smiling and nodding in thanks. "I'll reach out to you when we're through here."

The doors to the auditorium closed as Ini-herit guided Clara Kate to the room waiting for her. She sagged against his side when he put an arm around her shoulders, so he reached down and picked her up.

Gasping, she said, "Put me down, Harry! I can manage on my own."

"You've more than proven that," he said. "But you'll have to indulge my need to keep you close for quite some time yet, I'm afraid. At least a century or two."

That made her snort out a laugh. Although she shook her head at him, she couldn't hide her smile.

They reached the room a couple of minutes later. He set Clara Kate on her feet once they entered it, then closed and locked the door behind them. She looked around the nicely appointed bedroom with wide eyes, still unused to the level of opulence often seen at Central. Her family's home was comfortable and lovely, but many spaces here would put all human magazine pictures to shame.

Reaching into his pocket, Ini-herit pulled out the gift Sebastian had crafted for him. The two rings were silver. Hers resembled a vintage style from the human plane, the metal looking almost like lace with its delicate pattern. The diamond and deep blue-green gems comprising the center stone sparkled in the light. The men's ring bore a solid silver band with the same center stone.

"What's that?" Clara Kate asked, finally glancing at him. Her brows lowered into a considering expression as she stepped closer.

"These are rings that I asked Sebastian to craft for us." He watched her eyes widen as he held them up. She brought a hand to her lips and caught his gaze. "I'm hoping, since I've gained your father's permission, that you'll allow me to fulfill my second promise to you." Closing the distance between them, he tipped her chin up and lightly brushed his lips over hers. "Clara Kate, will you exchange vows with me?"

It took her a moment, but she managed to nod. Her eyes glistened as she took a deep, centering breath.

"Thank you, Angel." He handed her the men's ring and took her left hand into both of his. His throat tightened as the words he wanted to share with her entered his mind and his heart. "Clara Kate, when you entered my life, I had no idea how much it was going to change. Because of you, I know a love more precious than anything I ever imagined. You give meaning to my existence and I'll cherish what we have forever. I offer you this ring as a symbol of my love and my unbreakable commitment to you."

He slid her ring onto her left ring finger. She then took his left hand and said, "Ini-herit, I knew how much my life was going to change when I met you. Because of you, I now have a love that is every bit as precious as I ever imagined. You give meaning to my existence and I'll cherish what we have forever. I offer you this ring as a symbol of my love and my unbreakable commitment to you."

Once she placed the ring on his ring finger, they linked their hands so their rings touched. Then he leaned down and captured her mouth in a kiss to seal the vow.

Unexpected pain seared over his body, culminating in a longer, deeper pain on his right bicep. Clara Kate inhaled sharply, likely feeling similar pain as her avowed markings were created. Knowing better than to break the kiss, he pushed past the pain and focused on enjoying the moment. He wanted to preserve this memory forever.

Finally, they parted. He realized that the three deep blue-green estoile markings around her eyes now had silver crescents curving around them. She would have a matching symbol on the back of her right shoulder blade.

Your markings!

Her distraught thought entered his head as clearly as though she had spoken it, another effect of the avowing. He glanced down at his arms and realized his skin was now unmarked save for the marking on his right bicep that matched hers.

Don't be alarmed, he thought back to her. Her troubled eyes moved to his as she heard the thought. *The only marking that matters to me is the one that calls me yours.*

That had her concern easing into delight. *I love you,* she thought, reaching up to encircle his neck with her arms.

I love you, too.

Show me.

It would be my greatest pleasure.

Chapter 29

E IRIK GLANCED UP FROM HIS CONVERSATION WITH FRIEDRICH AS THEIR informant approached. The spy made appearances several times a day in an effort to keep Eirik's Mercesti from intersecting with Harold and Derian and the rest of the party searching for them. It had worked flawlessly so far, but today, the spy looked anxious.

"What news do you bear?" Eirik asked.

"I fear that my efforts to aid you have not gone unnoticed. It seems Derian and Harold have begun to suspect that the only way you could be eluding them is through the help of someone aware of their plans."

Frowning, Eirik exchanged a look with Friedrich. This was actually the concern they'd been discussing before their informant arrived.

"Have you received an update on the return of Tate and Ariana from Central?" Friedrich asked.

"Not recently. Harold and Derian are withholding more information now. The last I heard was that the Lekwuesti pairing ceremonies would take place today. Because I know they wish to stop you from acquiring the remaining piece of the artifact, I imagine they will return to the mainland within a day or two."

Eirik paced as he considered this. "Will you continue to aid us until they return?"

"For as long as it is possible without getting caught."

That had Eirik suppressing a growl. He wanted to grab the spy by the throat to try and gain compliance, but the truth was, he couldn't fault the other being's focus on self-preservation. He would have said the same thing if he was in their position.

"Fine," he snapped. "Then tell us where we need to go now to remain undiscovered."

"I will." The other being hesitated. "There is something else I thought might bear mentioning."

"What is that?"

"One of the Kynzesti was attacked while at Central."

Eirik stopped pacing and stared at the informant. His hands slowly closed into tight fists as he sensed the news to come.

"The details are vague, but from what I understand, a Mercesti somehow made it to Central and nearly killed the Kynzesti. Why I felt this was worth mentioning is that I learned the name of the Mercesti. It was the shapeshifter, Metis."

"You're *avowed*?"

Clara Kate blinked as she absorbed Alexius' shocked expression. She stood with him in the hallway outside of her bedroom at Central. He had stopped by after she and her family returned from the pairing ceremonies and asked to speak with her alone. No sooner did she greet him than he saw her new avowed markings and staggered a full step away from her.

"I, well...yes," she replied, trying to understand his behavior. "Harry finally remembered our relationship from the human plane. Once I told him I was pregnant—" She cut herself off as he jerked back again. Battling a wave of unexpected guilt, she said, "Alexius, didn't Uriel convey any of this to you?"

She knew the answer to her question even as she asked it. She hadn't ever seen him look so pale. So defeated. A sick feeling blossomed in her stomach.

"But I love you," he whispered.

Now she was the one who stumbled back, needing the wall behind her for support. She wasn't sure who looked more stunned as they held each other's gazes.

He loved her? Alexius, a being from the class that fought emotion at every turn—a being she had seen face terrifying enemies without batting an eye—*loved* her? When had this happened? How hadn't she known?

She watched helplessly as the male whose heart she had just blown to pieces slowly collected himself. The sick feeling unfurled in her belly and spread painfully to her chest. Hadn't she just endured weeks of this kind of anguish? How could she, of all beings, have missed the signs? She realized that she had been so absorbed in her own emotional turmoil that she failed to recognize the depth of his feelings. She had to be the most self-involved being on either plane.

"I'm so sorry, Alexius," she said, fumbling for the right words. "I should have told you sooner. I wish things were different. I wish—"

He cut her off. "I understand, *archigos*."

The use of her new title made her flinch. She stopped herself from begging him to use her first name when she saw his expression.

"*Archigos* Ini-herit deserved the honor of learning about his coming child before anyone else," he continued in a monotone. "Congratulations to you both."

She had no idea what to say. What to do. Alexius was such a good friend. Losing that relationship over an imbalance in their affection for each other was too devastating to consider. Wanting to convey this to him, she reached out and touched his upper arm as she started to respond. He took another step away from her. The action lanced through her like an arrow tip.

Letting her hands fall to her sides, she blinked back tears and said, "I can't begin to tell you how difficult these past couple of months have been, Alexius. I couldn't have gotten through them without the support of my family and friends. That includes you."

When his burnt orange gaze met hers this time, she read nothing there.

Feeling him slipping away from her, she hurried to explain, "I turned to you as a source of comfort. You're a wonderful friend. I'm so sorry for any pain I've caused you."

"You have nothing to apologize for, *archigos*. You made no promises or declarations of emotion to me."

Lord, he wasn't making this any easier by offering excuses for her. "No," she agreed, "but I wasn't entirely honest with you, either. I hope you know that it was never my intent to hurt you, Alexius."

He nodded once. "I understand, *archigos*. Thank you for taking the time to speak with me."

She took a deep breath, recognizing the dismissal. She knew he wanted to remove himself from her presence. He needed time.

"Of course," she said, and it about slayed her.

He started to turn, then looked back at her. "If I might make one request, should it not be too disrespectful of your position?"

Her heart lightening with hope, she offered him a grateful smile. "Anything."

"Please address me as commander Alexius from now on."

Her throat seized. Knowing words wouldn't get past the hot pain caused by his request, she nodded instead. Then she watched him walk away.

She wanted to break down and bawl, but she knew that Ini-herit now experienced at least a part of everything she did. The last thing she wanted was for him to step into the hall to find her in such a state. He'd learn soon enough how this conversation went.

Taking several deep breaths and pulling herself together, she turned the door handle and entered her bedroom. Much to her surprise, her bed was occupied.

"Finally," Tate said. "You were taking forever out there."

"Ah..."

Unable to manage more than that, Clara Kate looked from Tate, who was lying on her stomach in the middle of the bed with her feet in the air, to Sophia and Ariana on either side of her. They had all changed into lounging clothes since they weren't planning on traveling back to the mainland until the following morning. A tray containing an assortment of finger foods sat in front of them.

"Are you all right, C.K.?" Sophia asked with a concerned frown.

Smoothing her features and clearing the lingering emotion from her throat, Clara Kate shrugged. She wasn't about to lie with Tate sitting right there. "Where's Harry?"

"We kicked the guys out," Tate answered, reaching for a chocolate-covered strawberry.

Clara Kate's stomach grumbled despite the knot residing there. She moved closer to the bed. "You did?" She glanced around the room. "There's no way Zachariah left you unprotected."

Tate grinned. "He's standing on the other side of the adjoining door."

"Oh."

Ariana lifted the tray with a pointed look, beckoning Clara Kate even closer. Unable to resist, she climbed onto the large bed and sat beside the other females. She reached for a pink-frosted petit four. When she looked at it more closely, she realized that it was decorated with a white baby's bonnet.

"Okay…what's this all about?" she asked.

"We wanted to do a little something to celebrate," Sophia said.

"Yeah," Tate added, lifting a mini-cupcake topped in blue sprinkles. "We're going to be second cousins. Kind of like honorary aunts!"

Ariana smiled. "It's a baby shower. Well, a prelude to the one we'll have for you when we get back home."

Clara Kate didn't fail to miss that Ariana had referred to the Kynzesti homeland as her home. She also finally realized that they were celebrating her pregnancy.

The stark difference between this reality and the one she had endured only a day ago had Clara Kate losing her hold on her emotions. When she looked again at the tray of colorful treats, tears blurred her vision.

"Thanks, you guys," she managed to say. "You have no idea how much this means to me."

"Aww, we're happy for you, C.K.," Tate said, moving into a sitting position so she could put an arm around her. "And I have to admit, we figured we'd have more success in pumping you for details when we had you in the midst of a sugar high."

"Details about what?"

All three females leaned closer, making Clara Kate's eyebrows rise. Tate spoke for them.

"Details about sex."

In his bedroom, Ini-herit sat on the sofa and studied his medallion, trying to ignore the emotions swirling through him as a result of his connection to Clara Kate. Funneling and processing everything she felt was a kind of invasion of privacy, he thought. He also tried to close his mind to the stray thoughts she allowed to filter through. It would take her some time to get used to their mental bond.

"What do you suppose they're talking about in there?" Tiege asked.

Tate's twin sat at the table with Quincy, playing cards. His gaze kept moving to the closed door between the bedrooms. Since Zachariah leaned against the wall right beside the door, it looked like Tiege was staring at the Mercesti.

"Who knows?" Ini-herit said, keeping his tone vague. "Probably just boring girl talk."

Zachariah raised an eyebrow as Quincy snorted out a laugh. Knowing the other two males were likely intercepting thoughts from their avoweds, Ini-herit fought a hot flush of embarrassment. They surely knew exactly what the topic of conversation was.

"You could have the decency not to tune in," he muttered, looking between them.

"You take all the fun out of everything," Quincy said, staring at his cards and struggling not to smile. "At least all of the feedback from C.K. is positive."

"Good Lord." Ini-herit rubbed the back of his neck, swearing it was about to burst into flame.

"Feedback about what?" Tiege asked.

When Quincy opened his mouth to respond, Ini-herit shot him a look. "I'm still your elder," he warned.

Quincy closed his mouth. His silver eyes were alight with humor, though. Tiege frowned.

"Well, this all got rather awkward," Zachariah mused dryly, pushing away from the wall. He strolled over to Ini-herit. "How are your efforts to decipher the medallion's map coming along, *archigos*?"

"They're not." Ini-herit handed the medallion to Zachariah when he reached for it. Catching the Mercesti's gaze, he said, "I don't suppose I could get you to stop with the formal title?"

"Not likely."

"You could if you ordered him to," Quincy interjected from the other side of the room.

Both males looked at him. He shrugged with a "You know it's true" expression.

"All right," Ini-herit said with a nod. "Then I order all of you to address me as Harry or Ini-herit from now on. If you're more comfortable using my title among unfamiliar company, that's fine. Otherwise, knock it off."

Quincy and Tiege nodded their agreement. Zachariah stared at the medallion and didn't comment.

"Zachariah?" Ini-herit prompted.

"As you wish," he said at last.

"Thank you."

Lifting the medallion by its chain, the Mercesti walked back to the door and watched it twirl, his face expressionless. Ini-herit knew there was something significant the other male wasn't saying. Having spent centuries of his own existence not only expressionless, but emotionless, Ini-herit recognized the difference.

Zachariah lost his rank and his title. Maybe he doesn't understand why someone would treat theirs so dismissively.

Clara Kate's thought reached him as he studied the Mercesti. He realized she was right. He also realized he was conveying as much to her as she was to him.

Thanks, Angel.

Rising and approaching Zachariah as Tiege and Quincy resumed their game-play, Ini-herit said, "Zachariah, do you understand my request?"

"It doesn't matter if I understand it," he answered, his eyes on the flashing metal.

"Oh, I think it does." Crossing his arms over his chest, he also leaned against the wall. "When you avowed with Tate, you became a member of Clara Kate's family."

Zachariah looked over at him.

"That means, since I'm avowed to Clara Kate, that you're part of my family, too."

As Zachariah processed this, the medallion swung, forgotten, in his fist. Ini-herit's gaze moved to the spinning metal.

Then he reached out and grabbed Zachariah's hand. "Damn. That's it."

"What?"

"The map," Ini-herit explained, glancing at Tiege and Quincy as they got to their feet. "It isn't only on one side of the medallion. You have to twirl it to see it. And it isn't a map to the location of the scroll piece."

When the other males approached, he once again looked at the medallion and said, "It's the key to getting through the traps that surround it."

Chapter 30

THEY RETURNED TO THE MAINLAND THE FOLLOWING MORNING. HAROLD and Derian halted their search for Eirik in anticipation of the arrival of the others and waited in a forested area about thirty miles north of the ancient library.

Zachariah sought out Derian shortly after they reached the forest. The tattooed Mercesti male stood talking with Melanthe, peering at an ethereal map of the plane that must have been produced by a Waresti. Melanthe spotted Zachariah first. Derian followed her gaze and then turned to greet him.

"Welcome back, sir," he said.

"Thank you. I heard through Uriel that you've had difficulty tracking Eirik. I wanted to get your thoughts on that."

Derian caught Melanthe's gaze. She nodded and stepped away, excusing herself. Zachariah watched her approach Tate and her family, who had gathered a few feet away. She issued enthusiastic congratulations to Clara Kate over her pregnancy and ascension to elder.

"Best to speak of this privately," Derian said in a low voice.

Before stepping away, Zachariah glanced at Tate. She was angled away from him, so his gaze brushed the back of her head. Due to the weather and their travels, she had decided against wearing her usual hair accents. Instead, she had pulled her colorful curls back at the temples and secured that part of her hair with a red jeweled comb. The rest of her curls spiraled down her back. His focus was on her safety, but he couldn't help but notice how her hair drew attention to her trim waist and the curves of her hips.

I'll be right here, she conveyed, not stopping her conversation with Tiege.

Talk to Derian. My thoughts are open to you.

Nodding, Zachariah walked a short distance away with the other male. Although they were out of hearing range of the others, they could see everyone from their positions.

"I apologize, but this topic is one I've discussed with commander Harold at some length," Derian began. "In light of our failure to find Eirik or his closest followers, we've deduced that someone with knowledge of our efforts is aiding him."

Although he'd come to the same conclusion himself after speaking with Uriel, Zachariah frowned. Once again, he glanced at Tate. The traitor could be only feet from her.

"I suspect it's one of us," Derian said, following his gaze.

He meant a Mercesti. "I'm certain of it," Zachariah said. "And it's someone in a position with access to specific details about our plans."

Derian's eyes shifted to him. His usually fierce expression sobered as he absorbed the words and their implication. Zachariah knew what the other male intended to ask before he even opened his mouth.

"Of course it isn't you," he said, and watched the tension in Derian's shoulders ease. "Bloody hell. You should know I'm a better judge of character than that."

Clearing his throat, Derian said, "Aye, sir."

Both of the males looked around the camp. Because the temperature had dropped, the crisp air plumed white around everyone's heads as they breathed. Several fires burned in an effort to ward off the chill. A mix of Mercesti, Waresti and other classes moved around the area, seemingly united. The reality that they weren't was even more chilling than the weather.

"We need to identify the traitor before we leave this place," Zachariah said.

"How?"

"Simple. We'll ask."

Looking again at Tate, he thought, *I need your help, Beautiful.*

She turned from her conversation with Tiege, a bright, dimpled smile on her face resulting from whatever her brother had said. When her brilliant blue-green gaze latched onto him, Zachariah felt the breath seize in his throat. He wondered if he would ever be able to look at her and not have this reaction. When she started in his direction, her hips swaying with each step, he knew the answer.

Ariana was clearly trying to provoke him with her wardrobe choices for his avowed. Tate's black pants conformed to her feminine curves, as did the deep blue-green, long-sleeved top she wore. Her black leather boots reached all the way to the middle of her thighs, just above which she wore black leather holsters bearing her blessed nunchucks. Glittering red jewelry decorated her ears, wrists and throat. Tate insisted on wearing the accent color now, seemingly wanting the world to know to whom she was paired.

I thought you'd never ask, she thought, stopping beside him and brushing his bicep with her fingertips. She couldn't seem to be near him without touching him. He pretended not to notice. She grinned, knowing his thoughts. Then she looked at the other Mercesti.

"Hello. You're Derian, right? We never got the chance to officially meet. I'm Tate."

She extended her hand. Derian stared back at her. His face bore no expression, but his red eyes moved from her hair to her eye markings to her vivid wardrobe choices.

"Thank you for saving Sophia and risking so much to save me and Ariana," she said, seemingly unperturbed by his lack of response. When he still didn't return her handshake, she started to lower her arm.

He reached out and took her hand in both of his. "Nay, milady. Thank ye for bringing commander Zachariah back to us."

Blinking at the power behind his response, Tate looked at Zachariah. She smiled when she said, "Oh, he did that all on his own."

Derian squeezed her hand, drawing her attention. "We both know that's not true."

She held his gaze for a moment, her smile fading.

"And he picked an ideal female as his avowed," he continued. "One willing to risk her life to save the Estilorian plane from Eirik's evil."

Zachariah knew she was going to argue because she felt undeserving of Derian's praise. To avoid her argument and his resulting irritation, he reached out and took her hand from Derian. He held the other male's gaze for a long moment until Derian stood straighter and nodded.

"Right, then," Derian said. "How do ye want to go about it, sir?"

"Ask them."

Not questioning the order, Derian turned to face the encampment. He raised his voice and asked, "Have any of ye fed information to Eirik about our efforts to find him?"

A series of negative responses ensued. Tate's gaze moved around the campsite as she watched for the reaction generated through her lie-detecting power. Zachariah tapped into her thoughts. He was sure Derian was curious about what they were doing. They had been deliberately vague about Tate's abilities as they got to know the new Mercesti. All Derian really knew was that she could shatter illusions.

After a moment, Zachariah exchanged a look with Tate.

"Well?" Derian prompted.

"Who is away from camp?" Zachariah asked.

"Verrell, Alys and Oria have gone to meet with our allies to recruit their aid. Why?"

"Because one of them is the traitor."

Metis found that her time alone after her botched plan to kidnap the Kynzesti elder gave her more perspective on things. Although she loathed to admit it, she wasn't the most brilliant strategist. Yes, she had inherited some impressive mental abilities, but those weren't enough to get her close to the Kynzesti elder and the last scroll piece. Thanks to her limited time outside of Tethys' lair, she wasn't experienced enough to blend among the other Estilorians. Just her manner of speech had aroused suspicion and she had no way of knowing what other blunders she might make. While she knew she could follow thoughts to get to the last scroll piece, she knew she couldn't do it alone.

She needed Eirik.

Oh, how she hated that fact. For the past few weeks, she had wanted nothing more than to best the Mercesti male. He'd treated her abominably, contributed to Deimos' death and most certainly planned to kill her. But she knew he was the best chance she had at acquiring the scroll.

After her departure from the main base, she landed in the forest outside the ancient library. She figured Eirik wouldn't be there after all this time, but she could possibly find Estilorians nearby who could lead her to him. As soon as she landed, she opened her thoughts and searched for anyone near enough for her to hear.

She didn't identify any thoughts at first. After a few minutes, she moved north to continue her search. While trying to keep her thoughts contained enough to avoid detection by the Orculesti or Wymzesti elders, she scanned the trees and hoped to catch a stray mental signature.

She hadn't walked for fifteen minutes before she was grabbed from behind. She gasped in surprise as her legs left the ground. Instinctively, she sent a thought to her captor to release her.

"Your powers have no influence on me, Orculesti," a male voice growled. "I have had many centuries to shore up my mental defenses."

What were his intentions? Having borne witness to it numerous times, she knew all too well what Mercesti males enjoyed doing to females. Would she have to kill this male and assume his form to protect herself?

"Let's see what Eirik wants to do with you, shall we?" he said.

Where any other being might have cowered, Metis relaxed. She didn't bother fighting when the male put her on her feet and prodded her forward. If he found her compliance odd, he didn't mention it. She studied their path as they walked, trying to orient herself. If she had to flee for any reason, it would be best to have some kind of exit plan in mind.

They hiked for a number of miles before they finally reached their destination. Metis spotted Eirik the moment the Mercesti camp came into view. His height was accentuated by the spiked half-ponytail on his head. Despite the chill, he wore only his usual furred vest, pants and boots. Her gaze fell on the curvy black blades of his cursed krises, secured in a harness on his back. As though sensing her gaze, he turned and spotted her. She tried to intercept thoughts from him or those around him, but there was only silence. That was when she realized he had at least one mentally gifted Mercesti in his group. She threw up what defenses she had to keep that Mercesti from intercepting her thoughts.

"Look what I found wandering around the forest," her captor said.

The rest of the Mercesti standing around the campsite also turned to look at her. She couldn't prevent a hard swallow when she saw the expressions on some of their faces. When she'd had Deimos by her side, she'd been protected. Now, especially with her mental abilities serving her little purpose, she felt vulnerable.

"An Orculesti spy," one of the males said, shifting his gaze from her to Eirik and back.

Straightening her shoulders, she responded, "Do not be ridiculous. Eirik, it is me…Metis."

His gaze narrowed. "Is that so? You are incredibly stupid to present yourself to me, traitor."

"Traitor?" She lifted her chin. "I have been attempting to recover the two females to bring them back to you. Do you know what I have gone through in my efforts? What I have risked and sacrificed for you?"

He frowned.

"The females used trickery to escape," she continued. "They were already out of the cage when I returned from delivering you here. They incapacitated me and ran into the maze. In the end, I had no choice but to change forms and do what I could to make up for my—error in judgment." The last lie was hard to speak, but she thought she sounded convincing enough.

He studied her in silence for a long moment. Then he said, "Yet you come to me empty-handed?"

She dug her nails into her hands to prevent a biting response. "Yes, my lord," she replied. "I have failed. The females are too well-protected. I knew I had to return to you and beg your forgiveness."

"Is that what you call this?"

Unable to stop herself, she snarled, "It is as close to begging as you will see from me."

His scarred eyebrow lifted. He took a step closer, towering over her. "That sounds more like the Metis I know," he said.

He reached out and lifted a strand of her hair, rubbing it between two fingers as he held her gaze. Then he grabbed a fistful of her hair and dragged her closer. She bit back a cry of pain.

"And I do not believe you for a second," he continued. "You had better hope you are telling me the truth, female, or your death will go down as the longest and most painful in Estilorian history. Now, tell me why you went to Central and tried to kidnap the Kynzesti named Clara Kate."

Chapter 31

CLARA KATE DIDN'T ARGUE WHEN INI-HERIT INSISTED ON CARRYING HER as they flew toward the scroll piece. She wanted to try and retain as much energy as she could, uncertain about what lay ahead.

She didn't mind spending time in his arms, either. Every time he touched her, he made her want to grab him and kiss him until they forgot everything else. Adding to the impact he had on her senses, he had asked Sebastian to cut his hair the night before. It was now the length it had been when he was a human. He said he had done it because it was easier to maintain. She just knew he was hot as hell. Just being in the flight harness had her imagination working overtime.

As the afternoon transitioned to night, the temperature dropped. Sebastian generated special face shields to keep the cold air from burning their eyes or skin. The lavender energy glowed along with their many luminescent wings against the darkening sky. Clara Kate knew they'd have to land soon to avoid detection. Eirik and his followers were likely right behind them.

Harold and Derian had separated their forces from the rest of the group, hoping to intercept Eirik. Until they re-established communication with Verrell, Alys and Oria, however, they had no way of knowing how close the Mercesti was or how much he knew of their plans.

They took every precaution. Aside from her father, every elder flew with them. Malukali and Knorbis exercised their abilities as they flew, intercepting and masking thoughts. Hundreds of Waresti served as their escort, with many more working under Harold's command in search of Eirik. They even had Nyx back among them, the fully healed kragen having returned just before they took flight in pursuit of the third scroll piece.

Despite their efforts, the fact that there were so many unknowns about their path had Clara Kate more afraid than she could ever remember feeling. Yes, she had been scared for her cousins and Ariana during their recent rescue efforts. But she had been able to retain her focus. She had known that Quincy, Tiege and Zachariah bore the brunt of the fear for Sophia, Tate and Ariana, and she had known that she had to remain strong for them.

Now, her fear was for Ini-herit. It was for their unborn baby. It was raw and undiluted terror that she would lose the two things most precious to her. She had so much to fight for now.

We'll get through this, Ini-herit thought, his hold around her tightening.

I'm sorry that I can't contain my thoughts, she returned, giving his hand a squeeze.

It's all right. I want to share these things with you. We can handle anything together.

His thoughts comforted her, as did the confidence he conveyed. He was right. She needed to tap into his faith and exercise her own Corgloresti abilities. Something told her that it was going to take a lot more than just strength and strategy to defeat Eirik.

"We need to land," Malukali said.

No one questioned her. Within minutes, they touched down on a large, sandy expanse of ground without any nearby trees or buildings. Clara Kate heard the sound of crashing waves in the distance. The sun fell completely beneath the horizon as everyone gathered together. A biting wind whipped up grains of sand that struck Sebastian's shields like projectiles from a weapon.

At Uriel's command, the Waresti fanned out to patrol the area. Clara Kate briefly caught Alexius' eye before he turned to go. She couldn't help but worry for him. Looking up at Ini-herit, she drew again on his quiet confidence. Then she turned her focus to the elders and her family.

"I have picked up Metis' thought signature," Malukali said, making Clara Kate tense. "Knorbis has intuited that she's on the mainland and attempting to use her Orculesti abilities to find us. After all of these hours of flight, my energy is flagging. I need rest if I'm going to prevent her from picking up on our thoughts and coming right to us."

"Have you been able to interpret any of her thoughts?" Sophia asked.

"No, but I intend to apply my power to that task." Malukali looked at

Clara Kate. "We still don't know why Metis attempted to get you away from Central or what she intends to do, but it's safe to assume that she's also after the scroll piece."

"I also think it's likely that Metis will reconnect with Eirik, if she hasn't already done so," Knorbis said. "She'll know her greatest chance to succeed against us is if she joins with him."

"She'll use him as a distraction," Zachariah mused, his gaze narrowed in thought. "She thinks that he'll be our primary focus, and she considers him dispensable. As soon as she has honed in on the location of the final scroll piece, she'll do anything she has to—sacrifice anyone she has to—in order to get it."

"What makes you so sure of that?" Jabari asked.

"It's what I would do."

There was a pause as everyone thought about this. Clara Kate's gaze moved among the members of her family, ending on Ini-herit. Would Metis kill one or more of them in her quest for power? For that matter, would Eirik? It was terrifying to consider.

"We should heed Knorbis' foresight and Zachariah's strategic ability," Uriel said. "Assuming this is true, Metis is leading Eirik to us even now. Harold has yet to come across their path. According to the Waresti traveling with Derian, they haven't found any signs of him, either."

"So the real question is, where is he?"

Ariana made sure Tate and Zachariah had a weather-proof tent and comfortable cot to sleep in before she retreated to her own tent in hopes of resting. She highly doubted she'd succeed.

Her chest hurt from the intensity of her fear. She wondered if her heart could endure its constant state of agitation. It felt like it was bruised from slamming against her breastbone. Her trembling body had less to do with the weather than her raging emotions.

Stepping into her tent, she allowed the flap to fall behind her. She'd left a ball of light bouncing against the tent's ceiling, so she saw Tiege sitting on the edge of her cot. Her hand flew to her throat as she fought back a scream.

"Oh," she managed to choke out.

He got to his feet. "I'm sorry. I didn't mean to startle you."

She wanted to say that he hadn't, that it wasn't a big deal. Instead, tears filled her eyes. A loud sob burst from her.

"No," he said, hurrying forward and pulling her against him. "Please, Ariana. I'm so sorry. I didn't think."

His words made her feel even worse for her outburst, but she couldn't stop the flood now that he'd opened the gates. She wept against his chest, the feel of his protective armor against her cheek reinforcing the severity of what they faced. This was the third time she'd guided others to a piece of the Elder Scroll. Each time before had resulted in bloodshed and devastation. It didn't matter that she wasn't being forced to lead this group. In fact, it was worse. She felt like she was leading the family she had grown to love to their deaths.

Tiege stopped talking and just held her, stroking her hair, rubbing her back and kissing the top of her head. His tenderness intensified her heartache. How could she face losing him?

That thought finally helped her calm down. She couldn't lose him. She *wouldn't*.

She wouldn't let Eirik take Tiege from her. She wouldn't let him destroy the happiness she had found since he killed her best friend, Tisha, and abducted her. It didn't matter what it took. She was going to make sure Eirik was defeated once and for all.

When her tears dried, she pulled away from Tiege and caught his gaze. "Thank you," she said in a soft voice. "You didn't cause that, you know."

He brushed a strand of her hair from her cheek. The action sent pleasant shivers along her spine. "I do know," he said. "I still feel like an ass."

That brought a smile to her face. "Of course you do. You love me."

He returned the smile, revealing the dimple that matched his twin's. "You're right. As a matter of fact, that's what got me into trouble here."

Her brow furrowed. "What do you mean?"

"I mean that I came in here to ask you to avow with me."

Her mouth opened. For a moment, she couldn't even form a reply. Then she asked, "Now?"

"Yes." Holding her gaze, he reached into one of his pockets and pulled out two rings. "I didn't want to rush you, Ariana. I was going to wait until we returned home and Tate and Zachariah had their wedding. But the thing is, I know there are no guarantees that everything will go smoothly tomorrow. Everyone else is connected. Even if they're apart, they can communicate by thought and feeling. I want that with you, and I don't want to wait."

She felt another tear fall when she blinked, but it had nothing to do with fear. "I don't want to wait either," she said.

Without another word, he pressed his ring into her right hand. Then he took her left hand in his. Her heart swelled when he conveyed all that he felt with just one look.

"I, Tiege, love you, Ariana, with all of my being. You've captured my heart with your strength, generosity and kindness, and it will remain your willing prisoner for the rest of my existence. I give you this ring as a symbol of my love and my unbreakable commitment to you."

A current of energy flowed from her left ring finger when he placed her ring there, signifying his half of the avowing. It coursed through her with each beat of her heart.

Smiling, she lifted his left hand and said, "I, Ariana, love you, Tiege, with all of my being. You've captured my heart with your strength, generosity and kindness, and it will remain your willing prisoner for the rest of my existence. I give you this ring as a symbol of my love and my unbreakable commitment to you."

She slid the ring onto his finger. Then they entwined their left hands so their rings touched and kissed to seal the vow.

Pain flashed around her eyes, along her right shoulder blade and on the inside of her right wrist. Although the last pain surprised her, she ignored it. All that mattered was Tiege's kiss and the flood of loving thoughts that filled her mind as they fully connected. She had thought she understood the power of his love for her. She had been wrong.

She had also underestimated the power of his attraction to her.

Pulling away from his mouth to catch her breath, she held his gaze. She smiled as she intercepted the thoughts he couldn't contain. Running her hand along the hard muscles of his chest, she said, "You don't want to stop with just a kiss to seal our vow, do you?"

"No," he said roughly.

She felt his heart racing under her fingertips. It empowered her. Grabbing his hand, she led him toward her cot. "Do you want to know one of the nice things about being a full Estilorian female, my love? We can't get pregnant."

He blinked as she lowered onto the cot. Then he grinned. "Well, then…this vow is about to get one helluva seal."

* * *

Zachariah issued a curse as his wrist flared with pain. Beside him, Tate gasped and flinched. They both sat up in the cot and looked at each other.

"What the hell?"

He reached over and took her right hand, turning it so he could see the inside of her wrist. Tate tossed up a light so she could see, too. When his vision readjusted to the brightness, he studied the symbol that now marked them both. It was an infinity knot in the shape of a clover bearing four leaves, each a different color: deep blue-green, silver, lavender and red.

Tate gasped again. "Tiege must have avowed with Ariana!" she exclaimed, leaping from the cot. "I'll bet the others have this mark, too."

Zachariah grabbed her around the waist to keep her from sprinting out of the tent. "You know better than that."

Rolling her eyes, she said, "Okay, okay. Do your thing, Sparky."

He shook his head at her as he crossed the tent and eased the flap open. His senses didn't pick up any danger. Across the small clearing in the center of their accommodations, he saw Quincy and Ini-herit looking out of their tents, too. They all exchanged glances. He held up his wrist. The other two males nodded and briefly lifted theirs to show him the symbols that now appeared there.

Their attention all shifted to Tiege and Ariana's tent. Although the tent was dark, the soft sounds coming from it told them the couple wouldn't be emerging for a while.

"Well, is it safe to come out?" Tate asked from behind him.

He moved back inside the tent and resealed the opening. "Not really."

"What?" She looked at the tent flap. He sensed her warring with the urge to seek out her twin. "What's wrong?"

"Nothing's wrong," he said, tugging her back toward the cot. When she didn't immediately follow him, he picked her up and carried her. "Tiege is just otherwise occupied."

"But I want to know if he avowed with Ariana. Do the others have this marking? What does it mean?"

Laying her on the cot, he said, "I'm quite sure he avowed with Ariana, which is why the symbol appeared. The elders deduced that the eight of us are linked. It appears they were correct. And, yes, the others have the same mark. I saw Quincy and Ini-herit when I looked outside."

"But not Tiege?" She nibbled on her lower lip, drawing his attention to her lush mouth as he again settled beside her on the cot.

"No, not Tiege."

"Why wouldn't he and Ariana come out and tell us about their pairing? What could be more important than sharing such wonderful news?"

"I could tell you," Zachariah said, bracing himself above her. "But it would just be more bloody fun to show you."

Then he made sure that the last thing she was thinking about was her brother.

Chapter 32

EIRIK WAVERED BY THE HOUR ABOUT WHETHER OR NOT TO KILL METIS. He didn't believe her excuses in the least. As Deimos, she could have teleported back to the library after she realized she wouldn't be able to recapture Ariana and Tate. Her flimsy excuse of fearing capture by the Waresti near the library didn't convince him. She knew exactly where she was supposed to meet him to take him back to the females, but she hadn't done so. Her other story of trying to capture Clara Kate in an attempt to bring her to him as a bargaining chip was just as questionable.

He eyed her now as she sat bound and gagged against a huge boulder. Just feet away, the ocean lapped along the shore. Moonlight shone on the water and created shadows beneath the rocky overhang serving as their temporary shelter. Wind howled as it touched the nooks and crevices etched into the stone.

"Are you any closer to breaking through her mental barriers?" he asked the male Mercesti standing next to him.

"No, my lord. In truth, I may not succeed. Her mental signature is unlike any I have ever intercepted. She is even more difficult to read than the Kynzesti was."

That was bad news. Eirik knew that if his mentally-skilled Mercesti succumbed to exhaustion before Metis did, it would leave many of them susceptible to her Orculesti abilities. He wasn't sure how powerful she would be outside of the influence of a dampener. Although he was confident that he could resist her, he knew many of those Mercesti currently with him would not be able to do so.

More of his followers were on the way. He had held them off for days as he awaited word that he neared his goal. Not even an hour ago, his inform-ant revealed that the other Estilorians expected to reach the location of the scroll piece the following day. Upon receiving the news, he sent Friedrich to rally the others. He expected their arrival before morning.

The last thing he needed was a complication.

Drawing one of his krises from its sheath, he stalked over to Metis. Low-ering to one knee, he used the blade to remove her gag, scoring her cheek in the process. She glared at him, but didn't flinch as he held the weapon against her pulse.

"Give me one reason why I should spare your life," he growled.

She lifted an eyebrow. Then she said in a low voice, "The male whose mental abilities you are trusting is a monumental liar."

He stiffened, never expecting the response. Knowing better than to look at the male in question since he was surely observing the exchange, he returned, "Why should I believe you?"

"I have been deliberately projecting thoughts his way ever since I entered your camp. Which of those thoughts has he shared with you?"

Clenching his jaw, Eirik fought the urge to plunge his kris through her neck. If she was telling the truth, the male Mercesti was, indeed, a liar. The real question was how he could possibly determine who was telling the truth.

"You killed the Mercesti who was delivering you information about the other Estilorians," she said, turning his attention.

"I have no idea what you are talking about."

"You did so out of sight and sound of the others, wanting to keep your actions a secret." Metis said in conversational tones. "She projected a great deal of pain before she died. Those with mental abilities tend to do that, I understand. I sensed her conflict over her choice to feed you information even as she spoke to you. I imagine she realized she had been right to question her decision as you ran her through. Now…how much of that do you suppose your 'loyal' Mercesti mind-reader picked up?"

Getting slowly to his feet, Eirik turned from Metis and approached the male he had entrusted to protect him and his followers from mental intrusions. Seeing his approach, the male looked at the kris in Eirik's hand and stood straighter.

"Norman, are you in communication with the Mercesti traveling with Friedrich?" Eirik asked.

"You know I am, my lord," Norman replied, his gaze moving to Metis and then back to Eirik. He moistened his lips and added, "They are not far. What has the manipulative female told you?"

"Which one?" Eirik asked. "Metis? Or the female I killed earlier whose dying thoughts you surely received?"

Norman's eyes widened. "I did not believe you wanted anyone to know about that, my lord."

"I am certain. Yet it troubles me that you made no mention of it, even to me. Why is it you did not question my motives? Why did you not ask whether this was part of the plan?"

"B-because I know better than to question you, my lord. My loyalty is absolute. Whatever that female told you—"

"You surely already know," Eirik said. "She has been sending you thoughts since she arrived."

Norman's face drained of color. "N-no. That is not true, my lord. She is attempting to deceive you. I am ever your servant. You must believe me."

Eirik raised an eyebrow. "I must?" he repeated, reaching up and grabbing Norman's shoulder with his left hand. "That sounds very much like an order, *servant*."

Then he ran his kris through the male's heart, holding him up as he died. Norman's expression was a blend of surprise and confusion. Pulling his weapon from the male's chest with a liquid suction sound, Eirik turned and walked back to Metis.

"Everything you said was a lie, was it not?" he asked her.

"Does it really matter?" she replied. "Despite the fact that you killed him, I am not attempting to influence you with my abilities. We need each other, Eirik. We are united in our belief that the final scroll piece must fall within our possession, not anyone else's. If we work together, we can achieve that goal."

She had a point. But he wasn't a fool. He noticed that she left her proposal open-ended. She didn't say that the scroll should be in *his* position, but *theirs*. He knew that she wanted the Elder Scroll for herself.

Well, that was perfectly fine. He was quite content using her abilities to get the scroll for himself and then disposing of her at the first possible opportunity.

* * *

Ini-herit only slept for about an hour, but it was enough for him to regain his energy. Once he awoke, he lay in the oversized cot with Clara Kate pressed against his side. He ran his fingers through her soft hair as she slept, thinking of what lay ahead.

The other elders hadn't been involved in the creation of the various traps leading to the third scroll piece. It had been his responsibility to hide it, just as it had been Uriel and Gabriel's responsibilities to hide the other two pieces. Where Uriel had relied on a remote location and illusion enchantment to protect his piece, Gabriel had opted to hide his within the heavily enchanted ancient Estilorian library among thousands of other scrolls. Despite this, Eirik had successfully accessed both pieces using the second powers of Ariana and Tate.

Although his memories had been repressed for the protection of everyone, Ini-herit now remembered a little about where and how he'd hidden his piece. Malukali and Knorbis tapped into his subconscious after he remembered the purpose of the medallion. They helped him recall a few details.

As Ariana led them closer to the third piece, he realized where they were headed. He remembered the moment they hit the desert sands.

"You hid a scroll piece in one of the pyramids of Giza?" Clara Kate asked when she perceived his thought.

"Actually, I think I secured it near the pyramids rather than in the tombs themselves." He shook his head. "I should have considered it before. I was the one who designed them."

She was silent for a long moment. He sensed her awe and intercepted a few of her thoughts as she tried to process what she had just learned. Eventually, she grinned.

"Damn," she said. "You are *old*."

Remembering that now, he smiled. He hadn't bothered to mention that human historians were off on their timeline by a number of centuries. Now, he leaned down to kiss her cheek. She sighed softly and snuggled closer. While he had the chance, he reached under the covers and lifted her shirt so he could touch her abdomen. He pulled forth his power and listened to the swooshing heartbeat of their baby. The strong sound brought another smile to his face. Then he sobered as he considered the significance of what they faced.

If he could, he would send Clara Kate home to stay within the security of her homeland. He knew Gabriel would never let any harm come to her. But there was no way she would agree to that. As fate would have it, she was an integral part of this undertaking, something he couldn't deny or control.

He also knew, though she hadn't talked to him about it yet, that she wouldn't have Alexius enter this likely battle without standing by his side. But he was confident in her feelings and understood her heart. He just had to have faith that everything would work out okay.

After a while, he allowed his hands to stray from her stomach to other parts of her body. Then his mouth joined in. He loved how she responded to him even in sleep. She woke up at some point, but she didn't complain. In fact, she was rather enthusiastic about this particular wake-up call.

He wasn't surprised when she fell back asleep afterwards. The sun was only just cresting the horizon. He got up and put his clothes back on, then moved to the tent flap to see who else was awake. As he stepped out, he saw Quincy and Zachariah facing each other in front of Tiege and Ariana's tent. Zachariah held his black tank top in one hand and Quincy's arms were crossed. Beside them, Nyx lay on the ground and looked on with sleepy diamond eyes.

"I'm not going to find out that Tate's pregnant, am I?" Quincy asked. His Australian-like accent was more pronounced, revealing his agitation.

Zachariah quirked an eyebrow as he struck the top of Tiege and Ariana's tent twice. He responded, "You of all beings should know that there are many ways to offer a female pleasure without it resulting in pregnancy."

Ini-herit's eyebrows shot up. He snorted in amusement as Quincy's face flushed.

"Why *me* of all beings?" the Corgloresti sputtered.

"I imagine he means that you have the most in-depth knowledge about anatomy of any of us," Ini-herit explained as Tiege threw back his tent flap and emerged.

Tate's twin eyed the other three males, his gaze settling on Zachariah. He blinked when he noticed the Mercesti was only dressed in a pair of pants.

"I need Ariana's assistance," Zachariah said.

"What you need is to put a shirt on," Tiege argued. "Holy light, bro. You'll have the females stumbling into the campfire if you walk around like that."

Zachariah looked down at himself. Then he lifted a shoulder in a shrug.

He was tall and muscular, larger and more defined than any of them due to his base Gloresti form. Ini-herit thought Tiege had a point.

"I need Ariana to repair this tear," Zachariah said, holding up the garment in his hand.

Tiege frowned and lifted an edge of the damaged fabric. "How did it get…?" He trailed off and held up a hand. "You know what? Never mind. I don't want to know."

He grabbed the piece of clothing and retreated back into his tent. Ini-herit exchanged a look with Quincy as a flash of lavender light illuminated the area. They both grinned. Then, when Zachariah's tank top flew from the tent with a grumbled command from Tiege that he put it the hell on, they both burst out laughing.

"What's so funny?" Sophia asked, poking her head out of her tent. Her gaze fell on Zachariah, who had to walk several feet closer to her to retrieve his repaired garment. Her eyes widened and her jaw slackened.

"Nothing," Quincy said, moving to block her view. "We were just having a discussion about anatomy."

"Anatomy?" she repeated in a dubious voice.

"Yep. In fact, why don't we go inside the tent and I'll bring you up to speed? I've been told I'm quite the expert on the subject."

Chapter 33

CLARA KATE DIDN'T WANT THE BOWL OF OATMEAL AND FRESH FRUIT that Ini-herit served her for breakfast, but she knew she had to eat it. She sat with her family around a small fire that Sebastian created in the center of their circle of tents. A few of them were also eating. She figured if their stomachs were as twisted into knots as hers was, they were only doing it so she didn't feel weird. That just made her love them all the more.

"So, should we talk about the markings now?" she asked as she lifted another spoonful of food to her mouth.

Several of them instinctively twisted their right wrists to once again view the marking. Tiege and Ariana exchanged grins, which made Clara Kate smile. She had congratulated them earlier on their avowing and couldn't be happier for them.

"Each of us has now avowed as pairs," Quincy said. "After what Saraqael told us about our fates being tied to the scroll, I guess this isn't really surprising."

"Our parents all share markings on their right wrists," Sophia added. "As most of us know, the markings formed after they made a commitment to each other. But they had to be in physical contact at the time."

Clara Kate considered this as she scooped the last of her breakfast into her mouth. Her mother and her aunts were half-human, half-Estilorian, while their fathers were full Estilorian. Thus, their children were only one-quarter human and three-quarters Estilorian. Quincy had reasoned that the Kynzesti didn't menstruate because there had been an evolutionary leap in their reproductive development. What if that leap extended into things like bonding with others?

"That's exactly right," Ini-herit said out loud, catching her gaze. "The Kynzesti class has demonstrated capabilities more advanced than other Estilorians. It's likely that you can extend a vow of commitment—at least in part—without physically touching another being, just through strong enough emotion. Your human blood may be the key to that."

"Sure," Tate said, looking at Zachariah. "I was able to avow myself to Sparky in a dream."

Zachariah nodded as he met her gaze. "But our connection grew stronger after we avowed in person."

"How so?" Tiege asked.

Tate reached out and squeezed Zachariah's hand. "Well, before we avowed in person, we could hear each other's thoughts and feel some of what the other felt. Now we share everything."

Clara Kate understood that. She saw that everyone else did, too. Setting her bowl to the side, she said, "I think we should join hands and seal our connection."

A pause followed her announcement as everyone processed the idea. Then Tate smiled and took Tiege's hand in her free one, joining her to her twin and her avowed. Tiege nodded and took Ariana's hand in his. She reached out to Sophia, who sat beside her. Sophia clasped Ariana's hand and then joined her other one with Quincy's. Since Ini-herit stood beside Quincy, he reached out and took the other male's hand, then Clara Kate's. She reached out to Zachariah beside her.

The Mercesti hesitated, looking at Clara Kate's hand.

"Come on, Zachariah," Quincy encouraged. "This will work."

"Yeah," Sophia agreed. "If it worked for your avowing, it'll work for this."

When he still didn't move, Ariana urged, "Take C.K.'s hand, Zachariah. We need you to make this work."

"There's no reason we shouldn't do this," Ini-herit said. "It's just going to confirm what the markings already tell us."

"Yeah, bro," Tiege added. "We all know how you feel about us. No need to deny it now."

Clara Kate noticed that Tate's gaze didn't move from Zachariah. Her cousin was likely communicating whatever she wanted to convey through her thoughts. When she realized that Tate's eyes glistened with tears, she suddenly understood.

"Zachariah," Clara Kate said, not lowering her hand, "we're all family now. None of us is perfect. We've all made mistakes. But we accept each other without condition. You're only strengthening us by doing this. Don't ever think that you're less deserving of our love than anyone else."

He met her gaze. Then he looked around the circle. Everyone nodded. Finally, he reached out and took her hand.

That was the last thing she registered before everything went dark.

Ini-herit had witnessed the bonding ceremonies between the daughters of Saraqael and their avoweds. Each time, all of the beings involved had lost consciousness. He'd been prepared for it...but it happened quicker this time than he'd thought. They hadn't even spoken.

When his vision cleared, he saw the blue sky above him. As he registered the fact that he was on the ground, he remembered what they'd been trying to achieve. Then he heard an unexpected thought and knew they'd been successful.

Wake up, Beautiful.

The voice in his head belonged to Zachariah. He felt the concern associated with the thought. Jerking into a sitting position, Ini-herit shook his head to clear it and glanced around.

Zachariah knelt beside Tate, leaning over her and touching the side of her face. His gaze moved to Ini-herit when he registered the movement.

They'll be all right, Ini-herit sent to Zachariah.

If the Mercesti was surprised that he could now hear Ini-herit's thoughts, he didn't show it. Instead, he nodded and returned his focus to Tate. Ini-herit moved closer to Clara Kate and pulled her into his arms. Her pale complexion worried him, so he brought forth his healing energy. She moaned.

Tiege sat up as Ini-herit got Clara Kate into a sitting position and then moved to Sophia and Quincy. Grasping their arms, he used more healing energy to rouse them. By the time he finished with them, Ariana and Tate had regained consciousness.

Does anyone else need healing? he thought.

Though there were some widened eyes and raised eyebrows among the group, everyone shook their heads. He moved back to Clara Kate's side and put his arm around her.

We're all joined in thought now, he sent out. *Some of us have more experience sharing thoughts than others.* He exchanged a look with Zachariah, who once shared a mental connection with his Gloresti leaders. *But we all know this is a learning process. Don't hold anyone accountable for a stray thought you might receive as we strengthen our mental filters.*

Guess it's a good thing we weren't connected earlier when Zachariah had his shirt off, Sophia thought with a grin. She exchanged looks with the other females and grinned widely.

Tate laughed. Clara Kate and Ariana looked intrigued, turning their gazes to Zachariah, who shook his head. Ini-herit strengthened his hold on Clara Kate in a chastising way, but couldn't prevent a smile. He knew Sophia had deliberately sent the thought to lighten the moment, and sensed everyone else did, too.

"Okay," he said out loud. "We all know how strong our bond is. Now let's go put it to the test."

Ariana was asked to once again take the lead in identifying the location of the final scroll piece. Although Ini-herit believed he knew where it was, he couldn't be absolutely certain. Her second power, on the other hand, was consistent and reliable.

The trails she perceived that led to the other two scroll pieces continued to be behind them, telling her Eirik was still following them. It was a concern, but she couldn't worry about that on top of everything else. She had to believe Harold and Derian would find him before he reached them…and if they didn't, that she was prepared to defend herself and those she loved.

For the first time, she wasn't afraid to be the guide on this quest. She no longer felt alone. She had a family, something she'd never dreamed possible. Just as importantly, she had the full support of that family behind her. Whenever doubt or fear crept into her mind, they bolstered her with their thoughts.

The previous night had been the most amazing night of her entire existence. Considering that spanned more than two centuries of being, it said a lot. She wasn't about to lose a lifetime of nights like that because of Eirik's power-hungry ambition.

Damn straight, Tiege mentally agreed.

She looked at him and smiled, unwilling to be embarrassed that he had intercepted her thought. He already knew how she felt. Love for him flooded her.

We're getting close, Ini-herit thought.

Ariana returned her focus to her second power. *Yes,* she responded. *The pull is very strong.*

Within minutes, a series of pyramids and buildings came into view. Her mouth opened as she absorbed their grandeur. She hadn't ever seen anything like this.

Then her gaze shifted to another structure, something that didn't resemble a pyramid at all. Her second power pulled her right to it.

What is that? she thought.

It's the Great Sphinx, Clara Kate conveyed with awe.

Actually, Ini-herit clarified, *back when it was constructed, we called it a* Ssp-anx.

Bless you, Tiege offered.

There was a round of laughter at that. Ini-herit grinned.

How is it possible that these things exist both here and on the human plane? Tate wondered.

We recreated them on this plane, Ini-herit answered. *We initially thought everyone would live on the mainland, so we began building here. Obviously, that plan changed when Volarius was killed. We created Central instead, but left the structures on the mainland.*

Ariana looked at Uriel and said out loud, "We're headed to that statue with the head of a male and the body of a large feline."

The elder nodded. The Waresti fanned out and began creating a perimeter around the area. It was a little disheartening, Ariana thought, to see that their numbers didn't measure up to much in the vast desert. It was a lot of territory to cover.

This Sphinx is more intact than the human version, Clara Kate observed as she studied their goal. *It still has the nose and beard.*

This version is protected from the elements, Ini-herit explained.

I thought the Sphinx was just a huge statue, Tate thought as they neared it. *I don't remember learning about any chambers or anything inside or underneath it. Is the scroll piece hidden inside one of the stones or something?*

The Estilorian version of this statue has many mysteries, Ini-herit responded. *It's larger and more complex. Let's hope the medallion and my spotty memory can help us.*

Ariana took a deep breath as she considered his words. The unpopulated landscape and enormous size of the surrounding pyramids made the enigmatic statue rather intimidating. She guided them to land in front of the structure. As she extinguished her wings, she found herself unable to look up at it. For some reason, she feared what she would see if she looked into the sculpture's all-too-real eyes.

It's enchanted to make beings uncomfortable, Ini-herit thought. *That's one of the reasons I chose to hide the scroll piece here.*

Tiege took Ariana's hand. She caught his gaze and gratefully allowed him to pull her into a hug.

"We're here," Jabari said in grave tones. "Now we must decide how to proceed to accomplish our goals and keep Eirik from achieving his."

Chapter 34

METIS' ABILITIES ALLOWED EIRIK AND HIS FOLLOWERS TO CONGREGATE without detection by their pursuers. They had several close calls, nearly getting caught more times than Eirik could count. He had a number of instances to regret his impulsive kill of Derian's unfaithful follower, but there was no undoing that now.

Friedrich's scouts had gathered the aid of hundreds of Mercesti over the past few days. Because meeting as one group would be impossible under the circumstances, they used a combination of Mercesti scouts and Metis' mental abilities to communicate about their plans.

They were close. In just a matter of minutes, Eirik expected to reach the Estilorians searching for the scroll piece.

"Why is it you intend to confront them now, my lord?" one of the Mercesti asked. "They have elders among them. Our numbers are strong, but their abilities are stronger."

Eirik stepped in front of the male and looked down at him. "If they acquire this part of the artifact now, they will surely destroy it. Then the artifact will no longer be of any use."

"How will this artifact help any of us?" another male asked. "You claim that you will inherit the abilities of an elder. How will that be any better than what we endured under Grolkinei's reign? Or Kanika's?"

They seek esteem and acceptance, Metis conveyed.

"Neither of them were elders," Eirik answered the male, glancing briefly at Metis and keeping his tone level. "They could not compete against the other elders. Therefore, our class continues to be ostracized. I would change that."

"Why you?" another Mercesti asked. "Why not one of us?"

"The Mercesti elder will have to be mentally and physically strong, with a history of effective leadership and the ability to generate loyal followers without relying on force. Can any of you boast as much?" There was a period of silence following that question. Eirik let his words absorb, then continued, "I want our class accepted by the others. We deserve that. Although it might take time to earn our equal place in Estilorian society, I am willing to invest it."

Another pause followed. Eirik looked at Metis, but she only shrugged. Either she was unable to effectively read the crowd, or she didn't care to try. He silently considered and dismissed various ways to kill her, not caring if she intercepted the thoughts.

Friedrich stepped forward and scanned the beings in the small encampment. "We are all here for a reason. If we did not care about our future and the future of our class, we would not have bothered coming. Many of you have done quite well at removing yourselves from Estilorian society for a long time now. Admit it. We desire change."

"Why must this be done with bloodshed?" the first male asked. "If the goal is to become a class accepted by the others, should we not attempt to reason with them first?"

Eirik's eyelid twitched. "Do you not think we have tried that?" he snapped. "They all believe us incapable of change. They fear us and they want the artifact destroyed to keep us submissive to them. This is our only choice."

Frowning, the male considered this, then asked, "What is your plan to acquire the artifact?"

"Come with me," Eirik instructed. "I will explain it to you and then you can help implement it. I will appreciate someone with your…sentiment on our side."

As Friedrich stepped in to communicate to the rest of the Mercesti, Eirik led the male through the surrounding trees to the edge of a system of caves. When he was certain they were out of sight of the others, he turned to the male.

"What is your name?"

"Corwin."

"Well, Corwin, our plan is quite brilliant," Eirik said, unsheathing one of his krises and giving it a casual study. "We intend to take out the majority of our opponents with weapons we will employ from a distance. The devastation will be remarkable. While we slaughter them, we will keep their Waresti and Mercesti reinforcements far away by engaging them elsewhere." He met the other male's gaze. "Did I fail to mention that there are Mercesti like you who are loyal to the other classes that I must keep from interfering? Disgusting, really."

Corwin's eyes widened. He reached for his weapon, but Eirik was faster. The other male's neck was slashed before he could offer a word of protest.

"Too bad you will be unable to see it," Eirik thought to add before kicking the corpse into the closest cave and walking back to lead the others to his victory.

"Where is your second power directing you?" Zachariah asked Ariana as they all stood and stared at the Sphinx.

She pointed in the direction of the statue's chest, between its long paws. "There."

They all walked the length of the alley between the statue's stone paws and searched for an entrance. They found a barrier of solid rock.

Everyone looked at Tate, who shrugged and touched the statue. "It's real."

Zachariah considered this, then glanced at Ini-herit. "Think the medallion can help?"

Removing it from around his neck, Ini-herit replied, "Anything's possible. Back when I hid this scroll piece, we figured it would only be retrieved for one of two reasons: one, we identified someone we felt would fill the role of an elder, or two, we would be attempting to stop someone who was trying to use it for the wrong reasons. I'm sure I considered that, in either of those cases, we would have to identify the eight beings tied to the scroll."

They all backed up a few feet and stared at the medallion as Ini-herit held it up in front of the statue. Sunlight reflected off the medallion's etched surface, the colorful beams touching the rock. Considering Ini-herit's words, Zachariah looked at Tate. She nodded.

Everyone else knew his thoughts, too. Clara Kate reached out and placed her hand on top of Ini-herit's. Sophia and Quincy followed suit. Ariana and Tiege piled their hands on, then Tate and Zachariah.

As soon as their hands were joined, the beams of light reflecting from the medallion no longer winked in and out of visibility. They remained strong and steady.

Aim the beam at that glowing gap in the rock, Tate thought.

When everyone sent her confused thoughts, she focused intently on what she saw with her second power, conveying it to everyone else. Zachariah moved his hand with the others until the light touched the spot she saw.

A resounding crack resulted. Several of them jumped, making the medallion sway. They watched as a rectangular hole formed in the center of the Sphinx's chest. The rock seemed to dissolve.

"Cool," Tate breathed.

"All right," Ini-herit said. "I've got the medallion and I hid the piece, so I'll lead the way. Stick close and don't veer from my path."

He stepped into the doorway and cast a light, looking around as he walked further into the dark interior. Zachariah decided to guard the rear, keeping Tate with him as the others approached the door first. He glanced to the side as Nyx perched on one of the statue's paws.

"You need to stay out here," he said to the kragen. "The interior of this thing surely wasn't designed for creatures your size."

She blinked at him. When she leaned down to rub her snout against his arm, he gave her a firm pat on the side of her neck. Then he sent her off to join Uriel before turning to follow the others into the statue.

Tiege had remained near his twin. Ariana walked beside him. Clara Kate entered the statue after Ini-herit. Sophia followed her cousin, and Quincy went in next. When Tiege attempted to follow them, he struck a barrier. Zachariah stopped him from falling as he staggered back.

"Son of a—" Tiege cut himself off as he rubbed his chest. "What the hell?"

Frowning, Zachariah approached the open doorway and tried to put his hand inside it. He encountered an invisible barrier. When Quincy turned around to see what happened, he tried to reach out to them, but he encountered the same barrier on the other side. Tate and Ariana also tried to breach it without success. Ini-herit, Clara Kate and Sophia couldn't get through, either.

"We're going to have to find another way inside," Zachariah said to Ini-herit.

The elder looked confused. His mouth moved as though he said something, but they couldn't hear him. Zachariah then realized that he could hear the thoughts of Tiege, Ariana and Tate, but not those of their family inside the statue.

"Something's wrong," he said with a frown.

"Well, maybe it's not," Ariana responded. "We're now split, four and four. Maybe it's a part of this puzzle."

Before they could discuss it further, sand and rock spewed into the air not even twenty feet from them. The ground trembled. Pieces of the statue crumbled. Zachariah grabbed Tate and hauled her back as large rocks thudded to the ground just feet from them. Beside him, Tiege did the same with Ariana.

When they looked again at the doorway, they realized it was halfway collapsed.

"C.K.," Tate gasped. "Sophia!"

Zachariah looked around for signs of further threat, then approached the opening. He saw movement inside the structure, so he tried to calm Tate with that thought as he wondered what had caused the blast.

"What was that?" Tiege asked, also looking around. "I've never seen or felt anything like it."

Ariana wasn't focused on the doorway, Zachariah realized. She was frowning and looking back down the alley toward the distant horizon. When her frown eased and her eyes widened, he retrieved his tomahawk from its holster.

"It's Eirik, isn't it?" he asked.

Ariana swallowed and nodded. "I feel the pull to the other two scroll pieces. He's here."

Zachariah watched as Tate and Tiege reached for their weapons. They wouldn't last long if Eirik had many more weapons like the one he had just launched at them. Although they were all armed and wearing armor, they were no match for such destructive power. He didn't bother mentioning that to the others. He figured they already knew.

Just as they knew that the only two beings who could possibly heal them were now sealed inside the statue.

Chapter 35

CLARA KATE NEVER FELT THE CHUNK OF STONE THAT KNOCKED HER unconscious. She blinked back awake and watched the silver glow of Ini-herit's healing power fade. Only when she saw his expression did she realize something serious had happened. A quick look around the chamber made everything clearer.

"Did the statue collapse?" she asked, sitting up. She realized Quincy and Sophia stood a safe distance from the debris, brushing sand from their hair and armor.

"We're not sure," Ini-herit replied as he helped her to her feet. "There was something like an explosion, but that doesn't make sense. There aren't guns or explosives on this plane."

"There weren't," Sophia said, "but maybe there are now. Estilorians have the ability to produce many things without the machines or special equipment that humans need."

"If Metis rummaged around in C.K.'s mind while she was unconscious, who knows what memories about humans she found and shared with Eirik?" Quincy added.

Clara Kate felt lightheaded over the idea that she had somehow contributed to this. She rushed closer to the chunks of stone blocking the statue's doorway. Jumping on top of one, she peered through the opening.

"They've drawn their weapons," she said.

Her gaze moved to where Ariana pointed. A shadow gathered on the horizon beyond the nearby buildings. Sunlight glinted off rows of approaching beings bearing shields and weapons. She gripped the rock to keep from falling to her knees.

"Oh, my God. Eirik's coming. We have to get out there!"

The others hurried up behind her and found gaps to look through. Clara Kate watched a contingent of Waresti led by Alexius run up the alley to her family. Her heart throttled into her throat as she watched them converse and gesture with their hands, mapping out a plan to defend themselves. Alexius glanced toward her. He caught her gaze.

"Alexius," she whispered.

He must have read her lips, because he gave her a reassuring nod. Then he turned his attention back to the others. After a few more words, he waved some of the Waresti after him and started toward the approaching Mercesti at a run.

She caught Ini-herit's gaze. *I should have blessed everyone's weapons before we came in here*, she thought.

They've got no one to heal them, Quincy added.

Then another explosion rocked them off their feet.

Metis not only gave Eirik the idea for the high-impact weapons, she created them. It had been a challenge to make something like what she pulled from the Kynzesti's mind without knowing exactly how it worked, but she did it by combining some of the Waresti and Scultresti traits she had managed to retain. Of course, she couldn't be certain how many of the weapons would actually work, but she didn't care as long as they occupied Eirik.

All that mattered was getting the scroll piece. If she was fortunate, someone would injure Eirik enough that she could get the two pieces he carried. For now, she had to focus on acquiring the third piece so she had some leverage.

She did her best to mask her thoughts as they approached their goal. Even with that, she felt the presence of the Orculesti elder in her mind. She realized that Malukali was trying to reason with her. Even after all that Metis had done to the elder, she still thought she could redeem her. It was rather laughable.

The chill in the air dissipated as the sun rose. Metis kept a cloth over her face to block the biting grains of sand whipped up by the wind. Eirik's skin was protected by a form of energy generated by one of his followers. It was meant to deflect projectiles and weapons. She didn't bother requesting the same type of protection for herself, knowing it wouldn't be forthcoming.

Finally, they neared their destination. Metis looked at Eirik as he came to a stop.

"Dampeners, use your abilities to prohibit flight," he said. "For our primary weapons to work, our opponents must be on the ground. Stay as far from the battlefield as possible." His gaze moved to another group. "Incapacitate the Orculesti and Wymzesti elders with the darts. We do not want their interference, but they may be needed to activate the artifact."

A handful of males broke away from the main group to fulfill the command. They carried weapons that shot poisoned darts across distances. Metis had learned that the dart guns had been modified to travel farther and more accurately than traditional ones.

Eirik issued several other orders before his gaze turned to her. "I have a number of mentally talented Mercesti using their abilities to prevent mental intrusions. You need to do the same."

She nodded and applied her mind to the task. These Mercesti were the key to achieving her goal. She would do whatever it took to protect them for the time being.

Eirik once again started moving, so everyone else followed. As they reached the top of a sand dune, Metis saw what awaited them. Massive pyramids, temples, statues and other stone structures filled the landscape. Waresti soldiers covered much of the area in regimented patrols. Metis spotted the kragen walking among them. Fortunately, thanks to the traitorous Mercesti informant, the creature's survival wasn't a surprise.

"Do not let the kragen score you with its tail or you will not rise again," Eirik said loud enough for everyone to hear. He turned to several males beside him. "Launch the first weapon."

They did. The resulting noise and wave of energy had the sand shifting beneath Metis' feet.

"Get your shields ready," Friedrich called out a moment later. "Their archers are taking aim."

Metis looked around the active battleground and tried to determine where the third scroll piece was hidden. She switched from using her abilities to guard their thoughts and instead tried to pick up the thoughts of the Waresti. After a moment, she realized there was a barrier in place. She frowned. Sparks of lavender light flared around the battleground, several from behind buildings. Eirik noted them with narrowed eyes.

"Sebastian has generated shields," he announced. "The darts will not reach their targets until those shields are destroyed. Find anyone shielded and attack them first."

A contingent of Mercesti charged, deflecting arrows as they ran. Metis debated what to do. Without her mental abilities, she was defenseless and unable to find the scroll piece.

"Prepare more of the explosive projectiles," Eirik told the group of males carrying them. "Aim at the pyramids and larger statues. The artifact is most likely in one of those locations."

There was no getting around it, she decided, watching the Waresti approach. She was going to have to change forms. It was just a matter of deciding which one to assume.

"Fire," Eirik ordered.

Ariana saw the second volley of destructive weapons hit the air only seconds after Alexius and his Waresti hurried away to engage Eirik's Mercesti. Even though she hadn't seen the first attack or the weapons used in it, she knew that the glowing, red balls headed in their direction weren't just arrows or crossbow bolts.

Alexius had stopped to tell them that *archigos* Sebastian would provide them shields as soon as he could. In the meantime, the Waresti second commander intended to set up a perimeter to protect them. He told them to stay near the statue in case Clara Kate and the others needed them.

She realized that he spotted the aerial weapons headed toward the statue just as the rest of them did. As he reached the end of the alley, he turned to issue orders to the soldiers standing near him. She watched as the warriors lifted their un-empowered shields just as one of the glowing weapons hit the ground of the alley only feet from Alexius.

Only yards from her family.

She didn't have time to think. Even as Tiege knocked her to the ground and Zachariah threw himself on top of Tate, Ariana brought forth all of her Lekwuesti energy and pushed it out with a silent and desperate plea.

The explosion deafened her. She couldn't breathe. Darkness ringed her vision, but she dared not lose consciousness. Around them, sand and debris settled to the ground without touching her.

It could have been seconds or minutes later when she next became aware of what was happening. Tiege lifted her. He was talking to her, but she heard only a dull ringing sound. Beside her, an uninjured Zachariah held Tate by the waist so she wouldn't run from him. She strained against him, screaming something as her eyes shone with tears. Ariana turned to see what had so upset her.

When she shifted her eyes, she saw death.

Ini-herit couldn't remember the blocking enchantment placed on the entrance to the statue, but he knew it had saved their lives.

The concussion of the boom had all of them staggering back. When Clara Kate lost her footing, he reached out and grabbed her before she fell to the ground. He lifted her and carried her away from the crumbling rock at the entrance, joining Quincy and Sophia further inside the chamber. He wanted to get Clara Kate away from danger, but he was only too aware of the fact that their friends and family were outside where the blast occurred.

I'll check it out, Quincy thought. Ini-herit nodded.

"What happened?" Clara Kate asked, sounding dazed.

When Ini-herit looked at her face, he realized a rock had managed to strike her. Blood dripped from a wound along her temple.

"There was another explosion," he replied, healing her with his power.

"Oh, no," she said.

Her wide eyes moved to Quincy, who stood and looked through the only opening left by the rockslide. Sophia stood near him, her face pale and her hands clenched together. Ini-herit lowered Clara Kate to her feet, but kept an arm around her.

When Quincy turned away from the opening, they all saw the emotion on his face. They felt his horror and his despair. Ini-herit's grip on Clara Kate tightened as she sagged against him.

"Our family is okay," Quincy said in a quiet voice as Sophia hurried up to him. "Somehow, the blast didn't affect them." His gaze moved to Clara Kate. "But a number of Waresti were killed."

Ini-herit experienced his avowed's flash of fear and disbelief. He heard her stop breathing. They both watched Quincy collect himself before he delivered the blow.

"Alexius was among them."

Chapter 36

IT TOOK ZACHARIAH PRECIOUS MINUTES TO CALM TATE DOWN WHEN SHE saw the results of the explosion. The Waresti remains were scattered everywhere. Alexius' sword had embedded itself in the stone only a few feet away. For some reason, Tate seemed to think that she could do something to change the outcome of Eirik's attack. She was trying to get to the place where they last saw the Waresti second commander.

"Tate," he said, finally grabbing her and shoving her against the statue so he could hold her in place. "Look at me." She continued fighting for her release, shouting Alexius' name. Grabbing her by her jaw and forcing her to face him, he repeated, "Look. At. *Me.*"

Finally, she focused on him. Her beautiful eyes dripped tears. He felt every bit of her shock. Every bit of her pain.

"No," she whispered. Her breath hitched and she shook her head. "No, Sparky. He was trying to protect us."

"I know. Now we have to protect ourselves. Don't let Alexius die in vain."

He watched her process this, watched the shock ease. Anger took its place. Wiping her cheeks with brisk strokes of her hands, she nodded. Then she shoved away from him and checked to make sure her weapons were still intact and ready for use.

Was it any wonder that he loved her so much?

He looked on as the surviving Waresti regrouped and positioned themselves to hold their defensive perimeter. Turning to Ariana, he gauged her status. Although she leaned heavily against Tiege's side and had lost much of her color, she appeared steady enough.

"You shielded us against that weapon," he said as he approached her.

"Yes."

"Can you do it again?"

"I'm doing it now," she replied.

He walked up to her and put his hands on her shoulders. Once, she would have cowered from him. Now, she just held his gaze.

"When we survive this, Lekwuesti, it will be because of you," he said. Tightening his grip, he added, "Don't ever think of yourself as weak or inferior again."

Her mouth opened, but she didn't speak. Tiege nodded at him, communicating what they both felt without words.

"All right," Zachariah said, looking from Tate to the others. "Since we all share these damned emotions now, I know you're afraid. I know you're upset. But we're the last line of defense between Eirik and this scroll piece. Between him and our family.

"We will *not* bloody fail."

Eirik watched the launch of his newest, most innovative weapons with interest. Their first test release had resulted in considerable damage. What devastation would the release of five more cause?

The cacophony of sound when the weapons struck their targets was reassuring. The Waresti scrambled to identify the sources of the blasts and tried to locate where their offensive weaknesses lay. It was enough to make Eirik think they could win without any effort at all.

Then he realized that not all of the weapons had detonated.

Frowning, he looked at the Mercesti who deployed the failed missiles. "What did you do wrong?"

"N-nothing, my lord," one of the two males replied as his counterpart nodded jerkily beside him. "I did everything just as you instructed."

"Then why did your weapons not react the same as the others?"

"I am not certain, my lord. Perhaps it was not designed the same way?"

Eirik's jaw clenched. He kept his focus on the field of battle as he replied, "All of the weapons were created by the same being. They should all react the same way."

"I cannot argue, my lord," the male replied, exchanging a look with his counterpart. "Yet ours did not."

"You are suggesting—"

Cutting himself off, Eirik turned to confront Metis. She was gone.

Clara Kate didn't react to Quincy's news at first. She clutched Ini-herit's arm and let the shock and grief roll through her.

She pictured Alexius training her when she was younger, helping her become proficient with her blessed butterfly swords. She pictured him enjoying a holiday feast beside her in her family's home. She pictured him laughing at one of her terrible jokes. She pictured him standing over Tate's grave and then helping them search for her. She pictured him offering her whatever support she needed after she learned of her pregnancy.

She pictured his expression when he told her he loved her.

A wave of nausea made her gag. She pushed away from Ini-herit, stumbling to her knees.

"C.K.," Sophia said, hurrying to her side. "Come on, *archigos*. Keep it together. We have to get this scroll piece and get out of here. Our friends and family need us."

Ini-herit touched her shoulder and sent her some of his healing energy. It helped reduce the bile that threatened her, but it didn't make her feel any less wretched. This wasn't a physical ailment. This was crippling emotional pain.

"Another strike could come at any time," Quincy said. "We're leaving them vulnerable out there the longer we're in here."

Nodding, Clara Kate took a deep breath and allowed Sophia to pull her to her feet. There would be time for her to succumb to her emotions. Now wasn't that time.

"Hand me your weapons," she said.

She drew her butterfly swords. Pulling forth her second power, she imbued the weapons with extra holy light. The etchings along the blades glowed bright white, lighting the chamber. When she was done with her weapons, she imbued the swords carried by the others.

"Let's hope that lasts long enough to get us through this place," she said.

"Let's hope we don't need them," Sophia added. She rarely used weapons and looked a little odd with one strapped in a scabbard around her slim waist.

Clara Kate silently agreed with her. When Ini-herit touched her arm, she caught his gaze. The emotion she saw there almost had her losing her composure.

I'll be okay, Harry, she thought. *You'll give me strength.*

He nodded. "Okay." Looking at all of them and lifting the medallion, he said, "Follow me."

It didn't take Metis long to sneak away from Eirik and his followers. Getting safely to one of the guarded structures in the distance was another matter, however.

Eirik left a stretch of land between them and the rest of the Estilorians. Although Metis knew his shield prevented weapons from harming him, he was still vulnerable to physical contact from other beings. To cross the battlefield, she had to hide among combatting groups of Waresti and Mercesti, using their larger forms for cover. She wore a long cloak and the concealing cloth over her face, so she wasn't easily identifiable. A few Waresti caught sight of her, but since she bore no weapon and was running in an apparent bid to escape the turmoil, they let her go.

She took care to avoid the kragen as the creature swooped nearby and struck several Mercesti with its tail. Apparently, Eirik's dampeners couldn't prohibit an animal from flying.

Finally, she reached the side of a statue standing fifteen feet tall. It was one of several in front of a large ancient temple. Pressing herself against the warm stone, she made sure she wasn't being observed. Then she moved carefully among the shadows cast by the stones so that she could watch the battle.

Patience had never been one of her strengths, but she waited. Her timing and the circumstances had to be just right for this to succeed.

When a large group of battling Mercesti and Waresti neared her position, she straightened with interest. She watched events unfold with a careful eye, seeking the precise moment to make her move. Some of the combatants moved into the empty temple, their weapons clashing. She moved into the darkened interior of the once-sacred structure, keeping hidden.

Then she saw it. A Waresti male took a strike to the arm. His weapon flew from his grasp, landing near her. His Mercesti attacker went in for the kill, but the Waresti dodged the blow, stealing his opponent's weapon and killing him with it. Then he turned to rejoin the fight outside the temple.

And Metis ended his life.

* * *

"They are too skilled, my lord."

Eirik's gaze moved sharply to the male who had issued the statement. He wanted to pound him to dust him, but instead replied, "You are wrong, Ivan."

"Our numbers are diminishing," Ivan argued, his eyes darting across the battlefield. Sweat dripped from his hairline. "It is all we can do to prevent the elders from breeching our mental defenses, never mind us having any hope of breaking through their block. That kragen is shielded and targeting our forces. I have watched numerous Mercesti fall. The Waresti are nearing our position, and we have no idea where the artifact is."

"On the contrary," came Friedrich's voice. "I know exactly where the artifact is."

With a surge of satisfaction, Eirik turned to watch the other male approach. "You completed your mission?"

"Yes, my lord. It didn't take much searching to find the group you seek."

"Which group is that?" Ivan asked, looking between them.

"The other group searching for the artifact," Friedrich answered. His gaze settled on Eirik. "I saw two Kynzesti, one Lekwuesti and Zachariah."

"Wait—Zachariah?" Ivan repeated. "The Gloresti second commander? But I thought he died."

Eirik's lip curled. "That just tells us how uninformed you are," he said. "Now stop issuing complaints and get back to your tasks. Trust that your leaders know what they are doing."

Ivan bobbed his head and hurried away. Eirik debated whether to shove him into the nearing fray with the Waresti, but couldn't make up his mind before the male scurried out of sight. Shaking his head, he unsheathed his krises.

"Where are they?" he asked.

"In front of the largest statue. The one with the body of a lion."

"Excellent."

Without another word, Eirik started walking down the sand dune. Friedrich reached out and took his arm.

"My lord," he said, "Ivan was not completely incorrect in his interpretation of our situation. It does appear we are sorely outmatched on multiple levels."

"Fear not, Friedrich," Eirik said, removing his arm from the other male's grasp. "Reinforcements will be here any moment." As he turned to head to his goal, he added, "In the meantime, make use of the last of our special weapons. They should afford us as much time as we need."

Chapter 37

INI-HERIT WASN'T SURE HOW THE MEDALLION WAS MEANT TO HELP THEM. IT was unresponsive as they moved through the interior of the statue. They even joined hands to make sure they did the most they could to invoke the medallion's power. Still, nothing.

They didn't talk as they walked down a series of ramps leading far belowground. Speech wasn't necessary when they could share thoughts. He knew that, like him, they were all terrified for those outside the statue. How many of those deadly weapons did Eirik have? How long could their forces withstand the blasts? How many of them had already fallen?

They were equally worried about the unknown traps leading to the final scroll piece. He had created the medallion to serve as a guide and form of protection. Protection from what?

Finally, they reached the bottom of a ramp that led to a long, narrow corridor. He couldn't see the end of it from where they stood. Something about the darkness beyond made him hesitate.

"Creepy, isn't it?" Clara Kate said, squeezing his hand.

"Times a hundred," he replied.

Once again, he held up the medallion and twirled it, willing it to help them. He took a couple of steps closer to the corridor. This time, the metal glowed.

"That can't be good," Sophia said.

They all stopped walking. Ini-herit looked more closely at the medallion as it dangled in front of him. He realized that only a couple of the markings were illuminated. One was a triangle with a flat top that resembled the entrance to the tunnel in front of them. The other was a wavy line.

"What does that mean?" Clara Kate asked.

"I have no idea."

They all stared at the entrance to the tunnel. Something told him that they should exercise caution even though everything looked normal.

Let me try something, Quincy thought, reaching into his satchel of healing supplies. He rummaged around until he came up with a slat of wood used for setting broken bones. Then he tossed it into the tunnel.

Spikes shot out of the floor, walls and ceiling at a variety of depths and angles. After remaining there for a few seconds, they withdrew, leaving the tunnel looking completely innocuous once again.

Ini-herit exchanged glances with his family. Clara Kate's eyes were huge. Quincy frowned. Sophia stepped closer to the tunnel.

"Fascinating," she said, looking at the walls. "It's got to be enchanted. You can't see where the spikes will come out. I wonder if they erupt from the same locations each time." Glancing at Quincy, she asked, "Got any more of that wood?"

Shrugging, he reached into his bag and produced a couple more pieces. When Sophia turned her gaze back to the tunnel, she nodded at him. He threw one of the pieces, producing the spikes. Although the tunnel looked like a jumbled, unpredictable mess of deadly violence to Ini-herit, he saw Sophia's eyes glow as she studied the layout. He imagined she was enhancing her abilities by channeling an animal's senses. After the spikes retreated, she nodded again. Quincy threw another piece of wood and the spikes shot back out.

"Got it," Sophia said after a moment. "The spikes emerge the instant anything physically crosses the threshold. They don't change pattern. I can get to the other side."

"How?" Clara Kate asked. "You have to shift into an animal about your same size, which would be too big to avoid getting hit. You can't fly because the corridor is too narrow and the spikes practically touch in the middle."

Sophia smiled and patted her cousin on the shoulder. "Have faith, *archigos.*" Then she looked at Ini-herit. "Do you think there's a way to disarm this thing on the other side?"

Ini-herit looked at the medallion. "Probably. I'm guessing you'd have to use this."

"Okay. When I shift, put the chain in my mouth."

They didn't have time to argue. One second they were looking at Sophia, and the next she disappeared. Ini-herit glanced down in confusion. He realized a long, blonde-colored snake was emerging from Sophia's armor.

"Holy light, Soph!" Clara Kate exclaimed, leaping behind Ini-herit and making a squealing noise. "Totally gross."

Despite the intensity of the moment, Ini-herit smiled. "Some badass you are," he said with a shake of his head. Then he squatted and told Sophia, "Open wide."

She did, revealing long fangs that had Clara Kate shuddering. Ini-herit settled the medallion's chain in the snake's mouth and thought, *Be careful*.

She turned without a sound and approached the tunnel's entrance. Clara Kate took his hand. He felt the dampness of her palm as he twined his fingers with hers. They stayed back, but Quincy crept closer to Sophia, his face reflecting his fear for her. Ini-herit tensed as Sophia stopped less than an inch from the threshold.

Rather than put her entire head across it, she extended her flickering tongue despite the medallion in her mouth. The spikes erupted. As soon as they did, she slithered into the tunnel, her body winding fluidly around the deadly protrusions. Her movement kept the spikes from retracting. They were enchanted to remain out until all motion ceased. It didn't take long until she had gotten all the way to the darkened end of the tunnel.

Casting another ball of light, Ini-herit threw it as far into the tunnel as he could. Fortunately, it was enough that they could see the far side. He saw the last of Sophia's tail disappear through the doorway.

Clara Kate released a breath. "She made it."

"Of course she did," Quincy said, turning to collect Sophia's clothes and weapon.

"The coast is clear," Sophia called out.

They moved into the tunnel and hurried to the other side. Quincy jogged ahead so he could assist Sophia in getting back into her armor. Although it was a special lightweight design that resembled a black bodysuit, it wasn't simple to don. Giving them privacy, Ini-herit retrieved the medallion from the niche beside the door. Clara Kate looked at it over his shoulder.

"A wavy line," he murmured, thinking of Sophia's snake form. "I'll be damned."

"How did you know there would be a being capable of transforming into a snake when you created the medallion?" Clara Kate wondered.

"I'm not sure I did," he admitted. "I may have only known what kind of maneuvering would be needed to safely pass through the tunnel. The actual *how* of it might have been up in the air."

She considered this in silence. A moment later, Sophia and Quincy joined them. Clara Kate pulled her cousin into a hug.

"Great work, Soph."

"Thanks." Sophia looked at Ini-herit. "Any idea what's next?"

He shook his head. "We won't know until the medallion tells us."

Muted thunder reached their ears. A light rain of dirt fell from the ceiling. Ini-herit knew Eirik's forces had deployed another weapon. He looked at the others.

"So let's hurry up and figure out what challenge we have to overcome to end this."

Ariana hadn't ever been able to generate shields like those she produced for her and her family. It was a skill developed by the most experienced Lekwuesti, and even then, it was rare.

She thought she knew why she could do it now, though. Before, she didn't really have a need for the ability. Now she did. The beings standing with her meant more to her than her own life. If her family's safety depended on her, she would continue generating the shields.

The Mercesti were nearing. Ariana watched the Waresti gather to meet them. The numbers of Mercesti flooding around the statue seemed impossible. She wished she had any kind of skill with a distance weapon, like a bow.

"Or a throwing weapon," Tiege said out loud.

"What?" Zachariah asked.

"Ariana was thinking that a bow would be handy to shoot some of the Mercesti before they get here. I added the idea of throwing weapons."

Zachariah hefted his tomahawk, giving it a considering glance. They all knew the weapon would only work for one throw before he had to retrieve it. Lowering the axe, he looked from Tate to Tiege.

"How about icicles?" he said.

The twins exchanged glances. Ariana's eyes widened. Icicles could be thrown. If they were thick and pointed enough and thrown accurately, they could kill or incapacitate a being.

Tate and Tiege moved close together. They used their elemental abilities, Tate producing water as Tiege froze it. But they couldn't get the icicles to form consistently.

"Here," Ariana said after a moment. Using her power, she produced a rectangular metal object. "You need a mold."

Soon, they had a small pile of the icicles. Then they put them to use, taking down as many of their opponents as they could. Ariana stood back and focused on maintaining the shields. It was hard not to flinch when arrows rained down on them, but she managed it. She knew she had to protect all of them.

She saw Nyx flying from one point to another, taking down Mercesti with wide sweeps of her tail. Despite their efforts, though, they weren't making headway. More and more Mercesti entered the battle, outnumbering them at least three to one.

"Eirik brought in reinforcements," Zachariah said.

Reinforcements? Ariana fought panic. She struggled to control her fear as the Mercesti fighters grew closer and closer.

"Maybe you should use your invisibility illusion on us," Zachariah said to Tiege.

"Can't," Tiege replied as he threw another icicle. "I can't use my power on Tate."

Ariana knew Tate naturally shattered any illusion with which she came into contact, so Tiege couldn't make her appear invisible.

"Heads up," Tate said, reaching out and putting her arms around Zachariah. She caught Ariana's gaze, her face pale. "Bomb's away."

Glancing up, Ariana saw one of the weapons that had killed Alexius falling in their direction. She knew that even if the explosion didn't affect any of them because of their shields, many of the Waresti battling nearby would either die or get seriously injured.

She flung out her power, hurling it like a physical object. The shield she generated collided with the weapon. Instead of striking near them, the explosive ricocheted into a large sand dune piled against a temple.

When it exploded, sand blew everywhere. But there were no casualties.

Ariana sagged against Tiege as the drain on her energy caught up with her. She questioned her frame of mind when she realized she was happy that the Waresti were now able to battle with their more conventional weapons, on equal footing with the Mercesti, rather than wishing there was no battle at all.

"That was brilliant, Ariana," Tiege said, giving her a quick kiss. "*You're* brilliant."

Though she was exhausted, she actually felt rather brilliant. Knowing she was helping to spare lives gave her added strength.

That feeling lasted until she glanced up and spotted Eirik heading right toward them.

Chapter 38

IN THE FORM OF THE WARESTI, METIS MADE HER WAY ACROSS THE FLOOR OF the empty temple and approached a doorway on the far side. Sounds of battle reached her from beyond the door. She had to decide whether it was worth risking her safety by entering the battle without knowing how to properly wield a weapon, or waiting for an opportunity to leave the temple unnoticed.

She watched two Mercesti fall just feet away. Maybe Eirik's followers were as incompetent as she was when it came to fighting. That would give her a chance.

As she neared the doorway and prepared to step out, she spotted Eirik in the distance. He was approaching the large statue with the head of a male and body of a lion. Her gaze moved to the base of the structure.

Tate and Ariana.

Metis ran back to the spot where she had killed the Waresti and picked up his sword. It was large enough that she expected to struggle with it, but her muscular male form had no difficulties. It made her think that if it came down to a battle against Eirik, she might have a chance to at least injure him so she could retrieve the scroll pieces.

When she reached the doorway where she had seen Eirik, she paused to make sure she wasn't stepping into the middle of swinging weapons. Then she felt a presence behind her.

"Hello, Metis."

Turning, she faced her opponent. "Malukali."

The Orculesti elder's expression was calm, her eyes fathomless. Her dark hair was secured behind her head, an indication that she was prepared to fight. She even wore the same conforming black armor that Metis had seen on Tate and Ariana, a short sword strapped to her side. The contradiction between her ensemble and her unruffled demeanor puzzled Metis.

"Your mental signature is quite distinctive," Malukali said. "I only wish I had been able to find you before you killed Aaron."

Metis scanned the temple. "Where is the Wymzesti? He would not have left you to confront me alone."

"I'm surprised that you've developed that level of insight into relationships, Metis," Knorbis said from behind her.

She shifted at the sound of his voice so she could keep both elders in view. She assessed his posture and potential threat to her as she responded, "I have learned that you develop sentimental attachments to each other that can be used as leverage. You are all fools."

"What is it you hope to accomplish here?" Malukali asked.

"I am sure you already know the answer to that. You two are supposedly the most intuitive beings on the plane."

"We know you want the scroll," Knorbis said in the same level tone that his wife used. "You've been working with Eirik and he's made his goal clear enough. What we don't understand is why you're going about acquiring it this way rather than working with Eirik. Traveling to Central on your own? Trying to kill the Kynzesti elder?"

"You know it was not my intent to kill her," Metis snapped. "She is the key to acquiring the scroll...or activating it." She lifted her chin. "I intercepted your thoughts."

"Parts of our thoughts, perhaps," Malukali allowed. "But certainly not all of them. Your primary weakness is your failure to think things through before acting. You form judgments with very little information upon which to base them."

Knorbis moved closer. "Because you can change forms, you feel you have an understanding of each of the abilities and base personality types of those you assume. But you only absorb portions of those abilities and you have little insight to apply to them. Your arrogance leads you to believe you are stronger and more intelligent than you actually are."

Fury burned the back of her throat. She focused on harnessing the instincts of the Waresti. Not as strong or as intelligent as she thought? She would show them.

Bending, she retrieved the dagger hidden in her boot, throwing it at Malukali in one smooth movement. It deflected off an invisible barrier with a spark of lavender light. Growling, she raised her sword. She would get around the shield somehow.

No sooner did she lift her sword than it flew from her hand—her hand along with it. She stared at the garish injury, not even feeling it. A moment later, she fell to her knees.

"For example," Malukali said, walking up to her. "You considered the fact that my husband wouldn't leave me to face you alone." Knorbis joined her, looking down at Metis without expression. "But you didn't consider that our 'sentimental attachments' extend to more than just one being at a time."

Metis' gaze shifted to the Lekwuesti and Waresti elders as they joined Malukali and Knorbis. Uriel's blade was stained with her blood. None of them conveyed any emotion.

"It's over, Metis," they said at the same time.

Ini-herit stopped walking again when the spinning medallion glowed. They stood in front of an open doorway leading to a small chamber. On the far side of the chamber was an elaborate carving of a tree. There were no furnishings or other obvious signs of the room's purpose.

"What symbols are highlighted this time?" Clara Kate asked.

Holding the medallion up so he could see the lit markings more clearly, Ini-herit studied it as the others crowded around. He deciphered the symbols. One resembled a dripping leaf and the other a single eye. As he interpreted them and part of his memory about the trap returned, his curiosity transitioned to dread.

He looked up and caught Quincy's gaze. The other male's brow was furrowed as he also reasoned through the meaning of the symbols. His gaze moved to the etching of the tree on the back wall of the small chamber.

"What do they mean, Harry?" Clara Kate asked.

Although Ini-herit was tempted to lie, he knew that wouldn't help. Tightening his hold on the medallion, he said, "It means there's poison involved and healing required to get through this trap."

Quincy issued a soft curse, shaking his head and looking again into the chamber. "That's the Bahun Upas tree, isn't it?"

"Yes."

Sophia swallowed hard. "Isn't the poison derived from that tree fatal?"

Ini-herit nodded. "I remembered creating this trap once I saw the symbols. At the time, I thought I'd only be coming down here with another elder. That elder would have to go into the chamber first. Then, once the poison was ingested, I would heal him or her."

"I didn't think your healing abilities were that strong," Clara Kate said. "My mom mentioned that she once brought Aunt Skye back to life, and that no one could believe it because they hadn't seen it done before."

"When it comes to the connection between the elders, our abilities are enhanced. Sebastian can pair to all of us at once rather than just one being, for example. Uriel's offensive skills are enhanced when put to the task of rescuing an elder. Gabriel's defensive abilities are similarly heightened. So the belief is that my healing abilities will also permit me to bring an elder back from the brink of death."

"You didn't save Volarius," Sophia pointed out.

"Volarius was dead for too long before I learned about it. Besides, I said on the brink of death. I haven't ever brought a being back from the dead."

There was a long pause. Then Clara Kate said, "So a fellow elder needs to go into that chamber and allow him or herself to be killed by the poison, then you go in and bring that elder back to life?"

He knew where she was leading and shook his head. "You aren't fully connected with all of us yet, Angel."

"But you're avowed to me," she said. "Our connection should be at least as strong as the elder bond."

Panic set in as he realized what she was suggesting. "But the baby—"

"Look," Quincy interrupted. "Just heal me before I die, all right?"

Then he ran into the chamber. The door slammed behind him. They all stared at the closed door for a moment, frozen in shock.

"Quincy!" Sophia cried, running up to the door and searching for a handle. It didn't have one. She pounded on the wood. "No!"

"What has he done?" Clara Kate asked in a hoarse voice, her hand pressed to her chest. "Holy light…what has he done?"

Ini-herit walked up to Sophia and pulled her away from the door. When he saw the tears in her eyes, he wanted to go back in time and punch himself in the head to stop from creating such a dangerous and unpredictable trap. It was truly amazing how experiencing no emotion affected one's judgment on such things.

"What he's done is put his faith in me," he said, looking at Sophia. "You told Clara Kate to have faith in you before. Now I ask you to have it in me."

Although tears trailed down her face, she nodded. He hugged her. After a moment, he reached for Clara Kate's hand. She stepped closer, then took over hugging Sophia so he could position himself outside the door.

The wait seemed interminable, though it was probably less than a minute. Finally, the door clicked open.

Ini-herit ran inside and fell to the ground next to Quincy. Not even bothering to check for a pulse, he brought forth all of his healing energy and placed his hands on Quincy's chest.

Nothing happened.

Closing his eyes, he focused on his new bond with Quincy and the others. Sweat beaded on his brow as he concentrated. If his abilities were heightened for the elders, it sure as hell should be heightened for his family. And that's exactly what Quincy was now.

After several long minutes, Quincy's heartbeat resumed. Sophia sobbed and joined Ini-herit on the ground. Clara Kate placed a hand on Ini-herit's shoulder as he slumped in exhaustion.

He opened his eyes and met Quincy's gaze, sharing a silent understanding. He knew Quincy had sacrificed himself rather than risk Clara Kate and the baby. He wouldn't ever be able to repay that. He didn't even know what to say.

But Quincy did.

"Took you long enough, Harry."

Chapter 39

EIRIK IGNORED THE BATTLE AS HE ADVANCED ON THE STATUE. HIS SHIELD protected him against weapons and his followers kept the Waresti occupied, so he had no concerns. As he passed a temple not far from the statue, he spotted the kragen. A lift of his hand had his followers casting the enchanted net he had brought along for just this purpose. It brought the creature down.

Perfect.

He wasn't surprised when Zachariah walked out of the alley leading to the statue. The space was too confining for a fight, and there was no avoiding one now. The Waresti guarding the alley were currently engaged in battle with swarms of Mercesti, so Eirik didn't have much of a challenge getting through their defenses. In fact, this entire undertaking was proving ridiculously easy. He knew he would soon have the third scroll piece.

Although he expected Zachariah to meet him alone, he watched as Tate, Ariana and a Kynzesti male lined up behind him.

"Relying on reinforcements to try to defeat me, Zachariah?" he asked as he came to a stop fifteen feet away from them. "It is hard to blame you, considering you would have died the last time we faced each other if not for your former elder. I do not suppose Gabriel is here this time, is he?" Glancing to each side, he shrugged. "It appears not."

Zachariah stared back with a bland expression, his arms crossed over his chest.

Eirik shifted his gaze to Tate. He scanned her form, then said, "I see your avowed is healed. She appears in excellent shape, as a matter of fact." Looking back at Zachariah, he asked, "Did you feel it when my followers attacked her?" Seeing the other male's eyes narrow, he tilted his head. "It was a delight to watch. Next time, I have even better things planned for her."

None of them replied. They hadn't moved from their positions since stopping to face him. He clenched his jaw, fighting his growing rage.

"You must be Tate's brother," he said to the male Kynzesti. "As I see that Ariana now bears Kynzesti-colored markings, I will assume you have avowed with her." He looked at Ariana, who met his gaze without flinching. "She and I had a lot of private time together before she met you. I can attest to what a...*special* female she is."

He expected outrage. He expected loud protests defending the Lekwuesti's honor. He received neither.

They were toying with him. He gripped his weapons and calculated the best way to use them to cause the most damage. "Where is the third scroll piece?" he asked, his tone promising death if they didn't answer.

They didn't.

He took a step forward. A loud commotion stopped him. Glancing behind Zachariah, he watched as the battlefield flooded with Waresti and Mercesti reinforcements led by Harold and Derian.

Impossible. His forces should have stopped them.

Finally, Zachariah spoke. "In regards to the first question you asked, you bloody bastard...you can take that as a yes."

Clara Kate didn't want to know what other surprises awaited them inside the statue's depths. Just thinking about it made the low ceiling and narrow corridors feel as though they were pressing in on her. Since she knew the power of the Elder Scroll, she understood the need for having these traps in place. But disarming them was a terrifying prospect.

According to the markings on Ini-herit's medallion, there should only be one more trap. She supposed she should thank heaven for small favors. Instead, she was uncomfortably aware of the fact that everyone besides her had now done something to get them to the scroll piece. Judging by how these things typically went, there was a balance and reason behind why the four of them were allowed into the statue while the others weren't. In all likelihood, her abilities would be needed.

In other words, she thought, *batter up.*

After walking back up several ramps, they approached another chamber.

By now, they knew that they only encountered rooms when a trap was involved. Sure enough, Ini-herit's medallion began to glimmer as they neared it.

"Well, this is it," he said. "The last trap."

"I don't suppose your memory is returning to you?" Clara Kate asked, glancing from the dark chamber to meet his gaze.

"I wish it was." He turned the medallion to study the lit markings. "All I know is this symbol is a flame, and this one is the ankh."

"The Egyptian symbol for eternal life," Sophia mused.

"While that's true," Ini-herit agreed, "this symbol is the only true sign of faith among Estilorians. It's because we are long-lived and once placed such importance on this symbol that the ancient Egyptians adopted it."

"Okay. Faith and fire," Quincy summed up.

They all looked at the empty chamber. Then they exchanged glances.

"Is someone about to get barbecued?" Sophia asked.

"I wouldn't have created a trap that a being couldn't survive if approaching it the right way," Ini-herit said, but they all sensed his hesitation. They knew he wasn't sure.

Clara Kate's skin tingled with fear when she envisioned walking into fire. She pictured her skin roasting, her hair burning, her lungs filling with heat as she screamed. Just thinking about it brought a light sheen of sweat to her brow. But she knew her turn had come.

"Well, I'm no stranger to fire," she said out loud. When everyone looked at her, she held up her hand and produced a ball of flame. "It's my elemental ability. If I can summon it, maybe I can control it."

"You've never tried to before," Sophia argued. "You don't know that you can do it."

"No, I don't." Clara Kate agreed. "None of us do. But I know I have to do this." She met Ini-herit's gaze. "I know you, Harry. I know your core traits and those characteristics that you've contributed to your class. All of this is about faith. These traps center around it. Faith in one's self, faith in others..." Her gaze moved to the dark chamber. "And faith in the unknown."

After a moment, Ini-herit reached for her. She expected him to argue. Instead, he kissed her.

She didn't bother protesting. Pushing past her fear, she tapped into his mind and allowed his love to fill her as she enjoyed his kiss. She would use both as motivation to get her through this.

The kiss was over before she was ready, but she knew there was much more riding on this than a single moment with the male she loved. She parted from him, touching the side of his face and communicating her feelings without words. Then she turned and entered the chamber, allowing the resulting flames to engulf her.

Ariana's breath came too quickly as she stared at Eirik. Her heart beat so fast that she felt it throbbing in the sides of her neck, prohibiting speech.

This was a good thing. There was much she wanted to say to the evil male standing in front of them, but she knew Zachariah wanted all of them to keep quiet. He conveyed that their silence would provoke Eirik. As usual, the Mercesti's strategy was correct.

He's off-stride now, Zachariah thought. *Be prepared in case he opts to throw a weapon. I'm the only one the curse on his blades won't kill if he happens to get through the shields.*

They all issued mental nods.

"It appears my time to acquire the final scroll piece has arrived," Eirik said as he watched the new arrivals take over the battlefield. "You will have to excuse me."

As he started to walk past them to the statue, Zachariah mentally conveyed his intentions. Responding to the thought, Ariana shifted with Tate and Tiege until all four of them blocked the alleyway from Eirik.

"Looks like you could use a few reinforcements yourself," Zachariah observed.

Eirik quirked an eyebrow. "Perhaps you are correct," he replied.

Then he raised a hand. No less than twenty arrows struck the barrier that Ariana generated. She felt the blows like slices to her skin and flinched. She realized that Eirik watched her.

"Ah, Ariana," he said. "You have all sorts of secrets, do you not? It is a wonder that anyone would trust such a deceitful bitch."

Tiege started forward, but Zachariah stopped him with a loud, commanding thought. Ariana swallowed the anger and fear that threatened her and focused on reassuring Tiege. He didn't look at her since they all had to watch Eirik, but she felt him calm down.

"Very well," Eirik said. "We will test your abilities. My Mercesti have countless arrows. With such specific targets, it should not take long for them to weaken your shields." His gaze met Zachariah's. "Once they do, I will wait until they kill you and then walk over your dead forms to get the scroll piece. Or maybe I will have them focus their efforts on you and the Kynzesti male so that I may further enjoy Tate and Ariana."

Zachariah uncrossed his arms and approached Eirik. Ariana felt his blistering anger in response to Eirik's threat, but his casual stride and unemotional expression offered no insight into the reality that lay beneath.

"By the time you finish blathering, you pompous ass, the bloody battle will be over," Zachariah said. "Let's bottom-line this. You have to defeat me to get anywhere near that scroll piece, and I have every intention of killing you. We're both shielded against weapons, but the being who is shielding me is far more loyal than the being shielding you."

Eirik snorted. "Why would you assume that? You are a Mercesti just like I am. She has no reason to be loyal to you."

"I am nothing like you."

That was all the explanation Zachariah was going to give. Ariana knew, like he did, that Eirik didn't understand a thing about true loyalty, and most especially nothing about love. Presenting those as arguments would be a waste of breath.

"Fine," Eirik snapped. "What do you propose?"

In response, Zachariah broke his nose.

Ini-herit joined hands with Sophia and Quincy as he watched his avowed step into the raging inferno. He swore if he was ever called upon to devise traps again, he would flat-out refuse.

What the hell had he been thinking?

The heat emitting from the open chamber had all of them stepping back. He watched the outline of Clara Kate for as long as he could—a matter of seconds—until it appeared the fire had disintegrated her to ash.

Only then did doubt enter his mind. Had what he thought he'd just seen actually happened? Was she really gone?

Have faith, Sophia and Quincy thought at the same time.

He squeezed their hands harder. They were right. If anyone was meant to deactivate this trap, it was Clara Kate. The fact that her elemental power was fire was impossible to ignore.

He couldn't deny the compelling pull of fate as everything sank in. Knorbis had applied his foresight to the creation of the Elder Scroll. In it, he identified the eight beings meant to activate the scroll's power. Somehow, Ini-herit had created traps that also involved those beings, though he'd had no idea who they would be at the time.

Clara Kate was right. It all boiled down to faith.

As that thought flashed through his mind, the fire died. He stepped forward, not releasing Sophia or Quincy. After viewing the bright fire, the chamber was especially dark.

"Clara Kate?" he called out.

A moment later, she came into view. She held something in her hand. When she met his gaze, she smiled.

"I'm here," she said. "And I have the last scroll piece."

Chapter 40

ZACHARIAH COULDN'T DENY THE INTENSE SATISFACTION HE GOT OUT OF hearing and feeling Eirik's nose splinter against his fist. It had been increasingly difficult to subdue his murderous impulses as Eirik spoke. Only Tate's quiet reassurance kept him in check.

Now that he'd spilled Eirik's blood, however, all bets were off.

He followed up his right hook with a quick jab to Eirik's throat. The combo had Eirik gagging and staggering back. When Zachariah again advanced, Eirik sheathed his weapons so he could defend himself. He likely knew that he wouldn't stand a chance of breeching Ariana's shields if he was armed.

He deflected the next punch Zachariah threw, so Zachariah followed it up with a roundhouse kick. Eirik grabbed his boot and twisted, sending Zachariah spinning. Zachariah managed to remain on his feet, but couldn't block the punch to his kidneys. Pain radiated up his spine.

Taking advantage of Zachariah's stumble, Eirik brought his knee up into his abdomen. All of the air left Zachariah's lungs.

Lurching forward, he rammed his shoulder into Eirik's midsection. Dust flew as they hit the ground. They landed in the middle of the ongoing skirmish between the Mercesti and the Waresti, scattering a number of beings. Zachariah ignored them as he drove his fist into Eirik's face once, then again.

Eirik used his legs to dislodge Zachariah from on top of him. A second later, they were both back on their feet.

They circled each other. Zachariah feinted with a punch. When Eirik moved to block, Zachariah kicked him in the ribs, following it with a blow to the side of his head.

Then he was grabbed from behind. It took a moment for the violence to lift from his mind so he could absorb the fact that the fight had been interrupted. Looking to either side, he realized that Eirik's followers held him. The large swarm of Mercesti that had preceded Harold and Derian's teams had proven too much for the Waresti trying to hold them back.

Then he noticed that Tate and Tiege were also engaged in combat, trying to keep their opponents from reaching Ariana and disrupting the shields she generated. When he saw Tate facing six Mercesti, the violent haze returned.

Pain shot through him as Eirik struck him in the jaw. He turned his gaze back to his opponent.

"Your advice about reinforcements was sound," Eirik said, spitting blood from his mouth. "Looks like it will gain me the victory. But not before I destroy you."

Ariana didn't know how things slid sideways so quickly. One minute, she was relieved because Harold and Derian had finally joined the fight and Zachariah was standing strong against Eirik. The next, they were facing so many Mercesti she didn't see how any of them could survive.

Her gaze darted around the landscape, seeking assistance. She couldn't believe that the elders would leave them unprotected. The statue behind her housed the final scroll piece. On top of that, two of their fellow elders were within that statue, one of those elders being the daughter of yet another elder. If nothing else warranted their intervention, this certainty did. Yet all she saw was Eirik's followers.

She knew she couldn't focus on that. She had to maintain the shields. Direct physical contact was possible through the shields, but she prevented Tate, Tiege and Zachariah from taking a hit from an arrow or other weapon.

It wasn't going to be enough, she realized now.

Zachariah was currently restrained by six Mercesti. Two males held each arm and two held his legs. He was essentially defenseless in the face of his enemy.

Ariana wasn't surprised by Eirik's cowardly maneuver. She had seen and experienced far worse in her time under his thumb. That didn't make it any easier to watch him hurt Zachariah. Remembered terror had her shaking as she witnessed it.

Tate and Tiege had their own problems. Each Kynzesti faced a growing group of Mercesti. For each opponent they defeated, two more took his place.

The siblings fought well, though. Years of precision developed by working with their large family on offensive and defensive maneuvers now came to their aid. Because the Mercesti were unshielded, Tate and Tiege could use their blessed weapons against them. Just a brush with Tate's nunchucks or a slice from Tiege's kamas was enough to cause their opponents excruciating pain. Since the Mercesti weapons couldn't get past the shields, many of them backed off. It didn't take long for Ariana to realize that the siblings could hold their own.

Zachariah, on the other hand, was another matter. Surrounded and held down by Eirik's followers, he looked utterly alone. He had even closed off his mental connection to them, probably not wanting any of them to experience what he was, even if only in thought. She had caught one thought before he brought up the mental barrier, though. He knew that by keeping Eirik focused on him, he was giving everyone else a chance.

She had been in his position before. She wouldn't let him endure this alone.

As Eirik continued his attack, she ran from her position near the statue's entrance. Although fear had her chest aching, she silently reassured the twins with her thoughts when they tried to get her to return to safety. She needed them focused on protecting themselves and keeping any more Mercesti from surrounding Zachariah.

"Stop it, Eirik," she commanded, throwing herself in front of Zachariah when Eirik reared back to strike again. "This isn't getting you any closer to your goal."

"Get back to the statue, Lekwuesti," Zachariah ground out from behind her.

She heard a rattling sound with each of his breaths. *Stop talking, you stubborn Mercesti*, she thought back, swallowing hard as she met Eirik's gaze.

"Get out of my way," Eirik warned.

"No."

He drew back his fist. "It will be you or him."

"Damn it, Ariana—bloody move," Zachariah hissed.

She didn't. Fighting a whimper, she held her arms out to the sides to keep

Eirik from trying to get around her to hit Zachariah instead. For a brief moment, she saw surprise in his gaze.

Then he struck. She took the punch. Staggering back, she fell against Zachariah. Pain had stars dancing before her eyes, but she maintained her focus and stayed on her feet. She had a great deal of experience being on the receiving end of Eirik's abuse. It would take more than one blow to bring her down.

"Ariana!" Tiege shouted.

She sensed him trying to get to her, but their opponents were too many. She wondered how long it would take Harold and Derian's reinforcements to reach them. She wondered why the elders had abandoned them. She wondered how long she could maintain the shields while keeping Eirik from hurting anyone else.

"What are you doing?" Eirik growled. His gaze had moved behind her.

Confused, Ariana wiped at the blood on her mouth and glanced over her shoulder. She realized that the six Mercesti holding Zachariah had released him.

"You said all of the other classes hate us, that they want to keep us from being equals," one of the males responded. "Yet this Lekwuesti just allowed you to strike her to protect this Mercesti, and I see an avowed marking on his arm that bears the coloring of a Kynzesti."

Ariana realized that this Mercesti didn't know who Zachariah was. She also realized that Eirik had lied to his followers. His hold over them had just been shattered.

She met Zachariah's gaze as they reached that conclusion at the same time. He surged forward and tried to grab her, but he wasn't fast enough. Eirik snatched her from behind and dragged her away, his hands encircling her throat and squeezing.

Gasping for air, she clawed at his hands. He lifted her from the ground by her neck, making her spine pop. Agony ratcheted through her. Her vision went in and out of focus as she tried to remember what to do to escape. The voices of her family clamored in her head, confusing her. Her lungs screamed for air.

She felt him change his hold. He wanted to break her neck before Zachariah reached them.

No. He would *not* kill her.

Survival instinct kicked in. She brought forth her power. When she felt the handle of the kitchen knife in her hand, she stabbed backwards with all of her strength.

He let her go. They fell to the ground. She gasped for breath, shaking so hard she almost dropped the knife. It took her a moment to realize it was covered in blood, as was her hand. She had gotten through his shield. The being generating it had either died or chosen to stop.

Before she could look at him and see what she had done, Zachariah reached her. Taking the knife, he lifted her to her feet, positioning himself so she couldn't see Eirik. He held her gaze.

"I killed him, didn't I?" she asked numbly.

"Yes."

Tears filled her eyes. Tiege and Tate ran up to them, the Mercesti no longer trying to keep them back. She looked at the blood dripping down her arm and stumbled away from them. They couldn't touch her. She was a murderer.

"Ariana." Zachariah gripped her shoulders and forced her to look at him. He lifted a hand to hold Tiege and Tate back, then said, "You're not to blame. You acted in self-defense."

Tears clung to her lashes. "I k-killed him."

"Yes, and he damn well needed killing," Zachariah said. When she looked at her bloodied hand, he lifted her chin so she focused on him. "Your soul is untainted, Ariana."

Two tears dripped down her face. "How can you know that?"

He didn't reply at first. Two more tears fell. Watching them trail down her cheeks, he finally said, "Because for a long time I thought mine was, and now I've learned the difference."

It took forever to get out of the statue. First, they had to make their way back along the path they took to get to the scroll piece, then they had to deal with the rocks in the entryway. Clara Kate worried over the fact that she still couldn't hear the others in her mind. She had hoped that once she defeated the third trap, it would lift all enchantments over the statue.

As they finally made a hole big enough to see through, she took in the sight of the battle raging beyond the alleyway. It alarmed her that she still couldn't hear it.

"Holy light!" she exclaimed, her heart rate accelerating. "Tate and Tiege are seriously outnumbered. I don't even see Zachariah or Ariana. We have to get out there."

Her words were unnecessary. They were all working as fast as they could to clear the rocks without bringing the doorway crashing down. Ini-herit refused to let her do any heavy lifting due to the baby. Since there wasn't much she could do, she watched her cousins fight.

Damn, they were good. Pride warred with fear as she observed them. She longed to be by their sides. She felt more and more useless by the second.

Then something curious happened. The Mercesti who had been fighting the twins suddenly stopped. They lifted their hands and eased back, indicating that they meant no further harm. Tate and Tiege exchanged glances, then hurried somewhere out of her range of vision.

Clara Kate frowned. "What in the world…?"

"Nearly there," Ini-herit said, working with Quincy to shove one last, large chunk of stone away from the entrance.

Sophia could have gotten out by shifting, but Clara Kate knew she was remaining behind because of her and Quincy. She gave her cousin's arm a squeeze as they stood beside each other.

"There," Quincy said, brushing his hands off on his pants and retrieving his satchel from the ground where he'd left it. "We should be able to get out now."

"*Should* being the operative term," Sophia added, giving the entrance a wary look.

Clara Kate hurried forward, clambering over a few rocks to reach the opening. Ini-herit rushed up to steady her. Since she slipped and nearly clipped her face on a jagged rock, she supposed she couldn't blame him.

"Oh, I'm getting out of here," she declared. "Right. *Now.*"

She jumped from the top of a rock out into the alleyway. The moment she cleared the threshold, the outside noise resumed. She turned to make sure the others got out safely, then ran for the end of the alleyway, drawing her weapons as she went. Her gaze moved quickly across the horizon. Seeing no threats, she didn't pause before emerging from between the statue's paws. The others were right behind her.

Then she stumbled to a halt. The Mercesti who had been battling Tate and Tiege now all stood watching something. She couldn't see beyond them.

Tate? Tiege? she thought.

Over here, came their joined thought.

She hurried around the Mercesti. When she finally saw what they were looking at, she lowered her weapons. Eirik lay on the ground, his throat a bloody mess. Tiege reached for Ariana, who stood beside Zachariah, and pulled her into a hug. Zachariah took a few steps over to Eirik's unmoving body, a bloody knife in his hand. Then he went to one knee and stabbed the knife next to Eirik's head, burying it in the sand all the way to the hilt.

Clara Kate got a brief mental recap from Tate as she watched her cousin bend down and touch Zachariah's arm. She murmured something to him. Pushing her way through the crowd, Nyx also appeared, settling beside Tate and studying Zachariah with her diamond eyes. After a moment, he got back to his feet.

That was when Clara Kate noticed that all of the elders stood behind Zachariah. Blinking in shock, she even saw her father.

"Dad?" she asked, hurrying forward. She expected him to look at her, but his gaze remained on Zachariah. "What's going on?"

Seeing her expression, Zachariah glanced over his shoulder. Then his red gaze returned to her. "Who are you talking to?"

"My dad," she said. Then she reached out to touch the image she saw. Her hand passed right through it. "All of the elders except me and Harry are standing right behind you."

Ini-herit nodded. Now, everyone looked at where they pointed. Shrugs and confused expressions followed.

"You haven't seen an elder since Eirik approached the statue, have you?" Ini-herit asked, having read their thoughts. When Tate and Tiege shook their heads, he said, "I'm willing to bet that they transitioned to these forms the moment we recovered the third scroll piece." His gaze settled on Clara Kate. "Normally, we would have done the same."

"What's different about us?" she asked.

"We're part of the eight."

Derian and Harold approached, followed by hosts of Mercesti and Waresti. They looked around the group. Derian heard what Ini-herit said and repeated, "The eight?"

"The eight beings needed to activate the Elder Scroll," Ini-herit clarified.

He walked over to Eirik and reached inside his furred vest. After a moment of searching, he pulled out the two pieces of parchment that had caused all of them such pain and trouble.

Holding them up and scanning the growing audience, he said, "I don't know how much Eirik shared with all of you, but he was seeking the Elder Scroll in hopes that he would ascend to the position of the Mercesti elder. He sought power, not caring who he hurt to acquire it. What he didn't understand was that we created the scroll with the loophole that only the elders can select the being to whom it will be applied."

His gaze moved to Zachariah. Clara Kate's breath caught. That was why all of the elders—in whatever form they were in at the moment—now stood behind him.

Frowning, Zachariah glanced over his shoulder as though expecting to find that Ini-herit was looking at someone else. Then his head lifted and he took two steps back. She realized that he could now see the other elders. His stunned reaction made her smile.

Stepping forward, she produced the third scroll piece. "So…what do you say, Zachariah?" she asked.

"Bloody hell," he replied.

Chapter 41

ZACHARIAH CAUGHT THE STEADY GAZES OF THE ELDERS. SOMEHOW, HE could read their expressions even though their faces were still and unsmiling. What he saw confirmed Ini-herit's comments.

Running a hand through his hair, he turned and looked at Tate. He felt her awe as she processed what her cousin had just offered on behalf of the elders. A wide smile spread across her face as she held his gaze. Her thoughts told him that she believed this was the most amazing offer ever made and they were absolutely making the right choice. Of course, her opinion was rather skewed.

His attention shifted to Derian. The male who had served as the leader over the Mercesti allies for many years seemed a more logical choice to be an elder, in Zachariah's opinion. He had created and overseen a thriving community, a shelter for Mercesti who had been forced to convert like he had been. He had stepped in to aid the elders in their cause without hesitation, wanting only to do what was right for all Estilorians. Yes, Derian was worthy of the role.

Then, as he looked him in the eye, Derian crossed his right arm over his chest and went to one knee. The deeply respectful gesture was reserved for elders. He was offering his support of the elders' choice. His support of Zachariah.

One by one, the rest of the Mercesti in the area followed suit, all the way out as far as Zachariah could see. He couldn't process it at first. Less than three months ago, he was living on the run with Nyx, hiding from what he had done and who he had become. Now he was being offered the role of the Mercesti elder.

You are worthy.

The cacophony of voices whispered through his mind, addressing his unvoiced doubt. He sensed both his family and the elders offering their support. Their confidence in him was humbling and unexpected.

Then Nyx nudged him. He looked into her mysterious eyes and sensed her approval. For the first time, he didn't flinch when he saw his reflection in her faceted gaze.

He was a Mercesti.

"How does this work?" he asked at last.

A flurry of excitement resulted from the simple question. Ini-herit and Clara Kate set the pieces of the scroll on the sand, then held out their hands so the eight of them could create a circle around it. Zachariah took Tate's hand on one side and Clara Kate's on the other.

The moment the eight of them connected, the wind picked up. The scroll pieces lit with brilliant energy along every edge, each piece lifting from the ground. Ini-herit conveyed the contents of the last piece so that the words were in everyone's minds. Then he silently gave the order for them to recite the scroll.

> *"Should time and Fate both dictate*
> *That nine Elders become eight*
> *Let not their power and sway*
> *Fade like the light of the day.*
>
> ~ - ~
>
> *By this scroll may power flow*
> *So another's skill may grow*
> *And from eight will one become*
> *Mightier than anyone."*

As they spoke the last word of the first piece, it flared so bright that they all had to close their eyes. Zachariah felt a surge of energy unlike anything he'd ever experienced. It centered in his chest and pulsed through his body. Opening his eyes, he realized the first piece had vanished.

After exchanging glances with his family, he nodded. The wind whipped around them as they spoke the next words.

> *"To unfurl the force herein*
> *Eight journeys must now begin;*
> *Once separate and undefined*
> *Different paths somehow align.*
>
> ~ - ~
>
> *One most pure in blood and soul,*
> *One with too much self-control,*
> *One conceived of age and might,*
> *One who dwells 'tween dark and light."*

This time, they knew to close their eyes. Beyond his eyelids, Zachariah sensed the second piece light up and disappear, sending its power to him. He felt as though the energy cycling through him was going to burst from his chest. He didn't know how he'd ever contain it.

Once again, he sensed the presence of the elders in his mind. They told him that they understood, and everything would be okay. By doing this, he was making all of them stronger.

After taking a moment to center himself, he opened his eyes and nodded again. They spoke the words of the final scroll piece.

> *"One of two knows truth from lies,*
> *One of two the truth defies,*
> *One who finds what once was lost,*
> *One whose form with nature crossed.*
>
> ~ - ~
>
> *Should these eight ever unite,*
> *From this scroll shall strength ignite,*
> *Revealing the Elder new*
> *By whose actions they imbue."*

Zachariah braced himself for the last surge of power, hoping he had the strength to contain it. This time, however, the sensation that rushed through him didn't feel overwhelming or uncontrollable. In fact, it seemed to steady him. Now, the power coursing through him felt stable. More natural.

"That's because it is natural now," Jabari said.

Looking to his right, Zachariah watched the elders approach. He realized they were back in their normal forms and Gabriel was no longer among them.

"Gabriel will congratulate you when we return to his homeland and complete the elder bonding ritual with both you and Clara Kate," Jabari said. "He wishes he could be here."

Zachariah nodded. He started to reply, but Tate grabbed him and kissed him. He couldn't help but respond to her. Only after a minute did he register the cheering. He pulled away from her as the noise died down. She grinned up at him.

"So…this is what you look like with red eyes and markings," she said, trailing a finger along his bicep. "It's sexy." When his eyebrows lifted, she added, "I'm so proud of you, Sparky."

Her conveyed emotion had a corner of his mouth lifting. Then Derian echoed, "Sparky?"

Zachariah's gaze narrowed. He opened his mouth to respond, only to hear seven voices chime, "Don't *ever* call him that."

Blinking in surprise, he looked again at his family. They all gazed at Derian with serious expressions. Tiege even shook his head to punctuate the statement.

Zachariah couldn't help himself. He threw back his head and laughed.

Clara Kate slept during most of the trip back to her homeland. Due to the distance they had traveled to recover the last scroll piece, the trip took two days. She didn't remember most of it.

She spent time with her family and the other elders on the evening after they defeated Eirik and Metis. They all needed to discuss what they'd been through. Talking about it would help them work through it…eventually.

Grief still held her in its grip. There had been many more casualties than they'd anticipated thanks to Eirik's volatile weapons, but Alexius' death hit her most keenly. She would always bear the weight of guilt because Metis had garnered the idea of the weapon from her mind.

The elders revealed that Metis had been captured. They didn't go into detail about what they intended to do with her, but Clara Kate imagined she'd find out soon enough. Once she was joined in thought with the other elders, she'd have access to all of the information they retained.

"It wasn't long after we stopped Metis that we were called by the Elder

Scroll," Malukali explained as they all ate a meal together. "Once you all acquired the final scroll piece, we were summoned."

Jabari said, "We had decided to offer Zachariah the role of Mercesti elder prior to today, but we didn't anticipate that decision rendering us powerless until the scroll was imbued."

"We have never created anything as powerful as that scroll," Knorbis added, "or we would have prepared you. We're sorry that you were left without our aid while confronting Eirik."

Clara Kate didn't blame the elders for what had happened. She believed enough in the power of fate to believe that all of this had been outside of their control. In the end, Eirik had been defeated. It was just a shame it had come at such a price.

Ariana didn't speak much as they traveled. Tiege offered her comfort whenever she needed it, taking her away from the others when her emotions got the best of her. During those times, Clara Kate sensed Zachariah's sadness. The Mercesti elder felt responsible for the blood on Ariana's hands, though he couldn't have prevented that any more than she could have stopped Metis from invading her mind.

She hoped he found some solace while rebuilding his class in the coming years. Judging by his in-depth conversations with Derian, Melanthe and Verryl, he was well on his way to naming his core leaders. They would have quite the task ahead of them, rooting out potential dissention within the class like they had encountered with the traitorous Oria. Clara Kate was confident they could do it, though.

When she reached her homeland at last, she expected to be relieved. She wanted to feel safe and welcome, the feelings she always experienced when at home. Instead, anxiety continued to swirl like a cesspool in her heart.

Then she saw her parents. Her dad held her gaze as she neared. She couldn't read anything in his blue-gray eyes, but he opened his arms to her.

She threw herself against him and cried as though her life was ending. It took him and her mother several hours to calm her down. Outside of commenting that he was too young to be a grandfather—and finally making her laugh—her dad didn't discuss what had happened between her and In-herit on the human plane. She was eternally grateful for that.

She got to see how big her baby brother, Jack, had gotten even in the short amount of time she was gone. She talked to her mom about her wedding, which her mom said was ready whenever Clara Kate was. She seemed genuinely happy about her coming grandbaby. Clara Kate knew she'd be relying a lot on her mother's strength in the months to come.

As the sun set that evening, she walked with Ini-herit along the cliffs beside her parents' home. He held her hand and rubbed the ring on her finger.

"How are you feeling?" he asked after they had walked a while in silence.

Although he could easily sense her thoughts and emotions, she appreciated him asking. "I'm a little better," she said. "My parents are so supportive. I'm really lucky."

"I'm glad. But that's not what I meant."

She sighed. Coming to a stop, she gazed out over the vast moonlit ocean. "I know, Harry. In all honesty, I'm sad. I'll never forget what Alexius sacrificed for me…for all of us."

He pulled her against him, absorbing some of the chill that blew in from the water. "You shouldn't forget him, Angel. Alexius was a good guy. He loved you, and I can't fault him for that. I'll miss him."

A tear escaped and she wiped at her cheek. "Thanks for understanding, Harry."

"Of course." Tipping her face up so he could look into her eyes, he said, "I was thinking that you might even want to name our son after him."

"Our…" Her eyes widened. "You can tell?"

"Yep. Our baby's a boy."

Sorrow lifted from her heart as she absorbed the news. His smile reflected such happiness that she couldn't help but respond to it. She knew then that there would be no more room for grief with all of the love he had just generated.

Pulling him close, she kissed him, taking the moment to just appreciate what she had in him. They had suffered loss, yes. But life and love also awaited them. They had overcome so much to get where they were now. She had faith that whatever came in the future, they would get through it together.

Epilogue

CLARA BURKE HAD LIVED A FULL LIFE, BUT SHE KNEW HER TIME WAS near. She had been in the hospital for almost two weeks, hooked up to every manner of machine.

And she was tired. So tired.

When she wasn't having another test done, she enjoyed visits from her friends and loved ones. Her neighbors dropped by every time they were able, bringing her things that she enjoyed to make her days more comfortable and as filled with love as possible.

She especially enjoyed visits from the children she had fostered over the years. She wasn't sure how word got around, exactly, but she had seen young people that she never expected to see again. A few of them even traveled all the way to Newnan from across the country just to tell her goodbye. It made her happy to see how much they had all accomplished.

Now, she lay in her hospital bed and tried to sleep as the night darkened her room. The pain kept her awake. Although she disliked taking medication, she just might have to ask the night nurse for something to help.

A soft knock on her door had her turning her head. She saw the nice young doctor who had just introduced himself to her earlier that day. What did he say his name was? Dr. Quinn? No, that was a female doctor she had seen in television reruns. Her brow furrowed in confusion.

"Good evening, Mrs. Burke," he said as he walked into her room. She certainly remembered his Australian accent and lovely gray eyes. "Do you remember me? I'm Dr. Quincy."

"Of course," she said, offering him a smile. "Such a polite young man."

He returned the smile, his eyes crinkling at the corners. "I haven't been called young in many years, but thank you." He lifted her chart from its place at the foot of her bed and gave it a quick scan. His gaze moved to the beeping machines, assessing them with a knowledgeable eye. "How are you feeling tonight?"

"I'm tired," she said. "But I can't sleep."

"I see. Any pain?"

"Yes." She met his gaze. She was comforted by the true empathy she saw there. "I'm dying, aren't I?"

He started to speak, but he must have read something in her expression. He replied, "Yes, ma'am. I'm afraid so."

For some reason, hearing someone say it eased her fear. She nodded in acceptance. The relief she felt seemed out of place. She believed in living life to the fullest. But the time was right.

"I know this is a little unusual," he said, reaching out and touching her hand, "but there are a few people here to see you."

"Now?"

"Yes."

"All right."

He didn't even look to the door or call out, but the room was soon full of people. She looked at the first two and smiled.

"Harry...Clara Kate." She accepted their hugs, delighted to see them. "Thank you for coming to say goodbye."

"Oh, they're not here to say goodbye, Mrs. B."

Her eyes widened at the sound of a voice she hadn't heard in almost twenty years. Harry and Clara Kate stepped away and revealed the next two people who had entered the room. For a moment, she wondered if she was in the grip of a pain-induced hallucination.

"Gabriel? Amber?"

"It's us, Mrs. B," Gabriel said, stepping closer and bringing Amber with him. "We're sorry we didn't get a chance to tell you goodbye all of those years ago."

Tears threatened her. "I know you had your reasons. But...you still look so young."

"Well, where we're from, aging works very differently."

"I see," she said. And she did.

"We'd like to tell you more about it," Amber said. "We're hoping you'll want to come back with us."

Dr. Quincy took her hand. A sense of peace and rightfulness settled over her. Looking around and meeting the gazes of those she had nurtured into adulthood, she knew she didn't need convincing.

"I'm ready," she said. "Bring me home."

About the Author:

Raine Thomas is the bestselling author of a series of young adult fantasy/romance novels about the Estilorians. She has a varied background including such professions as wedding planning and mental health…two fields that intersect more often than one would think. Residing in Orlando, Florida with her husband and daughter, Raine is hard at work on her next books.

You can get more info about Raine, her books, and her upcoming releases by visiting her at the following sites:

http://RaineThomas.com
http://twitter.com/Raine_Thomas
http://facebook.com/RaineThomas

Made in the USA
Middletown, DE
15 March 2023

26824173R00161